The Italian Potion

The Italian Potion

Edward Bewley

ROBERT HALE · LONDON

© Edward Bewley 2010
First published in Great Britain 2010

ISBN 978-0-7090-8942-1

Robert Hale Limited
Clerkenwell House
Clerkenwell Green
London EC1R 0HT

www.halebooks.com

2 4 6 8 10 9 7 5 3 1

Typeset in 11.5/14pt Garamond Pro
Printed in Great Britain by the MPG Books Group, Bodmin and King's Lynn

Contents

CHAPTER 1

Monsieur Eustace Vouet

A hackney dropped me at the door of Lady Villiers' house in Pall Mall and I gave the insolent scoundrel sixpence for his trouble. A girl opened upon my knock.

'Mr Delaney, if you please,' I demanded shortly, the coarseness of the impudent fellow's tongue still stinging my wounded vanity.

'You're to go through, Mr Wyld, sir,' the girl told me. 'The gentlemen are in the long gallery.' She took my cloak and led me along a passage to the gallery door which was half-open.

'Ah, Mr Wyld.' Delaney was pacing agitatedly at the threshold. 'We are almost ready.'

The gallery was curtained against night though the evening was still light and candles from holders on the panelled walls sparkled like stars in the consequent gloom. As my eyes adjusted I spied half-a-dozen virtuosi gathered there, standing about a plain table upon which some instruments and glassware had been placed ready. Close by, in a hearth, a furnace was glowing ruddily and Delaney's assistant was at hand, I could see, to man the bellows. Of the virtuosi I recognized Mr Hooke from the back by his unkempt mane of hair; beside him were My Lords Brouncker and Moray. Mr Hill was there and Mr Southwell too. All were engaged in conversation with a gentleman whom I did not recognize, a figure of medium height and carefully dressed. The group turned as Delaney and I approached.

'Mr Wyld,' Delaney introduced us, 'this is Monsieur Vouet. He is recently out of Paris.'

I bowed and the foreigner reciprocated.

'Monsieur Vouet brings us news of the mathematical arts,' Lord Brouncker interjected, knowing my disposition in this regard.

'Indeed, My Lord. I shall be pleased to learn what progress has been made in Paris.'

'All in good time, Mr Wyld, all in good time,' Delaney cautioned impatiently. 'I'm sure your geometry can wait a while longer. Tonight we will, I believe, witness a wonder that few have been privileged to see. Monsieur Vouet has acquired a quantity of the powder of transmutation and he has agreed to demonstrate its powers of projection for us. We await but one further guest and then we can begin.'

As if these words were a cue, we all heard a gentle rustling of silks. Turning, I found a veiled figure approaching from the doorway.

'My Lady.' Delaney greeted the figure with great delicacy. 'I think you know all the gentlemen here with the exception of our guest, Monsieur Vouet.' The Frenchman bowed extravagantly while we nodded discreetly. I was, however, more than a little surprised. The veil concealed, as surely all but Mr Vouet recognized, a visage belonging to none other than My Lady Castlemaine, subject of a thousand whispered rumours each day at Whitehall. Why was she here? Was her presence at the King's bidding or at his expense?

Delaney was not about to essay an explanation. I divined that we were being invited to treat her presence as at once unexceptional and clandestine. 'Now, Monsieur Vouet,' he cried with barely suppressed excitement, 'shall we begin?'

Vouet nodded. From his pocket he took a small box, the size of a snuff-holder, and placed it upon the table round which we had gathered once more. Then, carefully, he removed the lid and showed us, one by one, the contents. When my turn came I saw a small quantity of powder, hardly enough to fill half a needle-woman's thimble. It was, as I perceived, a deep red in colour and of the texture of velvet. So this was the powder of which the alchemists made so much. It looked innocuous enough.

While we took our turns to examine the box, Delaney was busy with the final arrangements for the demonstration. His assistant had made ready a crucible into which his master now began to arrange several small ingots of that basest of metals, lead. Meticulously, as was his fashion, he weighed the crucible charged with the ingots on a balance. No doubt he had already measured the weight empty.

'Two pounds,' he announced with satisfaction. 'Two pounds of lead. Will the powder have the power for that amount, Monsieur Vouet?'

'The provenance of the powder is incontestable and of the finest quality. I have two hundred grains. That will be more than sufficient, I believe, Mr Delaney.'

'So be it.' And Delaney beckoned his assistant to place the crucible into the furnace. We watched as the crucible disappeared from sight and continued to observe as the man began to apply himself to the bellows, raising a glow from the charcoal and filling the room with its drying heat and acrid stench.

We waited for about ten minutes. Delaney paced restlessly once more while Monsieur Vouet appeared sanguine, confident. The other virtuosi whispered quietly but I waited in silence beside My Lady. Once or twice I surreptitiously examined what I could discern of the face beneath the veil but her expression was guarded. I sensed her gaze, however, falling on me for a few moments before moving on. I took care to avoid those eyes. There was, I well knew, danger as well as beauty beneath that veil.

The heat from the furnace was causing me to begin to perspire uncomfortably by the time Delaney, having examined the crucible several times already, pronounced himself satisfied. Carefully his man withdrew the container which now held a shining lake of molten metal. He bore it to the table about which we had gathered once more and lowered it gently on to a prepared clay slab.

'Monsieur Vouet, if you please?'

The Frenchman passed the small box containing the powder to Delaney, who lost no time in tipping its contents into the crucible, on top of the molten lead. It rested there awhile before the particles gently melted and coalesced then dissolved within the metal. In a minute it was gone. I watched, determined to miss nothing even though my eyes were beginning to ache in the heavy atmosphere of the room.

For minutes there was no change. Then gradually an extraordinary texture, like the skeleton of a leaf or patterning from the hoar-frost, emerged first from the centre of the silver puddle and then extended itself purposefully across the liquid surface towards the edges of the clay container. I can only describe this growth as organic, as if a living creature that had taken up home within the metal was revealing its presence to us. Imperceptibly this texturing – as I but poorly describe it – crept ever outwards until it had colonized the surface completely. Only then did I realize that the silver of the lead had taken on a reddish golden hue.

We watched, transfixed. The colour appeared to deepen and then lightened again until it matched the colour found in an early evening sky, close to the horizon and the setting sun. Then, more extraordinary still, the organic tendrils that had covered the surface faded and were gone. The metal lived no more.

Now we all began to mutter, each to another, impatient to know if the transmutation had taken place, and by what agency. Delaney would not be hurried. 'We must wait yet longer,' he insisted. 'The work is incomplete.' How he could tell, I know not. And so we waited, restlessly, for a further quarter hour by Delaney's new pendulum clock; in truth it seemed much longer.

At last Delaney signalled to his man, who lifted the crucible and carried it beyond the hearth where he plunged the whole deep into a barrel of water. There was a violent hissing and the man's head was momentarily enveloped in a rising cloud of steam. When the surface of the water was no longer agitated, he reached in and plucked out the ingot of metal – the clay crucible had shattered in the vat – and carried it back to the table where we waited.

'My Lady, gentlemen,' Delaney could not hide his excitement. 'If I am not mistaken we have indeed witnessed one of the great miracles of nature and art. Now we must put it to the test.' Then, with a sharp instrument he had put by, he carefully shaved two pieces of metal from the ingot and placed one into a glass vessel, the other beside him on the table.

'Aqua fortis.'

His assistant handed him a thick glass bottle from which Delaney poured a quantity of fuming, rancid-smelling fluid into the vessel containing the fragment of metal. He gently agitated the vessel while we watched. So far as I could see nothing happened. Meanwhile his assistant had heated a cauldron of water and Delaney used this to warm the mixture. The smell grew more rancid but other than that, nothing.

'Excellent,' Delaney exclaimed, pleased.

There was another small piece of metal – a portion of silver as Delaney now told us – about the size of an elderberry, lying ready upon the table. Delaney took up this slug of metal and dropped it into the same vessel with the shaving. Immediately the liquid frothed and within seconds the silver had disappeared. Yet still the shaving from the ingot remained inert at the bottom of the vessel. It was untouched.

'So,' he muttered. 'The aqua fortis is yet of excellent quality. It has entirely consumed the silver, and still not one particle of the other has been taken. By this we may conclude that our lead has now a nobility greater than that of silver.

'Only aqua regis has the capacity to touch true gold,' he added, by way of explanation for My Lady. 'Now we must try that too.'

Delaney's assistant had already brought another glass vessel and into this Delaney placed the second shaving of metal from the ingot. Meanwhile his assistant fetched another thick bottle the contents of which smelled, if such a thing were possible, even more malodorous than the first. As before, Delaney slowly decanted a portion of this fuming liquid into the vessel containing the shaving of metal. This time there was an immediate sign of activity; bubbles formed gently upon the metal before rising lazily to the surface and slowly the fragment dissolved, tingeing the whole a delicate pale green.

Delaney was ecstatic. 'Monsieur Vouet,' he declared. 'You have been as good as your word. I salute you sir.' The Frenchman beamed and bowed in acknowledgement of the compliment.

Putting the glass vessels aside, Delaney addressed us all. 'I have arranged one final test. Without there is a goldsmith of excellent repute. He knows not what has passed here. I will now ask him to join us and try the metal. If anyone can judge its metalline properties, 'tis he.'

This said he went to the door and called out a name. Moments later an honestly dressed artisan appeared in the doorway. In his hand was a leather bag which I guessed contained his tools. Delaney ushered Beauchamp, for that was his name, towards the table about which we were gathered and waved to his assistant to clear room for the man to work. Then he offered him the irregularly shaped ingot of metal.

'Take your time and do what you must. I wish to know if this is true gold or some counterfeit.'

The smith took from his bag a black cloth which he laid across the table. He placed the ingot at its centre. Then he arranged the implements he required. As I watched he hacked a piece from the ingot and began to work it, gently, with a tiny mallet. Slowly he beat and flattened the fragment of metal into a fine foil. Eventually he had beaten it so fine that the light of a candle could pass. The light that emerged, as I could see, was the green of a spring meadow.

Beauchamp folded the foil he had beaten and placed it into a small crucible. He added more from the ingot and then he took the container to Delaney's furnace. By this time most of the virtuosi had drifted away and I saw that Monsieur Vouet was taking up with My Lord Brouncker once more. Guessing they were to discuss the mathematical arts, I was on the point of joining them when I found My Lady approaching me.

'Mr Wyld,' she said pushing aside her veil. ''Tis a long time since we have seen your face at court. Have we lost your favour?'

'My Lady,' I replied hastily, 'you do me an injustice if you believe that possible. 'Tis but want of opportunity that has forced my absence. I have been detained elsewhere these last days.'

'Then I hope your detention will soon be at an end.'

'If you please, I have business this very Saturday that will bring me to court.'

My Lady smiled mischievously. 'Then I will be certain to carry news of your visit to the Duchess's chamber when I return,' she assured me, her eye fixing mine.

I felt a little colour in my cheeks, knowing that she referred to one who served the Duchess of York. 'You are very kind, My Lady,' I replied clumsily.

Her head bowed imperceptibly. 'I beg you remember, Mr Wyld, that you have other friends at court. Perhaps you will put time aside for them too?'

'My Lady, I am ever your servant.'

My interlocutor was on the point of replying when Delaney chose to interrupt our brief intimacy. Whatever riposte she had intended was quickly sheathed as she greeted our host.

''Tis a strange magic you have wrought this evening, Mr Delaney,' she told him. 'I'll warrant I have never seen its like.'

'I believe it to be no magic, My Lady, but a process as natural as the growth of a tree,' he replied.

'Then you cultivate strange trees in your orchard. Have you others to show us?'

'This evening is dedicated to Monsieur Vouet and his powder,' he replied. 'If you desire at another time to learn more of these arts I will gladly be your servant.' He glanced over his shoulder and then beckoned us. 'But Beauchamp is ready. Let us hear of his trials.'

In a few moments we had gathered around the smith and awaited his verdict. He brought it in swiftly.

'Mr Delaney, sir. This is as pure a gold as I have worked. If you feared you had been cheated, fear no longer.'

'Thank you, Mr Beauchamp,' Delaney replied, clapping his hands with delight. 'Thank you indeed.' And with that he showed the artisan to the gallery door and called a girl to take him to the kitchen where meat and ale was waiting.

'So,' he exclaimed, returning to the circle of virtuosi at the table. 'Beauchamp swears to the nobility of the metal which, until it was tinged by Monsieur Vouet's powder, was none but lead.'

'Are there not other tests?' asked My Lord Brouncker, ever the sceptic.

'An adept steeped in the arts might ask further questions,' replied Delaney. 'For myself I am satisfied. But perhaps I will inquire of Mr Starkey, if he is not in debtors' prison again. He has greater skill than I in these matters.'

After a few moments more of such talk My Lady departed our company to join Lady Villiers. When she had left the gallery, Mr Delaney cautioned us not to speak in vulgar company of what we had seen. 'Men not versed in our philosophy will take it to be the work of spirits, or worse,' he warned.

The main business of the evening was over, but we continued to discuss natural philosophy for most of an hour during which I found an opportunity to speak with Monsieur Vouet of Paris. Then My Lord Brouncker proposed we adjourn for supper. Delaney demurred, claiming he had further matters to discuss with Monsieur Vouet while he had the opportunity and My Lord Moray insisted he had business in Whitehall. So it was that Mr Hooke, Mr Hill, Mr Southwell and I agreed to make up a party to Will's by Covent Garden where I promised we would find some wits.

It being decided that we would convene again a week hence to hear what Mr Starkey's verdict would be, Lord Brouncker called his coach and we departed. My promise for our further entertainment was met in all parts for there were wits aplenty in the coffee house where we ate heartily on mutton in good company. I must confess, however, that our own Mr Hooke is quite as ingenious as any of the wits with whom we railled and makes of the new philosophy a true art.

So the evening ended. My Lord undertook to deliver Mr Hooke to his lodgings in the City and I strolled from Bow Street, entering the piazza of Covent Garden by the south and thence to my own door in the northern arcade, rapier at hand. In the event no one disturbed my passage. On the way I pondered somewhat upon the matter of the transmutation that we had all witnessed that evening and rather more upon My Lady Castlemaine. Had she some use for me, I wondered? If so, I would need to tread with care.

CHAPTER 2

A Death in Southwark

I have made my residence in Covent Garden these past eighteen months, that being the interval since I returned to London having concluded some affairs in the country beyond Calais. I took the place on the advice of my neighbour Mr May. Nowadays Mr May styles himself an architect but during the late troubles he acted as an intelligencer for the King and thereby secured himself considerable preferment. Mr Lely, the limner, makes his paintings from another dwelling close by while some of the wits who spend their days in Will's reside hereabouts too.

There is much to commend the fairness and proportion of these dwellings that give on to the piazza at Covent Garden, the latter being the Italianate conceit of the Duke of Bedford's late designer Mr Inigo Jones. The main misfortune is that the he made his piazza a place for public commerce. In consequence there is an infernal clutter by day of stallholders peddling their wares and a superfluity of riff-raff about the piazza by night. A straight back, gentleman's cloth and a well polished pommel are sufficient to keep all but the most truculent of these at bay. Those unfortunate few soon find the edge of a blade to be their reward.

The household I maintain in the northern arcade of the piazza is small, as befits my needs. I have a woman, Bridget, who keeps house and provides a middling fare at table when Will's proves inconvenient. This Bridget is a rotund, well-made woman, in age superior to me, who affects a matronly demeanour that is not unprepossessing. At her bidding I have also engaged her young nephew, Ned, as my boy. The boy is poorly schooled but eager and I have taken it upon myself to bring him on. With this in mind I have begun to provide him with the rudiments of the grammar. Besides these there is a third, Martha, who serves as my chambermaid. Martha still has the flower of youth upon her and with it an inclination to wilfulness and guile but she does her work well enough. Bridget would have her gone but it suits me yet to keep her about the place.

The boy was asleep when I returned from Will's after our philosophical supper but Bridget and Martha awaited me as usual. My head was still full of the evening's turns and Mr Delaney's reagents so I took a pipe of tobacco to clear the muddle from my mind while Martha removed my boots and undressed me. Then I sank wearily to bed, having no inclination this night to take up a book as was my usual practice.

I slept beyond my normal hour next day. When I finally rose and called for the girl the morning was already half spent. That morning was pleasantly bright, which was welcome for we had seen nought but rain so far this year, and I bethought to take a leisurely breakfast of beer and cold pie before stretching my legs as far as Will's in search of the latest news. This plan had hardly formed before it was interrupted by a rude banging at the front door. I sent the girl to find out who disturbed us, whereupon she discovered Lady Villiers' coachman.

'Here's a man from Mr Delaney, sir,' she called up to the parlour. ''E wants you to go with him. 'E's to take you now, sir, 'e says.'

'The devil he is, Martha. Send him up and I'll have it out of him.'

The coachman had been driving hard and his face was streaked with sweat and dust from the exertion. 'What is it, man?' I demanded, when he presented himself before me.

'I come straight from Mr Delaney, sir. I'm to take you to him sir. He says you are to come immediately, sir, if you please.'

'Why? Is there some trouble?'

'I can't say that there is, sir, but then I can't say there isn't. He's in Southwark, sir, where I took him this morning, first thing.'

'Southwark? Why?'

'We went to visit a gentleman, sir, a foreigner I believe.'

'Humph!' I muttered, for I had no wish to visit Southwark on such a day as this. 'Very well. Take yourself downstairs and get the woman to refresh you. I'll call you when I'm ready.'

No doubt I would have to do Delaney's bidding, but in my own time, I counselled myself irritably.

An excursion by coach to Southwark was not to be welcomed at the best of times but this was as inopportune a moment to chose as any. The City would be a throng and London Bridge barely passable, the clement weather having drawn half the population to sample the amusements found across the river. Still, Delaney had need of my presence so I put on my boots, took up a travelling cloak and made ready for the journey.

The voyage was everything I anticipated. Delaney's man had to use his whip more than once to clear a way past the beggars in Fleet Street while the bridge was a battlefield where the pedlars, hagglers, shopkeepers and travellers all fought for the same narrow causeway. The sun was well past the zenith by the time we stopped before an untidy looking timber-frame building located somewhat behind the pleasure gardens, on the south bank of the river and west of the bridge. Understanding this to be our destination, I alighted with caution. My boot heels were barely to the ground before I found Delaney at my elbow.

'Could you have come no sooner?' he greeted me, crossly.

I could see he was distraught and chose to let pass this ungracious reception. 'What is this matter,' I enquired, 'that demands my presence?'

In response he looked about him, somewhat furtively as I thought, and then bade me accompany him within.

The building which we entered was dingy and the room meagrely proportioned. I wondered briefly if this was a brothel in which Delaney had been pleasuring himself but quickly dismissed the notion. There were, laid about us, the appurtenances befitting a gentleman's residence. Some handsome volumes lay upon a table and writing implements were in evidence too. Yet the surroundings were too squalid to accommodate comfortably any gentleman I knew.

'Monsieur Vouet?' I guessed, recalling that the coachman had spoken of a foreign gentleman.

'He is upstairs,' Delaney replied, unhelpfully.

'These are his lodgings, then?'

Delaney seemed disinclined to answer, but drew me towards the back of the room where a doorway gave on to a small passage and a narrow stairway. As he hesitated, I took the lead and soon found myself in an upper chamber, the rear of which was taken up with a large bed. Upon this bed was a form that I soon identified as that of the Frenchman. Just as soon I recognized that he was dead.

'What has happened?' I demanded abruptly, not without alarm. 'Has Monsieur Vouet been taken with a seizure?'

'I know not,' Delaney answered, as he joined me before the bed. 'He was as you see him when I arrived. As was his chamber.'

At this I took a moment to look around and realized that the room was in complete disarray. There was clothing strewn about, papers clearly out of order and a large chest lay on its side, its contents spilled across the floor. It was difficult to imagine that any man could live in such a state by choice and I began to suspect the handiwork of another than the figure on the bed.

That thought having formed, I took time to examine the body more closely. Vouet's face was pallid and waxy to the touch. He had lain thus for several hours now. I began to feel the body carefully through the clothing, seeking any sign that might indicate the cause of his demise for I suspected his death was no accident. There was some marking about the neck, a slight bruising, but otherwise I could find no unnatural sign upon him. That, however, seemed to me sufficient.

'Have you called the constable?' I asked, turning once more to Delaney who had been hovering beside me. 'I'll warrant this man has been killed.'

Delaney looked uncomfortable. 'Francis,' he said, his voice wavering uncharacteristically, 'I need your help.'

Hearing those words my heart felt uneasy. 'Why?' I asked, cautiously. 'What do you know of this?'

'Nothing!' he exclaimed. 'Nothing. As I have told you, Vouet was as you find him when I arrived here this morning. But—'

'Would you have any reason to wish him dead?' I interrupted.

'None. I would wish him alive; I would wish him well and able to speak. We were to complete a transaction of considerable importance to me this morning. Now that is impossible.'

'Then how can I help you, Robert?'

'You can help me first by listening to what I must tell you,' he replied. 'And then if you will, you can help me further. I came to Monsieur

Vouet's lodgings this morning by arrangement. He had procured for me in Paris a manuscript that was both unique and of inestimable value. Today I was to repay him for his services and take possession of that manuscript.

'Please, Francis,' he cautioned, anticipating my question. 'I am not at liberty to reveal its name. But be assured that it is of an esoteric nature that would interest none but a select few.' Suddenly he looked forlorn. 'But now we cannot complete that transaction. And ...' He looked around the room once more in despair. 'And it is my belief that the manuscript has gone.'

'Then *you* have done this?' I scolded, indicating the chaos that surrounded us.

'In part, I confess. But with no such enthusiasm as the first instigator,' he added vehemently. 'Much was as you find it. This ransacking was the work of some other hand, a hand, I fear, which took Vouet's life and the manuscript that Vouet brought for me.'

'If this manuscript is gone, what have you to fear by the constable?'

'Will I not be his first suspect in this?' he demanded crossly. 'Besides, I cannot be sure the manuscript is not here. The Frenchman knew its worth. He may have secreted it beyond my skill of discovery. Unlike you, I am not fitted for such an enquiry as this.' Delaney's features betrayed a thorough, deep, misery. 'I fear, Francis, I am guilty of the unchristian sin of valuing this manuscript before Monsieur Vouet's life. It is unpardonable and yet I find I cannot help myself.' He paused, uncertainly. 'I must place myself in your hands,' he told me finally. 'What should I do?'

'Am I to understand that you would wish me to locate this manuscript for you, if that is possible?'

Delaney nodded.

'And do you give me charge in the manner of proceeding?'

'Of course. I have no experience in such matters.'

'Then do as I bid you. Go down and send the coachman for the constable.'

Delaney looked mindful to demur, then, with a shrug, his shoulders dropped and he adhered to my request, leaving me alone in that upper chamber. I examined it with my eye once more but the irregularity that had been wrought left me little hope that the missing artifact was to be simply located. 'Lay such thoughts aside,' I instructed myself. First, the Frenchman must be laid to rest in a fashion befitting a Christian. Upon that resolution I, too, descended, following Delaney down the narrow staircase.

There was, nevertheless, one matter upon which I wished to seek satisfaction immediately. I had spied a truckle bed beneath the main bedstead in the chamber above. Clearly there had been a servant, likely more. What had become of them?

From the narrow passage at the foot of the stairway there was a second opening giving on to a further parlour to the rear of the building. Entering it, I quickly discovered the evidence to confirm my suspicion, evidence of a household that had been violently disturbed. An upturned utensil hid a solidified brown mass which I identified as chocolate. Other items were in disarray. Here were the remains of food that had been prepared some time the previous day, and here the laundry waiting to be completed. Two servants, I divined, both now fled, or worse.

With this intelligence, the course that events had taken began to coagulate in my mind. The Frenchman had returned to his lodgings late the previous evening having left Delaney's some time after we had departed for Will's. He had commanded the beverage be prepared, a prelude to repose, and then the intruder had arrived. The body above was still clothed after the fashion Vouet had sported the previous evening. He had had no time to undress. Yet he was barely marked. There had been no immediate or violent altercation. Indeed it may have been that the Frenchman knew his attacker, was expecting him and invited him within.

Perhaps. Yet much remained obscure. One fact was quite clear, however: the testimony of the servants was vital. If they lived, they must be found. Pondering this, I joined Delaney once more in the front parlour.

The constable, when he arrived, was called William Hudson. This Hudson let it be understood that he was proprietor of a tavern beside the bear garden, a position for which he appeared admirably suited. He was a thickset, ugly-looking fellow clothed in a leather jerkin, with some coloured cloth tied about his neck. His trousers were of a course hemp and severely soiled. There was, besides, the stench of onions about him. I took him for a reluctant parish servant and was not surprised to find him but little concerned as to the fate of Monsieur Vouet.

As I anticipated, the sight of a sovereign soon raised a glimmer in his eye. 'I desire you to put a watchman by the door,' I ordered. 'Nothing is to be disturbed within until I have completed my work. There's a gold coin for you and ten shillings for the fellow who minds the place.'

'How long'ud that be, sir?'

'Good God, man, I don't know. Three days, four? If the work doesn't suit you I can easily find another.'

'Now don't you annoy yerself, sir, with that trouble. I'll put a fellow here as 'll keep the Devil hisself out.'

'Mind you see to it without delay, then. We'll be leaving promptly and I wish to be satisfied before I go. Besides that, there were servants in the house. I want to know who they were and where they can be found. Is that within your capabilities?'

'I wouldn't be surprised, sir, if I couldn't provide satisfaction,' Hudson replied.

I could see that the constable was trying to decide how much more this would be worth. 'Well, set to it, man,' I told him, curtailing his avaricious machinations. 'We don't have all day.' At that his brow furrowed and he ambled off leaving Delaney and me alone once more.

While we awaited the constable's return I put Delaney to the matter of an autopsy. For the manner of Monsieur Vouet's death was far from certain.

'I'll get Sir Charles Scarborough,' he proposed. 'He's the best cutter in London, they say.'

'Excellent,' I replied, for I knew Sir Charles myself, a dabbler in the mathematical arts. 'He'll see to matter on the morrow, I suppose?'

'I will encourage him to act swiftly, certainly.'

After this was agreed, we fell silent awhile and I began to feel the atmosphere within the house encroaching uncomfortably upon my reason for there is no peace to be found when the dead lie by.

'Let us take ourselves into the street,' I proposed. 'The air in here is becoming foul.'

Delaney was quick to concur and we stepped beyond the door. And thus it was from here that we discerned some few moments later the sound of a team approaching. Looking in the direction from which the sound came I perceived an elegant coach turning the corner. The pace of vehicle faltered briefly as it came within our view and then the driver picked up his stride so that the carriage rumbled past our position at a canter. Of the occupant we saw no sign for the interior was concealed behind blinds but there was no disguising the outlandish livery of Lord Illminster's servants.

'What business does his lordship's household have in these parts?' I asked Delaney, after the equipage had passed.

Delaney shrugged, his features betraying a troubled frown. 'His lordship has never shunned his pleasures,' he suggested with but little conviction. I was left with the uncomfortable notion that Delaney conceived some other motive which he chose not to share with me.

CHAPTER 3

The King's Physician Conducts an Autopsy

As we had agreed, Delaney and I called on the King's physician, Sir Charles Scarborough, that same afternoon where we found him engaged with The Reverend Dr Bathurst in a lively debate concerning the matter of the curing of the King's Evil. There is now a public superstition that the King possesses the miraculous power of healing by touch, but Dr Bathurst represented himself to be puzzled that His Majesty's brother, the Duke, should profess the similar ability, it being avowedly the gift of kings. The matter was in total, he proclaimed, a challenge to our natural philosophy. Sir Charles proposed that a history should be made to show by what means the touch could heal. Whether the King will agree, or no, to such a suggestion I am disposed to doubt. But I am inclined to that scepticism expressed by Lord Chancellor Bacon when he said that imagination was the next kin to miracle working.

Sir Charles, not being called into the King's presence the next day, allowed he would be pleased to examine the mortal remains of Monsieur Vouet when Delaney put the suggestion to him. The physician recommended that use be made of the chamber of the Royal College of Physicians for the purpose, to which Delaney acquiesced. This being settled, I took leave of the company in order to detail the college porters and supervise the removal of the body to the college. I was, in truth, minded also to test the trustworthiness of the constable, Hudson. I felt little confidence in the man's word. On this occasion, however, I took a boat as being the more convenient means of arriving by Southwark in comfort.

My misgivings regarding the constable were proved unfounded. When we arrived at the Frenchman's lodgings I found a stout young fellow ensconced within. It took a few words, indeed, to persuade him that I was his paymaster, after which I and the two porters were able to gain entry. Under my guidance they placed the body of poor Vouet into a sailcloth bag which we lowered carefully down the narrow stairway and so to a handcart brought for the purpose. That achieved, I was tempted to begin my examination of the premises straightaway, for my curiosity was quite aroused. The day being virtually spent, I conceded that this would have to be put off until the morrow. Instead I accompanied the body back across the river and, leaving the porters by the college, thence by hackney to Covent Garden.

The old mansion in Knightrider Street, the seat of the Royal College of Physicians, was a ferment of activity the following morning at the hour set for Sir Charles's examination of the body. Much to my consternation, the autopsy was to be carried out in public.

The chamber which served as an anatomy theatre to the college already contained fifteen or twenty gentlemen when I arrived. A few whom I recognized were virtuosi. For these few the investigation of the body offered an opportunity for inquisition. But for the majority, as I readily perceived, this would be not so much an opportunity for learning as one for spectacle. Such a public dissection was an invitation to the inquisitive and the vicarious. The atmosphere was already akin to that of a vulgar bear garden, or so it appeared to me.

'Monsieur Vouet is most popular this morning,' I observed caustically to Delaney, whom I found standing beside the slab upon which the body lay under a heavy cloth.

'Sir Charles thought fit to make of his examination a philosophical investigation,' Delaney replied, ignoring the tone of my observation. 'It is ever his wish to extend the work of his late friend Sir William Harvey regarding the regulation of the humours. Much remains of these processes to be understood.'

'No doubt Monsieur Vouet was a man of great curiosity too,' I retorted. 'Let us hope Sir Charles will not bare the dark secrets of his soul for all to read.'

Delaney was in no mood for such sarcasm. 'The seat of the soul is a matter of great philosophical concern,' he admonished me self-right-eously.

Sir Charles was already laying out his instruments, helped by a young gentleman student he had taken under his tutelage. Turning aside from Delaney, whose company I was finding wearisome, I addressed the physician instead.

'Have you taken time to examine the body yet, Sir Charles?' I asked him quickly. 'There is some discolouration about the neck which caught my attention.'

'Thank you, Mr Wyld. I have seen the marking of which you speak. I would say your Frenchman has a broken neck, eh? But the knife will reveal all.'

Having made himself ready, Sir Charles instructed his assistant to remove the covering over the body. This latter had now been stripped naked, revealing the imperfections which had accrued to the person of this gentleman of some forty years. The stomach was soft and somewhat bulging, exceeding in size the chest which was thereby rendered mediocre to the eye. The arms and legs were thin and almost hairless; indeed they appeared barely provided with the strength to serve the body adequately. The sexual organs were distended, and somewhat marked. Yet there were no further signs of injury, only the marking about the neck which I had already noted.

Sir Charles took up his scalpel. 'Gentlemen,' he began, 'if you will pay attention I will now begin my enquiry into the death of this gentleman who was found, expired, this day just passed. You will note, I hope, some bruising about the neck, here. This may represent the seat of an injury. So ...' And with a swift incision down the length of the throat, he began his dissection.

The niceness of Sir Charles's technique could not be doubted. He had soon revealed the organ of speech, then the tracts leading to the lungs and stomach. 'Ah,' he exclaimed, having laid back the skin from the spinal column. 'As I had predicted. Gentlemen, please observe the discontinuity between these two vertebrae of the neck. Here is the cause of death. This man's spine has been snapped like a rabbit taken for the pot.'

Having made this pronouncement, Sir Charles turned aside to speak to Delaney and I in private. 'This was either a strange accident, or murder,' he told us quickly.

'It was murder,' Delaney muttered.

'If that be so, the man you are seeking is a skilled practitioner and of, I would suggest, considerable strength. Do not underestimate him, I beg you.'

'Thank you for your warning,' I replied, for Delaney made no answer.

'And now,' said the physician turning back to his audience, 'we will continue.'

I have seen men split open before but only in the heat of a moment. Observing Monsieur Vouet as his entrails were spilled, stretched and measured in the name of philosophy left me, I confess, not a little affected. Indeed, I believed for a moment that the spectacle would turn my stomach, but, fortunately, I was preserved from that embarrassment.

Our philosophers showed no such qualms and they maintained a rapt attention as Sir Charles revealed organ after organ until it seemed all the secrets of the human body must be laid bare before us. Having overcome my own uneasiness I found, I must confess, much that was curious in the physician's demonstration. Nevertheless, I did not believe that anything further would be revealed of relevance to the Frenchman's death. In this I was proved to be wrong.

'Now, gentlemen,' Sir Charles, said, 'let me draw your attention to the stomach. It is, as you will already have observed, a capacious sac and if I make a quick incision, here ...' And with this Sir Charles made his incision. 'As I say, we will be able to discover what was the deceased's last meal.'

Sir Charles's face became, at once, both absorbed and puzzled. 'Gentlemen,' he announced after some moments, during which he examined the contents of that stomach intently, 'I fear there may be more to this matter than I had until now suspected. The man's stomach is quite fouled with quicksilver.'

Delaney hastened to the physician's side and made his own inspection of the contents of the organ. As he did so his face darkened. Then he turned away without speaking.

Sir Charles, meanwhile, had started examining the sexual organs. 'Ha,' he muttered. 'I think I may essay an explanation. Here I can find several barely healed sores,' he explained, indicating the testicles and penis. 'There is little doubt as to the diagnosis. This man had the pox and it would seem he has but recently taken a mercury cure. No doubt that accounts for the presence of such quantities of quicksilver. And now, gentlemen, I think we will make that do for today.' With that he indicated to his assistant to cover the body with the cloth. In truth, I think he too was somewhat perturbed.

Delaney was still frowning, distracted. While the others began to depart he approached Sir Charles. 'I should be pleased if it were possible to preserve such quicksilver as there is to be found in Monsieur Vouet's cadaver,' he requested. 'Can that be arranged?'

'I will do what I can,' he replied, and, beckoning his assistant, he relayed Delaney's request. 'If you should return after dinner, I will endeavour to have it made ready.'

It being well past noon, I proposed to Delaney that we make our way to Garaways, by Gresham College and the Royal Exchange, where we might hope to dine in the company of some learned men. He assented, but to what I fear he knew not for he remained deep in thought.

'What troubles you?' I demanded, as we made our way across St Paul's Yard and into Cheapside.

'This quicksilver. 'Tis the last thing I had sought.'

'But its presence presents no mystery, as Sir Charles has shown us. Monsieur Vouet would not be the first Frenchman to take a pox cure in Leather Lane.'

'Yes, yes. 'Tis perfectly reasonable. But you are surely aware what quicksilver signifies. It is symbolized by the Planet Mercury and in alchemical lore mercury is the female virtue, the begetter by sulphur of all that is in the material world. More pertinent I fear, mercury is the messenger. Was not Vouet a messenger?'

'What meaning do you draw from this?' I asked, somewhat perplexed. For I found Delaney's perambulation far from rational.

'I draw no meaning as yet. But you will have marked already that the manuscript Vouet carried was of an esoteric nature. I cannot but wonder at such a coincidence.'

''Twas not the quicksilver that killed Vouet,' I reminded him. 'His death was procured by means of a pair of strong hands.'

'I know,' Delaney snapped, impatiently. 'But you must give me leave to ponder whether there are other signs to be found.' After that we continued to Garaways in silence.

By the time we arrived all the best seats in the house were occupied and we found ourselves taking our meal in an inconvenient corner. Such an arrangement suited Delaney who had become poor company since Monsieur Vouet's decease. I, however, would have welcomed the opportunity of a spirited discussion in company. It was some compensation that the hare pie we consumed was as sweet as I have eaten this year. Fortunately, this and the claret improved Delaney's temper so that the time did not pass as dully and I had initially supposed it might.

After dinner I accompanied Delaney back to Knightrider Street where we found Sir Charles's student. The apprentice physician had served Delaney nobly, having managed to provide a goodly quantity of quicksilver from the stomach and gut of the French body.

"Tis another job for Mr Starkey,' Delaney told me. For the American chemist was quite the expert, when it came to quicksilver, of all that could be found in London.

Thus we parted, for I proposed to return to Monsieur Vouet's lodgings in order to make such enquires as I could there. Delaney, still much preoccupied I fear, declined to accompany me but took a hackney back to Pall Mall.

CHAPTER 4

Mr Wyld Makes Some Unexpected Discoveries

After parting with Delaney I made my way towards the river and took a wherry from Blackfriars Stairs, bidding the waterman carry me to Southwark. The sculler had to thread his way through a flotilla of barges making sail upriver but he charted a safe passage during which I dwelled somewhat on Delaney's preoccupations. The disappearance of this manuscript about which he pretended such coyness appeared to have begat a chimera which stalked his mind, or so I bethought. Some such beast must have roused these ill-formed alchemical mutterings he had but lately voiced.

Having paid the waterman sixpence for his trouble, I strolled from the stairs to the pleasure gardens where there was already much ribaldry in evidence, it being another bright June day. Thence by foot to the lodgings that had lately served Monsieur Vouet. The constable's watchman admitted me at my first insistence and I was pleased to find that Hudson had provided him with victuals for his sojourn.

'What is your trade?' I asked the young fellow, having ascertained that all remained undisturbed within.

'I'm by way of a man-at-arms for Mr Hudson, sir,' he replied. 'I keep the order if there be trouble about his tavern.'

I could see he had the strength and roughness for such business, which suited my purpose nicely. For now, however, I preferred the place to myself. 'You might take a respite while I'm about my work here,' I suggested.

'If you be tarrying, sir, then I'd be minded to take some air, sir, and a beverage.' And upon my confirmation he was gone.

When I was alone I began to put my mind to the business before me. There was much to be done and thoroughness was the key. My task was to locate Delaney's missing manuscript if it lay within the building; if not, then I must mark the thief's tracks in order to retrieve the artifact. The former appeared to me unlikely but that was where I must start.

My first thought was to pace the dwelling once more in order to form a stronger impression of its layout. There were, as I had previously observed, two small rooms forming the lower floor, these two separated by the stairway leading to the upper chamber. The front parlour was conveniently if somewhat sparsely furnished for a gentleman, with some seating, a writing desk and a table suited to the taking of a meal. The rear, meanwhile, was marked for the domain of the servants. Beyond, at the back of the building, was a yard with provision for the disposal of night soil and access from thence to a rear alley. Here was a route by which servants might have made an escape, I observed with some hope.

Returning within, I took the narrow stairway once more to the upper chamber. Save the absence of a body, this was as it had been the first time I saw it in Delaney's company. The chamber occupied the complete depth of the building with a bedstead at the rear and to the fore an area more carefully appointed for study. It was here that the intruder, abetted subsequently by Delaney, had wrought the most havoc. I picked my way cautiously through this disorder towards the front of the building and to a narrow window giving on to the street below. Only when I reached my goal did I spy the small opening in the side wall to the right of the window. There was a second staircase. This latter was built into the space of the adjacent building and its presence was almost completely hidden except from where I now stood.

The second staircase was narrower than the first and led to a low garret beneath the rafters. The room fashioned from this space was equipped with another truckle bed and other mean furnishings from which I deduced that I had found the sleeping quarters of a second servant.

It was while I was examining this garret that I heard a door creak below and then the sound of somebody moving cautiously. Thinking this was the watchman back somewhat swiftly I made no haste to return below and I suppose I made little sound as I perused the dingy upper chamber, so little indeed that after a few moments I heard a rustling in the chamber below and then the whisper of feet on the staircase. But instead of the watchman's, the head which appeared from the stairway was that of a young girl. We stared into each other's eyes, like animals crossing one another's paths in a forest, and then with a start she was gone. I raced down the stairs in pursuit, calling in vain to her not to fear me. By the time I reached the rear yard and the alley behind, she had disappeared. My sole consolation was the conviction that this girl was one who had served Monsieur Vouet. No doubt she had seen the watchman leave and had imagined it safe to return. I was confident that in time she would be found and I would learn something from her of the events of that evening first-hand.

I returned indoors again and being now upon ground level, I resolved to begin a closer examination of the premises among the utensils and paraphernalia of the rear parlour. There was disorder here too, but it was the child of slovenliness. I found a fowl so spoiled it must have been inedible ere Vouet's soul had been severed from its mortal body; other poorly preserved foodstuffs, too, betrayed themselves by their rank odours. Besides this there was an accumulation of detritus upon the floor, a history of carelessness. Rats had found rich fare amid this squalor and I heard several scuttle away as I made my examination. This was, I quickly convinced myself, no place to hide a thing of value such as Delaney sought. Vellum concealed here was as likely to be consumed as preserved.

The front parlour was a paragon of order in comparison with what lay behind in the scullery. There were books, including a handsomely bound Latin Bible and various works of natural philosophy; several indeed were in French and Dutch vernacular from which I deduced that Monsieur Vouet had been widely travelled. Clearly, though, Delaney's manuscript was not among them; if it had been he would have located it already without the need to call me. And, though I searched carefully, I could find no niche in which such an article might be secreted beyond his discovery.

The upper chamber had held the most interest for Vouet's intruder and it was to this that I next addressed my attention. I found several more books there, discarded carelessly upon the floor, as well as scattered papers that clearly formed a species of journal which Vouet had kept. These I collected and put in order that I might peruse them at my leisure for any clues they might contain. The upturned chest I righted and carefully repacked with the clothing and other traveller's artifacts that I found scattered round about it. Then, having returned the place to a semblance of respectability, I began to search for any secret hide-away. My search was in vain. Beneath the bed, between the joists, there was nowhere I could discover within the chamber convenient for the missing object to be stowed.

Finally I ascended to the garret. Again I found no manuscript, nor even a sheet of vellum, though I did find a small cache of coins, perhaps to the value of two sovereigns. This, I presumed, was the prize that had drawn the servant girl back. It was nothing of mine, so I let it be.

As I had supposed, my examination of the building had yielded no secret. My first presumption was correct: the intruder had taken the manuscript, exactly as Delaney had feared. But what clue was there to lead me to this intruder? What was the history of this crime? I resolved that if Delaney desired me to retrieve his artifact he would have to reveal to me its nature and background. Therein must lie the motive and the means.

So thinking, I made my way cautiously from the garret to the bedchamber below and was crossing the room to collect the sheets of Monsieur Vouet's journal when my progress was arrested. Perhaps the light had changed, or maybe my disinterestedness gave rein to some unconscious faculty; whichever, I saw Vouet's travelling trunk with different eyes. I recognized it for what it was. This was no ordinary trunk but the work of an artisan from Leiden whose craftsmanship I recognized in spite of its plainness. And knowing its author, I knew also that somewhere within there was a hidden compartment.

This revelation produced a quickening of my senses yet also a quiet-ness within me as I focused my resources on the trunk. There would be a puzzle to be solved before the hidden treasure could be revealed.

Quickly, I unpacked the contents which I had so carefully replaced a little time before. Then I examined the interior. My curiosity soon revealed that this interior was in depth some four inches short of that of the exterior. There was, indeed, a compartment within the base.

I upturned the trunk but the bottom showed no obvious means of entry. The key lay in the skill of the carpentry. Slowly I perused the exterior, searching for panels that would move this way or that. And finally I saw one that was not quite true. A pin held this narrow panel in place. When I removed the pin, the panel slid easily, then a second, third and fourth. Eventually the bottom panel was free. I slid it open with a sense of anticipation.

The space inside the compartment was packed tightly so that its contents would not betray their presence by their movement. From within this cavity I removed a small, bound Latin volume, surely the work Delaney sought. There was also another bound journal – at least I assumed it was such for it was written in a language which I could not immediately recognize – some correspondence and a little wooden box. Inside the box were two glass bottles, each carefully sealed. They contained a fine grey powder and upon each was inscribed the legend 'Manna of Saint Anthony'. I knew not what this meant.

I had seen an old leather bag in the parlour below. This I fetched and into it I placed all the items which I had discovered, along with the sheets of Monsieur Vouet's first journal. My afternoon's work has progressed satisfactorily after all, I congratulated myself, as I awaited the watchman's return. I had need to speak to him again.

I was not required to loiter long before the young fellow appeared, the smell of ale about him. I cared not. In truth his watch was no longer required but I charged him to locate the serving girl with as much haste as possible, promising to return in two days for news. It seemed to me, although my primary commission was complete, that the murder of Monsieur Vouet should be avenged with all possible haste.

Having thus delivered my orders I set out to return across the river and to Pall Mall. There I would be able to relieve Delaney of his present anxiety. I hoped he would thence recover his former humour.

It was evening by the time I was shown once more into the gallery in Lady Villiers' house, the same gallery in which we had met but two days earlier to witness an alchemical transmutation. Delaney kept an elaboratory here in which he pursued his chemical enquiries.

'I have it,' I told him at once, not wishing to prolong his distress one moment longer than necessary.

'Show me,' he replied excitedly, as I laid the leather bag upon a table and began to unpack its contents. But when I placed the volume in his hands his face immediately fell. 'This is not the manuscript I was to receive from Paris,' he told me without even opening it.

I was perplexed. 'You are sure?' He nodded. 'Then what is it,' I asked, 'that makes it worth secreting?'

Delaney perused the volume, but with no enthusiasm. 'I cannot say,' he replied at length. ''Tis esoteric, but a work of little merit. Perhaps this?' He indicated an inscription. ''Tis from the library of the great Van Helmont whose wisdom in the chemical arts remains legendary.'

'Then I have failed,' I admitted, crestfallen, my earlier elation completely drained.

'Not yet succeeded, I would rather say,' Delaney corrected me. 'But tell me how you came by this book.'

At that, I explained about Vouet's travelling trunk and then displayed the items I had found with the book.

The wooden box with its two glass bottles meant no more to Delaney than they had to me. 'They are almost certainly relics of the saint,' he suggested, taking one of the bottles in his hand. 'I have long suspected Monsieur Vouet to be of the Roman faith and he dealt in all manner of arcane and devotional objects.'

'Is not My Lord Illminster also of that faith?' I observed, but Delaney only nodded distractedly as he placed the bottle back into the box.

The correspondence he glanced at briefly then put aside, likewise the sheaf of papers upon which the Frenchman had written his journal. However he took somewhat more interest in the second bound journal. 'Have you examined this?' he asked me, at length.

'Briefly,' I replied. 'But I made no sense of it. Why do you ask?'

'I believe it to be written in a cipher,' he answered, handing it back to me. And when I examined the book again I found that there were elements that might fit that description. 'You must try your mathematical skills against it,' he added.

I nodded and began to pack all back into the leather bag once more, for I intended to study closely each of these several items including this journal. As I did so, I proceeded with my determination to question Delaney further.

'If I am to help you, Robert, I need more information,' I told him. 'You must confide in me. How am I to discern who would have designs on this manuscript if I know not what it is, nor what it contains?'

But Delaney remained obdurate. 'It is not possible,' he once more insisted. 'To tell you more would be to dishonour a trust I value highly.'

Hearing this, I was moved to throw the matter back into his arms. Why must he be so impossible? But judging him to be honest, and a friend, I allowed I would persevere a while longer.

'Then tell me at least about Monsieur Vouet,' I persisted. 'How did you come to make his acquaintance?'

'He was a traveller of renown, a frequent guest at courts across Europe, an especial friend of the learned. He has visited these shores three times, these three years since the King was restored, to my certain knowledge. I was introduced to him during one of those visits.'

'By whom?'

Delaney hesitated for a moment. 'My Lord Illminster,' he finally admitted.

'And did Lord Illminster have business with him this visit?' I asked. Though I did not mention the coach we had both espied he knew that was the purpose of my question.

'I cannot say,' he told me, but again there was in his voice a sense that he might say more if he chose.

'What was Monsieur Vouet's business?' I pressed. 'Was he an intelligencer?' For in truth I had began to wonder both about the man and about the nature of this esoteric manuscript he had been carrying.

'He was certainly an intelligencer among the virtuosi, but as to matters of government ...' He shrugged. 'It is possible. I know him only in the former light. Perhaps the cipher will reveal more.'

'Perhaps. When did he return to London?'

'He sent word to me three days ago, the day before we met here. That is all I know.'

'Tell me this at least, then. When were the arrangements regarding the manuscript made? How long has it been expected?'

'These three months.'

Three months. Time enough for a world of scheming.

There was much yet to be learned I could see. But no more, I feared, would be pried from Delaney, not today anyway. Picking up the leather bag containing the collection from Monsieur Vouet's travelling trunk, I prepared to leave.

'You must dine with us soon,' Delaney urged me as I made my farewell. 'My sister has especially requested your company. Tomorrow?'

'Please thank Lady Villiers and assure her I am ever her servant. But not tomorrow, Robert. Tomorrow I must be at court.'

CHAPTER 5

The Chambers of Whitehall

I dressed with care the following morning, having instructed Martha the night before to prepare apparel convenient to my attendance at court. She had put up a good linen shirt trimmed with lace, a fair pair of breeches and my new velvet cloak, all which pleased me well. I settled, then, upon plain leather boots which fitted neatly to the knee and showed a wide cuff as looking agreeable over my best silk hose. The outcome was, I do believe, becoming. By and by, I also told the girl to trim my hat with fresh ribbon for there was one with a discerning eye whom I wished especially to impress.

Of the latest enthusiasm for French periwigs I confess myself yet to be persuaded though the King and Duke are quite won over and where they go the court will follow. There is a clumsiness about this mode which offends my eye, not to mention a good deal of discomfort to the wearer. Or so I understand, not having ventured as yet thus far. Martha at any rate found no fault with my own curls for she boldly curtsied as nicely as any maid of honour before I sent her packing. I fear that girl's charms are ripe to bring trouble to some young man before this year is out.

There was business to be done and the time had come to do it. Taking up a long walking stick as more fitted to court than my rapier, I set off in search of a sedan. There was one to be had in Russell Street whence I was carried by Drury Lane and the Strand, past Charing Cross to Whitehall Palace.

The sedan brought me to the palace gate that stands hard by the Banqueting Hall. As I alighted I espied several coaches being brought out for a turn about the park. I was briefly minded to enquire who would take the turn, then resolved otherwise. My time could be spent more profitably elsewhere for I had much to achieve this morning. Though the day was still young there would already be found, beyond the palace gate, a bustling market in which intelligence was the object of trade. Here dukes and earls would touch their hats and speak in loud voices about matters of state; there lesser gentlemen, but maybe wiser, would keep closer council. As a matter of habit, I had need of such commerce.

As I crossed this first wide courtyard within the palace, I spied Sir Paul Neale who greeted me with warmth. Sir Paul was in company with Sir Robert Moray and they were both much occupied with the new society for natural knowledge to which the King has but recently granted a charter. I believe, too, that Sir Robert would have quizzed me about Monsieur Vouet's demise had I not excused myself with a flourish after a few moments. My immediate business was with Mr Killigrew, the comptroller. It was by his good offices that I hoped to secure payment of my pension.

This pension is no great matter, as I can easily explain. In the recent troubles there was need for men to make up their minds as to their allegiance. Being no lover of austerity and privation, I made up mine for the prince. I was subsequently able to be of some service to him during his exile and of greater use since his return. My pension, such as it is, is provided by His Majesty in recognition of that service.

I found Mr Killigrew in his chamber. As I had hoped, he was alone. There is a gloom about that chamber which I have long thought emanated from its occupant and I felt the same today. This latter was at his papers, a task which he was in that habit of proclaiming more onerous than any other man's. 'Tis a façade that serves him well.

'How goes it, Mr Wyld?' he greeted me, forsaking for a moment his chore.

'Well enough, thank you, Mr Killigrew. Well enough,' I replied, taking the chair which he proffered.

'Life in London is not too quiet for you?'

'No indeed. I find it quite refreshing.'

''Tis a shame, then, for I have need of a gentleman of your ability in Paris just now.'

'French business, eh? I wonder you haven't a dozen gentlemen of ability there already.'

'You know the business, Mr Wyld. There is rarely enough to be had, however many gentlemen are gainfully employed. But this is a matter of a particularly delicate nature which will require someone of your dexterity.'

'Nevertheless, Mr Killigrew, my presence is required here these coming days regarding a curious business of my own.'

'Ah, yes. I had heard something of the sort. Well, so be it. I dare say I can find another, more willing and more needful, to take the commission.'

'No doubt. But as you mention needs there is matter upon which we might touch. I mean concerning my pension. There seems to be no absolute routine for its settlement, but it would be convenient if some arrears could be made available if that should not prove too troublesome.'

Mr Killigrew waved an arm over his papers with a sigh as if to suggest the fault lay somewhere among them. 'You are remunerated by the Secret Service Fund, are you not?'

'By His Majesty's kindness it is so, yes.'

'I fear the fund is becoming so much subscribed there will be little left for our overseas business. The King finds he has many debts to repay. But that is by the by and for your ears alone.' He shuffled some of the papers before him, as if by such shuffling he would reveal the solution. 'If you could wait on me this day fortnight I believe I can accommodate you,' he told me finally.

'I will be at your service.'

'But I wish you were, Mr Wyld,' he admonished me with another sigh. 'I wish you were.'

I left the comptroller's chamber contented. Mr Killigrew would be as good as his word and I should be supplied with funds before the month was out.

There was much coming and going in the courts beyond his chamber as I emerged, the King having that moment returned from his morning perambulation in St James's Park. I quickly fell in with that part of his entourage in which I found some gentlemen with whom I was intimate. Among them was Mr Pemberton, a member of the Duke of York's household.

'His Majesty has outwalked us all this morning,' he confided to me in a low voice. 'Even the most eager of his subjects was left breathless in his wake.'

'Perhaps even the most eager considers it prudent that His Majesty should conquer in the field,' I suggested with a smile. 'The Duke did not join the party today?'

'His Royal Highness is not given to walking in his present mood,' he replied. 'I am sent instead as his eyes and ears. But you have been absent from court these last days so perhaps you are not privy to the most recent affliction to attach itself to the person of the Duke.'

'Is he unwell?' I asked.

'His spirit is troubled, certainly,' Pemberton replied. 'Come, walk this way awhile.' And with that he steered me towards the Stone Gallery in order that we might talk without being overheard.

'His Royal Highness fears he is to be deprived of the succession now that the Duke of Monmouth is at court,' Pemberton told me quickly, once we were beyond earshot. 'He has convinced himself the King has brought his son to court and created him Duke in order to teach him the life of a prince.'

'The boy was born out of wedlock,' I answered. 'How can he succeed?'

''Tis said there was a marriage. That the King married the boy's mother in secret and that he is the true heir. The King will not publicly gainsay the rumour and so all believe it to be true.'

'But if it is false, *why* will he not say so?'

'I imagine he considers it prudent to say nothing. Many fear that the Queen can bear no child and that the Duke or his heir must succeed. The Duke makes no secret of his communion and none outside the Catholic party welcomes a Popish succession. It suits the King to allow it to be believed that the Protestant Duke of Monmouth can one day take the throne.'

'And does he not confide in His Royal Highness?'

'He does. But the Duke is … the Duke believes he must suffer for his faith. He is, unfortunately, encouraged in this belief by the Queen Mother.'

I knew not what to say. That there had been no marriage I could vouch, but duty prevented me from repeating openly what I had learned while serving the King. Besides, this was not a matter with which I wished to be involved. Reputations were soon lost among the rumours at Whitehall and I had no wish for mine to be among them.

'The King is in rude health, as you have but recently witnessed,' I reminded him. 'Such talk of succession is premature. No doubt the Duke will find an understanding with His Majesty in due course. Now tell me, how fares the Duchess?'

Pemberton stopped and checked again that we were not overheard. 'She keeps her own council, but her father, the Chancellor's influence is in decline,' he whispered. 'The cavaliers rail against him daily. My Lord Bristol, who gains the ear of the King, has almost publicly vowed to bring him down. The Duke of Buckingham and My Lords Barkeley and Illminster, who are of the same party, have become the King's favourites while Sir Henry Bennet, much promoted by My Lady Castlemaine, is to become one with them now, it is said. This Catholic party has almost thrown My Lord Chancellor over.' He laughed. 'Now you know everything that has been spoken these last days except perhaps in respect of the one who truly interests you. But come, you are expected. We had news that you were to be at Whitehall today.'

I was on the point of demanding the source of this intelligence when I recalled the philosophical evening at Delaney's and My Lady Castlemaine. Then I laughed too. 'I must have become an important personage in my absence, Mr Pemberton, that news of my imminent arrival should be broadcast so widely,' I told him.

'Perhaps, Mr Wyld, perhaps.'

By now we were approaching the Duchess's chambers and I felt a flutter of anticipation. For as Pemberton well knew, 'twas not the Duchess that I especially admired but one who waited upon her.

The Duchess was seated with three of her maids of honour about her when we entered the chamber, appearing from afar like a cluster of silken roses. They feigned indifference to our approach, but I knew it had been marked. On reaching them Pemberton and I bowed deeply, I sweeping the floor with my hat.

'Mr Pemberton, Mr Wyld,' the Duchess exclaimed. 'What a surprise. How gracious of you to visit us.'

'The pleasure is all ours, Your Highness,' I replied.

'Then please be seated, Mr Wyld, and tell us of the world beyond these gates. We see so little of life from our narrow windows. Miss Hamilton, make room for Mr Wyld. You may leave as you please, Mr Pemberton. The Duke, I am sure, has need of your counsel.'

Thus dismissed, Pemberton bowed once more and I found myself alone with the Duchess and her entourage. Most pleasing of all, I discovered myself upon a settle alongside Miss Rebecca Hamilton, the most delightful creature to be found within the palace walls. For a moment I knew not what to say.

'How goes it with you, Mr Wyld?' the Duchess asked.

'Middling well, Your Highness, thank you.'

'But you have been about some matter of a Frenchman, I hear. Is it not so?'

'There is some business yes, about a Monsieur Vouet.'

'Then you must tell us all the details,' she instructed me gleefully. 'They say he was struck quite dead by some dreadful poison and that his heart within his body was black as coal. Is that not what they say, Rebecca?'

'It sounds quite horrible, Mr Wyld. Quite horrible.'

Upon this excuse I was able to turn briefly toward my companion on the settle. The silk of Miss Hamilton's skirts, which I found brushing my fingertips, was of a cornflower blue, matching almost perfectly the colour of her eyes as I caught them with my own.

''Twas not so bad as you imagine,' I reassured her. 'But 'tis true he was quite dead when I first came upon him. Sir Charles Scarborough has found that his neck was snapped by some brutish assassin. But his heart was of a normal complexion when his body was opened. I saw it myself. The mystery lay in his stomach which contained a prodigious quantity of quicksilver.'

'How perplexing,' the Duchess told me.

'Sir Charles was able to essay an explanation, Your Highness, for the poor fellow was riddled with the pox and had ingested quicksilver in an attempt to rid himself of the affliction.'

'I hope you did not touch him, sir,' she warned me.

'Fear not, Your Highness, for I have contracted no contagion.'

'And shall his murderer be found?'

'I judge it unlikely,' I told her.

'Well, let us hope King Louis can spare him.'

With this and other tittle-tattle we diverted ourselves for half an hour or so, upon which the Duchess took a notion to a game of cribbage. There had as yet been no opportunity of a private moment with Miss Hamilton, but now it seemed she would not take a hand at the game so I, too, begged to be excused for I had no wish to gamble away an hour's worth of sovereigns.

'You may entertain Miss Hamilton then, Mr Wyld,' the Duchess told me with hardly a trace of amusement. For I gauged well that this had been essayed before my arrival.

We moved aside slightly from the gaming, far enough that we might speak in hushed tones without being overheard. But before pleasure was to be mine I knew I must bear some reproach.

'You have been absent so long we feared you had quite forgotten us,' Miss Hamilton scolded, as soon as she was, privately, able.

'But I have not forgotten you,' I replied. 'How could I?'

'I know not but that you forget me as soon as my face is no longer before you,' she replied sharply. 'You have sent no message these three weeks and more.'

'And I am at fault. Yet I fear I had no choice for I was charged with an errand which took me beyond these shores and from which no message could return more swiftly than myself. Can you forgive me?'

Miss Hamilton looked at me directly, then dropped her eyes. 'I believe I am foolish enough to forgive you anything,' she whispered. 'To which country did you travel?'

'For your ears only, but 'twas to Holland, to Leiden and Delft.'

'I have heard that those towns are most pleasingly disposed as to aspect and proportion.'

'I found little pleasure within them myself for I was travelling constantly that I might fulfil my obligations with the shortest delay.'

'Well, I am pleased to see you safely returned.'

'And I am pleased to find your countenance fairer even than the one I implanted upon my mind ere I took to the sea.'

'Now you are making love to me,' she replied, blushing. 'And I have not given my consent.'

'Must I always ask your consent?' I replied, grazing the back of her hand lightly with the tip of my finger.

'Why, Mr Wyld, I believe you must,' was her response, but she made no attempt to withdraw her hand. 'Now for your sins you must tell me more of this poor dead foreign gentleman. Have you quite done with him?'

'My interest is not entirely concluded,' I admitted. 'For he was an odd fellow. But I would not talk of him. 'Tis you that occupies me chiefly. Now that I am returned I would serve you in any way that I can. Only tell me when I may wait upon you.'

'I am much obliged, Mr Wyld, but we are much confined these days. His Royal Highness is little disposed to pleasure of late and we are all under that spell. I fear you will have to content yourself with such stolen whispers as these.'

'I would be content that we might simply inhale the same air,' I assured her with a smile. 'For the most sullen chamber is sweetened by your presence.'

There was much more, indeed, that I wished to say, for in truth I felt myself in a heat of passion. And I believe I might have opened my heart had the Duchess not become bored with her gaming and sought other sport.

'Miss Hamilton,' she called some moments later. 'Mr Wyld, forgive me, but I must take this lady away from you or you will make her so soft as to be useless.'

And so I bowed, low as ever, and took my leave. For I was contented that our interview had passed with as great a success as I could have hoped.

CHAPTER 6

Lady Castlemaine's Table

I left the Duchess's chambers in high spirits intending to take a sedan back to Covent Garden, but I had barely found my way into the Stone Gallery when a page appeared at my side and placed a note in my hand. I thought – I dreamed briefly at least – he brought some pre-arranged token from Miss Hamilton, but when I broke the seal and as I read the contents, all images of love evaporated from my mind.

The note was from My Lady Castlemaine and in it she begged me attend her in her chambers at my earliest convenience. I understood at once that my passage through the palace had been marked; no doubt the boy had been instructed to await the conclusion of my audience with the Duchess before delivering his missive. There was no question but my presence was desired now. I would be a fool to ignore such a request. Yet that was my first thought.

My second was that my first was indeed foolhardy. It was said that My Lady was the most powerful woman in the land; I tutored myself to tread carefully. It was also said that intrigue was her metier and men were her meat. In what capacity would she desire my services?

My Lady had recently installed herself in the Duke of Ormond's lodgings, the Duke being about his business as Lord Lieutenant of Ireland. These lodgings were located close by, just beyond the Privy Garden which lay adjacent to the Stone Gallery. Folding the single sheet and tucking it into the pocket of my breeches, I walked slowly up and down the gallery, fondling again briefly the sweet memory of my recent interview. Then, upon a sudden determination of my mind, I strode out firmly through the garden, past the parterres and sundial to her door.

When I was shown into her presence, I discovered My Lady was preparing to dine. I was somewhat surprised to find she intended to sit down alone. That was but my folly, for I soon discovered that a second place was already laid. How finely she judged her position.

'My Wyld, how kind of you to come,' she exclaimed upon espying me at the threshold.

'I am ever your servant, My Lady,' I replied, bowing at the extravagant vision in which she appeared before me.

My Lady was indeed a wonder to behold. She was got up in crimson satin of the severest cut, pulled in about the waist and low across the bosom which was barely hidden by a gossamer shawl. With her oval face and dark eyes, surrounded by a sea of dark curls, it was no wonder the King was enthralled by her. Now, I feared, that charm was to be turned upon me.

'I hope you found the Duchess in good spirits this morning?' she continued, taking me by the arm and steering me across the chamber.

'Indeed, My Lady, I believe she was.'

'And Miss Hamilton has quite forgiven you, I hope?' she asked, somewhat mischievously as I thought.

'She was kind enough to spend some moments with me, by the Duchess's leave.'

'Then she is a lucky woman, Mr Wyld, for 'tis my judgment you cut as fine a figure as any gentleman to be found in London.'

'You flatter me, My Lady,' I replied, fearing I showed a little flushed.

'Fie. Were I so fortunate as to find myself in Miss Hamilton's situation I should be quite as pleased as she to whisper sweet words in your ear. Indeed I would.'

'Now you mock me,' I complained. 'For I should swiftly find myself despatched to the Tower, or worse, before that day was out.'

'You believe His Majesty would care a fiddle? Then you are sorely misled. He is so taken with Miss Stuart of late that I must find solace in needlework and quiet contemplation. Can you imagine that?'

'I cannot,' I confessed, and indeed it was impossible to imagine the lady before me pursuing such simple pleasures.

'But come, Mr Wyld. I am about to take some plain fowl and I beg you join me, for then I may for once not dine alone.'

Fowl there were indeed, though hardly plain. But before they were served I found myself entertaining a plate of crayfish accompanied by some fine French wine. And with the fowl arrived some cold beef and a bowl of Spanish oranges. In spite of her avowedly monastic existence, My Lady retained a healthy appetite.

'I am glad you found the Duchess in good health,' My Lady told me, as she broke apart the fowl. 'For I fear she must be much disturbed at the charges which are laid daily on the account of the Chancellor, her father. I would fain comfort her as her friend, but the Chancellor loves me not and I mark well that Her Highness must respect his wishes.'

'It is true then, that he is to fall?'

'Is that what you have heard?'

'I have heard said that My Lord is wise,' I replied cautiously, for it was my understanding that the regard in which the Chancellor held My Lady was reciprocated. 'But that there is no place for such wisdom as his at court.'

'They say many things, Mr Wyld, some more just than others. Nevertheless I find that the Chancellor has few allies and many enemies. 'Tis not a receipt for success.'

'And do they speak of a successor?'

My Lady eyed me a moment. 'Ha, you would make a fine courtier yourself, I see. But you shall not have it from me for I have heard no such talk. Perhaps that will be of some consolation to the Duchess.'

I began to muse over this awhile as the servants brought in another plate but my reverie was soon halted.

'Come, let us raise a glass,' said My Lady, lifting her goblet and catching my eye.

'To whom shall we drink?' I asked, raising mine likewise.

'Why, to His Majesty. Long may he reign and happily may he lie abed.'

Thus we continued for another hour in such a vein as My Lady chose, during which time I found that I had quaffed more than was my custom, though not so much as to leave me open to foolishness. Finally I bade farewell and stepped once more into the clear afternoon air. I drank of it deeply, hoping that I had remained uncompromised. For I knew, in all, that My Lady had a purpose by this meeting and yet its nature I could scarcely divine.

The day was still fair and I bethought to walk back to Covent Garden for I found there were fumes within my head which I had need to dispel. As I strode along Whitehall I could not but register a degree of uneasiness in respect of these recent events and what they might portend but by and by that passed. I had kept my wits and played my part with good humour, leaving as I believed, no hostages save one. My visit would soon be reported about court. Let it be so. Perhaps such speculation as it would engender could uncover the purpose that so far eluded me.

It took me about an hour to walk back to my lodgings during which time I was given cause to poke with my stick one or two scoundrels who thought to accost me. The exercise proved entirely beneficial to all and I arrived home quite restored. Upon arrival I called Martha to undress me and lay out some plainer garb for I had determined to return to Southwark before the afternoon was over.

Having wiped some dust from my face and refreshed myself with a glass of small beer I dressed, belted on my rapier and was on my way again, taking a wherry from steps below the Savoy Hospital on the south side of the Strand. The waterman took me swiftly downstream, the tide being on the ebb, and I was soon standing once again on dry land, close by Southwark.

My destination was the tavern presided over by the constable, William Hudson. 'Twas the constable himself I sought. If my instructions had been followed, he or the brawny fellow he had engaged to watch over Monsieur Vouet's lodgings would have intelligence for me concerning the servants that had waited on the unfortunate Frenchman.

The tavern was named the Boar and Bear and it was as filthy a den as you could wish to visit. The sawdust upon the floor was black and in my estimation had not been tended for a month; it stank both of the swill the establishment served and of the urine produced by its consumption. Yet the squalid nature of the surroundings appeared to have but little impact on its custom. I found the place to be a bustle of rowdy townsfolk. There were tradesmen and their stout wives mingling with harlots and gentlemen of a poorer sort while from the darker corners shone the bright eyes of some rogue seeking trade.

I found Hudson at a bar upon which glasses of beer and wine were being drawn by his servants. He was seated on a high stool, a perch that provided an outlook on every transaction taking place before him. His features, as he oversaw this business, were set in an ugly scowl.

The constable seemed not to recognize me at first but all at once his eye ignited briefly, the thought of his sovereign no doubt firing his mercenary imagination. Then his countenance resumed its normal appearance.

'I wus a' wondering when you might 'ave bin returning, sir,' he greeted me sullenly. 'Your business bein' over, as the lad tells me.'

'Here.' And I tossed two sovereigns upon the counter. 'For your troubles. Pay your man out of that, too, if you please.'

'Thank you, sir,' he grunted, surprised. 'And will I be getting you a beverage, sir?'

'I'll take a glass of sack, if you have one,' I told him.

He poured the wine himself and fetched the glass over to me directly.

'Now,' I said, not yet touching the wine, 'do you have the information I require concerning the whereabouts of the servants of the unfortunate Frenchman?'

'Well, sir. I can't say as I haven't. But to tell you the truth, sir, I had to put myself out, as it were, by way of payment for such information as I was able to acquire.'

'And what did your money buy?' I demanded.

'I believe, sir, I have intelligence of the present whereabouts of the wench that kept house for the foreign gentleman.'

'And where would that be?'

'Well, sir, if you could see your way to reimbursing me, as it were, I'll just get my lad to take you there straight away.'

'You are a rogue, sir,' I told him plainly, tossing another gold coin on to the counter. 'Next time I might wring your neck for your impudence.'

'Now, sir, there's no call to be intemperate,' he complained, snatching up the coin for fear I might take it back. 'The lad will be coming along, by and by.' With that he returned to his perch leaving me to quaff my measure of sack alone.

Hudson was a man of his word, his account having been settled. Within a short span I was without the infernal tavern, the young fellow who had watched over Monsieur Vouet's lodgings at my side.

'I suppose you can find a hackney?' I demanded shortly, being still mightily vexed at the constable and of a mind to serve the man a sound thrashing.

'If I might presume, sir,' my young companion replied, ''Tis but a short step and like as not you'll find the woman gone if you make too much of our arrival.'

'So be it,' I told him with, I fear, little grace, judging it nevertheless seemly to take his advice.

That decided, he led me away to the east, crossing the highway which ran south towards Canterbury and Dover, then beyond until we found ourselves among hovels of the more unfortunate sort. We stopped finally in the shadow of one such dwelling.

'It might be convenient that I make myself known first,' my companion suggested. 'This woman is mightily fearful, sir.' And upon my acquiescence he disappeared down the side of the hovel, leaving me to finger the pommel of my rapier.

My guide was gone but a few moments. When he reappeared he beckoned me follow him. The path led along the side of what was a primitive, single-storey structure composed of wood and mud. At the back there was a door giving on to a mean scullery and through this door we passed. The dingy interior contained a low deal table with stools and seated on one of the stools was a hunched figure. The woman, for 'twas her, was from her features no more than thirty years of age but life had squeezed such youth as she may have possessed from her long ago.

'Please. Trouble not to rise,' I instructed her, for I could see she was intending to do so. In spite of my instruction she continued, no doubt obeying an instinct for deference beaten into her since she was old enough to be beaten.

'This is the woman as served the Frenchman, sir,' my companion told me. The woman nodded but said nothing.

'I'll not trouble you longer than I need,' I assured her.

'Why, 'tis no trouble, sir,' she told me, suddenly finding her tongue. 'It's maybe all the best for the telling, as I've heard say.'

So I sat myself down on one of the stools, having adjusted my blade, and bade the other two follow suit.

'It was you tended for Monsieur Vouet,' I reiterated.

'Well it was, sir, yes. Me an' the girl.'

'And you were there the night he was murdered?'

'Aye, we was. Both, sir.'

'Then I'd be obliged if you would tell me what happened.'

'What was it as you wanted to know, sir?'

'Perhaps you will start when Monsieur Vouet returned home that night.'

'Aye, sir. 'Twas late, sir, but no later than often 'e'd be.'

'And how long after that before his assailant arrived?'

'Well, there was two of 'em, sir, you see. Not gentlemen, they wasn't, but rough and ready if you see what I mean. They was expected, sir, that was the thing of it. 'Sieur Vouet had one of his packets ready. But when they was come in and he's given it to them, they had some sharp words and 'sieur Vouet went up the stairs. Then the big fellow followed him. We could hear the rumour of a further altercation, sir. Then, of a sudden, there was a sharp cry, like of an animal in pain.'

'What happened next?'

'That's just it, sir. There was a terrible banging and a throwing about and the other one, him being still in the parlour, goes racing up the stairs too. They'd barely marked us, but I knew it was a bad business and told the girl so. Then I 'eard 'im coming down the stairs again, rushing and tumbling like the Devil was on his tail, and I knew it was time to go. He came tumbling out the back after us, the smaller of 'em, cursing like a man possessed but he didn't know where he was. Next thing he knew, we was gone.'

'Can you bring to mind the look of either of these ruffians?' I asked.

'Now that it comes to it, I'm not sure as I can, sir.'

'Nevertheless you'll favour me by doing your best.

'Well, the one, like I said, was a big, ugly-looking fellow with a beak of a nose. And now I put my mind to it, he had the mark of the pox about him, too, I do believe, sir. The other, sir, I can't say, but that he had a guileful, villainous air. 'Sieur Vouet wasn't given to dealing with such as these, as a rule, sir.'

'And what exactly was this matter of dealing in which Monsieur Vouet indulged?'

'Why I'm not rightly sure, sir, except that he brought all manner of relics and preparations from across the sea. There was a need for such comforts, as he said, and if he didn't serve it some other would. Maybe he was right, sir, for there was so much coming and going as you wouldn't believe of coaches. Fine gentlemen, sir, an' ladies too.'

'And did you recognize any of these ladies and gentlemen?'

'Upon my honour, sir, I can't say as I did.'

I detected something of evasion in this answer but let it pass. 'Was he a good master, Monsieur Vouet?'

'I believe he was, sir. I've been here these three years and he never beat me above twice. Not that I see'd him above a month out of each twelve-month. But' – the woman hesitated – 'I don't know as I should repeat this, sir, bein' as I don't know the truth of it but the thing is this. I've heard it said that 'sieur Vouet could supply to those as had the need and the means a potion to dispatch a body to their Maker as if by nature.'

'Meaning what?' I asked, somewhat perplexed.

'Why with poison, sir, 'tis said, that left no trace. That don't seem quite right, sir, do it?'

'From whom did you have this?'

''Twas from my gossips, sir, but like I said I don't know the truth of it.'

This was strange intelligence, indeed. There was, it appeared, much yet to be learned about Monsieur Vouet. 'Was your master a Papist?' I asked.

'Why, I couldn't say, sir,' she replied abruptly, obviously alarmed.

I felt into my pocket and slipped a shilling on to the table. 'You have nothing to fear from me,' I told her. 'Now tell me, finally. When did your master arrive from across the sea?'

'He was here these last three weeks, and more, but for much of that time he lodged elsewhere, sir. I wasn't to say where, but if he was needed I was to send to a Mrs Benn by Leather Lane.'

Ah, I thought, the pox house.

For now I had wrung the woman dry. As I took my leave the evening was already closing in and I thought it wise to hasten to nearest the stairs by the river before night fell. There I bade adieu to my guide with a further shilling for his troubles. It was, I judged, money well spent.

CHAPTER 7

A Cipher is Decoded

Upon my return from Southwark that night I found that Delaney's man had called with an invitation. I was to dine with Lady Villiers in Pall Mall on Monday next if I would find it convenient. I instructed my boy Ned that he should go in the morning to thank Lady Villiers for her invitation and inform her that I would find such an arrangement to be entirely to my convenience. After that I supped on pig's cheek and ale, which suited me well following my evening's exertions, then took up a pipe and some tobacco.

I had by me the leather bag containing Monsieur Vouet's various effects. From it I drew at length the octavo volume which I had found in the Frenchman's travelling trunk, that same volume which Delaney had declared to be other than the one he sought. Delaney had dismissed the volume as being of little merit and yet Monsieur Vouet had chosen to hide it from the world in a place he considered safe. Why? I opened the tome and began to examine it as I took my tobacco.

The work was by one Eirenaeus Philoponos Philalethes and purported to be a treatise on the preparation of that philosophical elixir which so occupies our alchemists. Whether it be the work of a charlatan or an adept I know not and such was the ingenuity of the metaphor that I would challenge any rational man to make a like judgement. Nevertheless is was nicely writ and showed by its content that its author had been schooled in the classical texts.

There was, as Delaney had noted, an inscription on an inside page indicating that the volume had at one time belonged within the library of Jan Baptista van Helmont, the great iatrochemist. Van Helmont was a scholar whose method Delaney particularly admired, as I knew. So if the text was without merit, why had van Helmont kept it by him?

I was pondering this enigma when another, at once more troubling and more interesting presented itself for my contemplation. The octavo volume had been published by a London bookseller in the year 1654. Yet I knew with passable certainty that van Helmont had been laid to rest in the year 1644. How was such an impossibility to be explained?

Clearly it was not. But it seemed to me that this very impossibility lent the volume some merit, a merit that lay not in the text itself but in something else. Yet by my candle, this night, I could not discern its nature. So, by and by, I put the volume aside and calling the girl, prepared myself for bed.

The next morning I awoke to a dull, leaden sky. I have seen such skies hanging cold above the polders in Holland in winter. There was, withal, the smell of rain in the air. This being a Sunday it was not, I estimated, a day on which to venture abroad.

Having determined to remain at home, I called Martha to dress me, then took some whey with what remained of the cold cheek for my breakfast. After that I called the boy, who had returned from his errand to Lady Villiers, minded to tutor him in his grammar. When he was sat down I put him to recite some Latin which he read to me so nicely I decided to try him with my *Euclid*. This was a mistake for he has no brain for mathematics. Having boxed his ears twice for his stupidity, I resigned to putting geometry aside and sent him away. Then I set myself to private contemplation.

Monsieur Vouet had been dead these three days. In that time his body had been opened up for all the world to see. And yet I knew little more of the man and his secrets than I had before the philosophical evening at Delaney's. But secrets there were aplenty, pressing secrets in need of penetration if I was to advance in the matter of Delaney's manuscript. It was time, I conceded, to make a thorough examination of the contents of the bag I had carried from his lodgings.

I took up first the alchemical text of Philalethes and perused it again with great intent. Yet I knew not what I sought and not knowing, was still unable to find it.

The loose sheets I had found scattered about his chamber I took up next. These were, as I had already surmised, some form of memo-randum by which he maintained a daily record of his life. Vouet wrote in the vernacular of his native land but fortunately I was acquainted with the French tongue and thus able to interpret this record with little hindrance.

What I found was a miscellany of daily rituals. The Frenchman was meticulous in recording his consumption of food and beverage with a philosophical precision as to both number and size. From this I deduced among other particulars a recent fondness for Thames eels and burnt brandy. There were details concerning his travelling arrangements and destinations so I was able to discover that he had arrived in London from Genoa by way of Paris and Amsterdam and had crossed the channel some four weeks previous to this very Sunday in a Flemish barque. There were accounts of men he had met; he had discussed the moons of Jupiter with the astronomer Cassini in Genoa and optics with Azout in Paris. In this vein his final entry, fatefully unfinished, recounted our alchemical evening at Delaney's where he noted the presence of a dark, English beauty whose mystery he found most alluring. My own humble pres-ence, I noted with a passing smile, merited no mention.

Vouet's afflictions made several appearances. He was troubled by noises in his head and to combat such attacks took laudanum while his stomach was a further source of anguish. But as to his trade, of this I could find no evidence unless it be in some cryptic initials and the occa-sional alchemical symbol. Frustrated, I set the sheets aside.

Hungry for something of value I started next to examine the corre-spondence which I had also found secreted in his trunk. This comprised five letters, all in the same hand and none of any great length. They were written from London, but with no more of an address than the name of the city. They were dated and the dates showed they had been directed to Monsieur Vouet while he travelled in Italy and France in the months before his final visit to London. As to the contents, there was about them an alchemist's conceit and subterfuge in which the truth was hidden behind a veil of metaphor. And yet it was clear that their purport was to engage Monsieur Vouet to procure and deliver a certain elixir to the author and to deliver it no later than this very month of June. That, most likely, he had done. Or so it seemed to me.

As to the author of this correspondence, therein lay a further mystery.

The signature was clear to read: Aurum. This I took to be further alchemical subterfuge and I assumed that it was an alias. But it was impossible to imagine who chose to hide behind such an lustrous title.

There was one further item to peruse, the bound journal from the trunk which Delaney believed to be written in code. I took it up with the intention of examining the contents but the mixture of numbers, letters and hieroglyphs I found there so deranged my mind that I soon put it away again. I was in need of company and the rain having held itself so far in abeyance, I decided to take my change at Will's.

The coffee house was quiet when I arrived. Seating myself at the main table, I took up the sheets from abroad but found little in them to entertain me. Fortunately my plight was relieved by the arrival of Mr Dryden and his entourage. He is considered chief among the wits that gather there and the liveliness of the establishment was quickly enhanced by him and those several who followed in his train.

The party was occupied with the art of the play. Mr Dryden had his first comedy put on at the new playhouse this February past and is taken to be an expert in the form though his own effort was not, if I be any judge, a complete success. Indeed I found it to fall some distance short of his much praised paeans to our monarch. He did confess to some shortcomings himself but that has not dissuaded him for, as he vouchedsafed to me at the table, he plans a second of a Spanish flavour for the spring.

In all I found him to be in good humour and appetite. While we took some beef he made much sport with a tale of My Lady Castlemaine and Miss Stuart playacting a mock marriage at court in the presence of the King, which I had not heard. He told me also with great amusement that My Lady takes Miss Stuart to her bed, betimes, but whether to tease His Majesty or to serve him he would not say. All in all, it seems the King would have Miss Stuart yet she will not be had and he is driven to distraction.

Such raillery as this raised my spirits after my morning's close study and the comestibles filled my stomach so that I returned to my lodgings with my vigour renewed. Settling myself in my parlour I sent the girl for my pipe and tobacco and thus equipped I began to do battle once more with Monsieur Vouet's cryptic journal.

This journal was such a puzzling affair that I could, at first, make no more sense of it than I had previously been able. That it was, indeed, a journal was made certain by dates written clearly at intervals on its pages. But what it recorded remained unintelligible.

Much of this record was composed of letters, grouped as if in words, yet these words made no sense in any tongue with which I was familiar. Interspersed with these letters were series of numerals which might have denoted numbers or might have been yet more words in cipher. And often, usually at the start or end of a line, would be placed a symbol. Some of these I recognized as alchemical symbols such as those denoting the planets, others were unknown to me.

I myself had often found need for the secrecy of a cipher yet I found that experience to be of little help in reversing the process and breaking the code. Somewhat of the art of cryptology was, as I recalled, delineated by the Reverend Wilkins in his *Swift and Secret Messenger*. I cursed my luck at not having a copy of his book by me. Then, by and by, I determined to try whether I couldn't indeed penetrate the cipher by my own wits and skill.

'Tis said that a simple cipher can be broken by counting which symbols or letters appear most often. The English tongue favours certain of the vowels and it seemed to me that the French must show a similar propensity. Taking up a sheet and a quill I began to test this hypothesis against a page of Monsieur Vouet's journal.

Down one side of my sheet I wrote the abece in order and beneath it the numerals. Then I started to determine, for each in turn, the number of instances on that page. To my surprise this revealed a clear pattern within the abece. Of the numerals, however, I could make no sense by this.

Upon a sudden insight, I realized that I was dealing with two different ciphers, the one made up of the letters of the abece and the second of the numerals. At this I discarded for the present the numerals and concentrated on the letters alone. What had I found?

There is a simple code I have myself exploited called the Caesar code because, as Suetonius tells us, it was used by Julius Caesar for his private business. In this code the letters of the abece are replaced by other letters in a regular fashion such that, at its simplest, a becomes b, b becomes c, c becomes d.

This scheme would perhaps have served Monsieur Vouet to prevent a casual observer understanding his private journal. I could see that the first, simple, variant could not be correct, but by and by I used my analysis of the page to try and determine if there were some other ordering of the letters. Fitting the most common letter on the page to the letter e, which I had reason to believe was the case for the English tongue, I was able to construct at length a transposition of letters which at once released words of the French language from the cipher.

After an hour's labour I had a page of the journal translated. Not in total, for there were still the numerals and the symbols to place, but in greater part. What I found was a tradesman's record of trade. The notation was still cryptic, a species of shorthand, I divined, and yet the import was clear. There were places and quantities and costs and prices, all laid out in a ledger so that accounts could be tallied and orders placed and delivered.

This success drove me to attempt a second page from a more recent part of the journal, for the first I had chosen came from the front. Alas, my joy was shortlived, for my new abece produced no sense from this second page whatsoever.

Somewhat chastened I returned to the front and began to translate the page following the one I had conquered. This revealed the continuation of the record I had already found but then, part way down the page, all sense was lost. The cipher had changed. But now I had a clue for this discontinuity took place immediately following one of what I had taken to be plainly written dates.

Monsieur Vouet was, I believed, a rational gentleman. If he thought it prudent at intervals to change his cipher he would most likely use another of the same species. Upon this, I started to prepare a sheet to test the letter frequencies again but my preparation was interrupted by a further notion. What if the date, plainly writ, was also the key to the cipher? All it needed to convey was either a quantity representing the number of letters by which the abece was transposed or the letter which substituted the first of the abece. From one or the other the rest followed.

Within moments I had it. The number of characters within this date gave the distance by which the abece must be transposed to create the cipher. I tested it upon the page before me, with immediate success.

Then I turned to the last few pages of the journal, the pages which covered Monsieur Vouet's recent journeying. If there was anything of value to be learned relating to his death, it was from these pages I would learn it.

Rendered sensible to the eye, the journal now told me of Monsieur Vouet's business these months just past. He had purchased much while in Italy and had ventured within the Empire too, to Bohemia and the court at Prague as well as passing into the lands of the Sultan. But now I began to understand the niceness of his method. His merchandise appeared nowhere except, as I now divined, in the form of symbols, those very symbols whose meaning I could not yet comprehend. And where precise locations should appear, as addresses, or where the names of his sources and clients would normally be placed, there I found numerals. In sum, without two further keys, I had gained nothing.

Upon this realization I put the journal aside for I had not the temperament to continue today. In truth I knew not how to proceed further. And yet I was determined that by further application I should finally know Monsieur Vouet's business to the full. With that understanding I called Bridget and had her bring me a bottle of claret from my store.

CHAPTER 8

Mr Starkey's Elaboratory

A desultory sky still hung over London the next morning but a westerly wind brought welcome motion to the sullen airs of the city and the promise of change. I looked forward to the fulfilment of that promise.

As I was to dine with Lady Villiers I ordered Martha put out my black cloth suit. My Lady has of late dedicated herself to a sombre sectarianism which finds much to despise in the more ostentatious show of popular fashion. Whether this new dedication be occasioned by the death of Lord Villiers, this two years past, I know not but I do suppose it to be so. And though I am no lover of sectaries, for the sake of friendship it behoves me forgive My Lady's conviction.

I had much to discuss with Delaney today, so, before dressing, I prepared for our engagement by transcribing the strange symbols from Monsieur Vouet's journal on to a sheet. Delaney was well versed in the alchemical arts and would, I hoped, provide some explication as to their meaning. I slipped this sheet, together with one of the two glass bottles of grey powder from Monsieur Vouet's hiding place, into my breeches. These phials had now assumed great import for they were all I had of whatever it was in which the Frenchman dealt. And in truth I could not dismiss entirely from my mind the gossips' tale repeated by his servant.

At noon I sent Ned to find a hackney. He returned forthwith and I gave instruction for Pall Mall. 'Twas but a ten minute ride by the Strand and Charing Cross and the coachman remaining civil the whole journey I gave him a shilling, which pleased him well.

I found Delaney pacing anxiously within the hall, awaiting my arrival. He took me straightway to the gallery in which he maintained his elaboratory, for he was impatient to learn what progress I had made in the matter of the manuscript. He continued to pace as I told him the servant's tale of the assassins and of the gossips' tittle-tattle but when I explained my progress regarding Monsieur Vouet's journal he stopped. The significance of this latter he quickly understood. If the nature of the final package and identity of its purchaser could be found, his manuscript would once again be in sight. Upon this, I brought forth the sheet of symbols but my hopes of him were not fulfilled. He was able to offer little more than I knew already; that the alchemical signs for the various planets as the sun, the moon or Venus signified metals, namely gold, silver, copper and others less noble. Of the remaining marks he had no knowledge.

'It is no language in which I am schooled,' he confessed. 'I fear, indeed, that it be of his own devising.'

This seemed to me entirely probable. 'Then 'tis upon the numerical cipher that everything rides. If I can master that we may yet learn something of his business from those with whom he dealt.'

Delaney concurred, but without much enthusiasm of success. He was not, by nature, of an optimistic disposition and I fear he believed his manuscript now surely lost for ever.

''Tis not intractable, Robert,' I counselled him. 'By my recollection The Reverend Wilkins has delved into these particular matters in his *Mercury*, though I have it not by me. Should you have a copy, it would aid my purpose.'

This raised his spirits somewhat and he took me directly to his library where he was able to pull down the book after a few moments' perusal.

'By the by,' he said as he handed it to me. 'I am minded to visit Mr Starkey this afternoon for I have yet business with him. Will you accompany me and take his opinion of these symbols? He has a greater depth of knowledge in such matters than I.'

This struck me a profitable arrangement but we could discuss it no further before a servant appeared and requested we join My Lady.

It was a short step to the chamber in which My Lady was wont to take dinner and we were there in a moment.

'Mr Wyld.' Lady Villiers greeted me upon our entry.

I bowed.

'How goes it?' she asked.

'Exceedingly well, My Lady,' I replied, for in truth I felt in good spirits.

My Lady Villiers was, as had become her custom, decked in black. She was two years older than her brother, Robert, but her black gown, unrelieved by even a hint of lace, lent her the air of some severe and elderly matriarch. She had retained the strictest mourning garb these two years without ever graduating to second mourning so that her brother feared she would continue thus imprisoned for the remainder of her life. I cannot say that his fears were without substance.

'Come, be seated,' she ordered. 'Robert, you will manage the turbot if you please.' And she proceeded to ladle soup from a great dish, handing the bowls to us as she went.

'What is the news at court?' she asked with no little interest, as we began to feast. For while My Lady shuns Whitehall and makes a habit of condemning its frivolity and lustfulness she hungers also, like any beast, and must have succour for her scorn. I gave her my latest resumé.

'The King's bastard son, the Duke of Monmouth, is much in favour, My Lady. This has cast a shadow on His Royal Highness who I hear is sorely afflicted. His Majesty, meanwhile, has found a new distraction in the form of Miss Frances Stuart who is admired as a beauty by all and exceeded only by My Lady Castlemaine.'

'My sister will have time enough, then, for her scheming,' she retorted.

My Lady Villiers and My Lady Castlemaine were related through the late Lord Villiers, he being cousin to My Lady Castlemaine. Thus they regarded one another as sisters.

'She tells me in her letters that the Lords Bristol and Illminster are thick about casting down Lord Clarendon, the Chancellor, he being the only courtier who advises the King against the excesses to which this court sinks. And I do much suppose from her intimacy in the affair that she schemes with them to have him on his back. No doubt he has sinned, as have we all, but I wonder who there will be who will understand the matter of government when he is gone.'

'I did not think My Lady Castlemaine harboured any particular sympathy for such conspirators as these,' I replied, puzzled.

'No doubt they find a bond in the common cause,' she replied. 'For I do suppose she would exceed beyond all others. She spoke this very week of articles being prepared as to impeach Lord Clarendon for treason. Besides, I do believe my sister expects Sir Henry Bennet to have the Chancellor's place and he will surely serve her well.'

This set me to contemplating. I had heard recently that My Lady Castlemaine had converted, though whether it be true or no, I cannot say. But if all be as My Lady has told us, and her sister truly does conspire with these Popish schemers, then maybe there is some truth in the rumour, strange as it seems.

The arrival of a dish of roasted pigeons served to interrupt my reflection and while I took one and broke it apart, My Lady found another subject to be more pressing.

'Has Robert told you that we will extend our house, for it has already become too small, what with an elaboratory here and his library there. Who will be best to do it for us, do you suppose?'

'I believe Mr May is much admired,' I told her.

'I had heard so.'

'You know, Margaret, I may do it myself,' Delaney reminded her, somewhat peevishly.

'But you never will, Robert. You know that.'

'Indeed I do not know but that I can turn my hand to architecture as well as any man. What do you say, Francis?'

'If he sets his mind to it, My Lady, then you can be sure he will do it. The question is, can he set his mind to it, or no?'

'I see you have put your finger on the matter,' she replied.

I do believe, after that, that Delaney sulked.

'My sister can be insufferable,' Delaney told me later in the coach as we made our way to Mr Starkey's lodgings. 'I do so wish you would not encourage her.'

''Tis but some jesting,' I assured him. 'She means no injury. Besides, she is right: You will not become an architect.'

'Humph!' Was his only reply.

Mr Starkey was something of a specimen having come out of the colonies of New England to set up his elaboratory in London. His skill in the alchemical arts was much valued by Delaney, as I knew, but his mastery of financial matters was less sure and in consequence he had languished from time to time in debtors' gaol. He was, for the moment, at liberty but reclusive, so that it was necessary to hunt him down from one address to another. However we did, at last, locate him as having set up his elaboratory hard by the Tower. Mayhap he thought this convenient as to his next incarceration.

'My dear Mr Delaney and Mr Wyld, too. How do you do?'

'We do very well, Mr Starkey,' Delaney assured him, 'having come directly from my sister's board. How do you do?'

'I should not say well, but at least I am alive and that must count for something.'

'And do you make progress in those arts in which you excel?'

'I cannot say that I make progress, but if I had more time I do believe I could complete the volatilization of the alkalies after the manner of Van Helmont for I conceive I have mastered his method. The Philosophical Mercury occupies me too, and I have made some advances as to its purification.'

'Then I have something that may interest you,' Delaney told him. So saying he withdrew the ingot of gold of transmutation that had been wrought by means of Monsieur Vouet's powder. 'This very metal is the product of transmutation as myself and Mr Wyld can bear witness,' he explained. 'You will, I believe, find it conducive to your own pursuits to examine it by means of analysis. I cannot tell it from true gold, but maybe you have the means to distinguish the two and thereby learn something of the art of transmutation and of the stone.'

We were by this time within Mr Starkey's elaboratory which proved a storehouse of strange apparatus. Besides his alchemical furnace there were tables bearing glass alembics of several sizes and other glass vessels, some containing liquids of various colours. Ranged about the walls were shelves upon which reagents and powders resided in prodigious numbers and the corners were darkened by strange metal contraptions whose purpose I could scarcely guess. And from the shadows I spied, also, a young assistant who was watching us.

Mr Starkey took hold of the ingot and carried it to a dusty window, the better to examine it. 'It has the lustre of gold,' he remarked, 'and I suppose the density. How was it wrought?'

'Why with but a hundred grains of powder.'

'Then I think I had better make a study of it with all possible haste. What was the provenance of this powder?'

'Ah. There you have me, for its provider was much given to secrecy in the matter. Besides, he can speak no more for his neck has been broken these three days.'

Mr Starkey placed the ingot carefully upon one of his tables.

'Then God have mercy on his soul.'

'I hope God will indeed be merciful but I fear he may not. The circumstances are darkened by uncomfortable portents.' Delaney now produced a small flask of quicksilver. 'This was found to pollute his body, his being cut open. I have purified it, but I would fain know of its philosophical nature for its presence has disturbed me.'

'Sir Charles ventured a pox cure was the source,' I interjected, knowing Delaney's confusion in this matter.

'Sir Charles is not an adept, Mr Wyld, and cannot know the meaning of such signs. To my knowledge no similar case has been recorded, eh, Mr Starkey?'

Mr Starkey nodded as he took the stoppered glass flask and shook the contents gently. 'I will try it as to its purity with the regulus,' he told Delaney. 'You shall have my reply the day after tomorrow, God willing.'

'Excellent,' Delaney told him. 'Now I do believe Mr Wyld has a query, also, with which to tax you.'

I brought forth the sheet of symbols from my breeches pocket and placed it upon a table for Mr Starkey to examine. 'These are a code,' I explained, briefly. 'Each stands for … For I know not what. I believe them to be symbols representing items in which the supplier of the powder of transmutation dealt. Can you aid me with their interpretation?'

Mr Starkey looked at the sheet carefully for several minutes without speaking. 'Are they accurately transcribed?' he asked at length.

'I believe so.'

'Then I must confess that excepting the metals, I can provide no positive identification. The fact is, I have heard of their like before, described in the Jesuit Semedo's account of the Great Monument of China, and therefore would suppose that they be oriental hieroglyphs but as to their meaning, well …' And he made an expansive gesture as if to suggest that only the King of China would be privy to such arcane knowledge.

'Can you say what weight of meaning they might carry?'

'I fear not, Mr Wyld.'

I thanked Mr Starkey and folded the sheet before tucking it back into the pocket of my breeches. In doing so I found the glass bottle which I had placed there that morning and on an impulse I withdrew it.

'Mr Starkey,' I said, 'do you perhaps recognize this?' And I handed the bottle to him.

Mr Starkey took the bottle and examined it closely, reading out the inscription. "Manna of Saint Anthony". He looked at me then, directly. 'What is its provenance?' he asked.

'Why, the same as the other, from the lodgings of the Frenchman who supplied the powder.'

'And what is the import of these queries, Mr Wyld?'

'The fact is, Mr Delaney was to—' But before I could finish, Mr Delaney chose to interrupt.

'The fact is, Mr Starkey, I have put Mr Wyld to discover who killed the Frenchman, if he will, as the least I could do to honour his kindnesses to me.'

For a moment a look of disbelief fell upon the countenance of Mr Starkey but then he shrugged. 'Then you are a Christian, Mr Delaney.' He turned back to me. 'Do you have any knowledge of this preparation?' he asked.

'None,' I told him. 'Unless, perhaps, it be some species of poison.'

'Is that likely?'

'I cannot say so with certainty.'

'I think I can, for this is come out of Italy, 'tis my belief, where the people are prone to poison one another so frequently it is often hard to know who dies naturally. Unless I am mistaken this is as potent and secretive a poison as gold might procure.'

'Can there be no mistake?' I asked, for I was more than a little surprised to have my suspicions confirmed thus.

'Well, we are natural philosophers, Mr Wyld, so we may not speak of certainty, perhaps, but we will try the experiment, eh?'

So saying he beckoned over his assistant and, begging a shilling from Delaney, sent the boy to procure a dog. 'Be sure to bring back a fit creature,' he instructed. ''T would be a pity if the animal should drop dead of its own free will.'

Thus we left it, that Mr Starkey would feed the contents of the bottle to the dog and in due course he would be able to confirm whether the powder was indeed toxic. I left his elaboratory deep in wonder that Monsieur Vouet had dealt in so deadly a preparation and anxious as to the use to which it was to be put by that person for whom it had been procured.

Delaney suffered no such consternation, for he was unmoved by the revelation. In his coach, as we headed back towards Covent Garden, his concern was more after Mr Starkey's inquisitiveness.

'I would have him know nothing of the business of the manuscript,' he insisted when quizzed.

As to the cause of this reticence, he did not enlarge. But I had now formed a clear impression that Delaney's esoteric manuscript was alchemical in nature. And I began to understand that the society of alchemists was not very sociable.

CHAPTER 9

A Pox House in Leather Lane

Parting with Delaney, who left me by my lodgings before he returned to Pall Mall, I found myself much troubled by the import of what Mr Starkey had conveyed regarding Monsieur Vouet's powder. I had hardly believed the gossips' tale of death-dealing but now I must learn to expect that it was true. And while it still required Mr Starkey's confirmation, I began to think that the addition of this venom to our brew mightily confused the confection. For if Monsieur Vouet dealt in death in addition to his other business, then his situation in regard of those with whom he dealt must become much more precarious.

I found, withal, that I could barely settle again in my parlour and by and by, the evening still being light, determined upon strolling to Lincoln's Inn Fields to observe how work progressed upon the new walks and gardens. I was pleased to discover that the toil advanced exceeding well and amused myself for above an hour, venturing so far as to visit the puppet theatre where I judged the clockwork to be both admirable and prettily done.

Thus distracted, I remained in the Fields 'til sunset when the cloud which had lowered upon us all day broke sufficiently to the west to allow the final glow from the firmament to penetrate the gardens, lending them an evanescent lustre of gold. This raised my spirits and as darkness fell, I hurried away, stopping by Will's from whence I finally returned to my lodgings much refreshed.

Next morning broke fair and I lay till late, being in no mood for early exertion. Having breakfasted and dressed, I purposed to seek out a Mrs Benn in Leather Lane that I might at last determine whether Monsieur

67

Vouet had indeed taken a pox cure. For I would, if possible, lay this delusion of Delaney's regarding the quicksilver to rest.

It being no great distance, I chose to walk from the piazza by Russell Street and along Drury Lane. Eventually I found my way to High Holborn and thence to Leather Lane which lay upon the northern side of that thoroughfare, close by Hatton Garden. These gardens marked the furthest extent of London. Beyond, the country opened.

Leather Lane, as I quickly discovered, served trades of several kinds. I found a coachmaker, two shoemakers and a chandler before enquiring at an apothecary's door where, after some hesitation and the exchange of money, I was finally directed to the house I sought.

This house gave the appearance of a simple dwelling with no outward sign of trade. Upon my knock a well-kept woman answered and enquired as to my business.

'I seek the house run by Mrs Benn,' I informed her.

'I am Mrs Benn,' she replied cautiously, her eyes alert.

'In that case you would do me a great favour if you would tell me of your dealings with one Monsieur Vouet, a Frenchman who has but lately died.'

At this the woman looked mightily alarmed. 'I have had no dealings with any such person,' she vowed with exaggerated emphasis.

'Do you not, in this house, treat the pox?' I demanded.

I watched her hesitate before replying. ''Tis an efficacious cure as I have perfected, sir, as many a gentleman will tell you as has swived at the wrong gate.'

'I have no doubt as to its efficacity,' I assured her, at once comprehending the source of her dismay. 'Monsieur Vouet died from a broken neck.'

'Then why do you come here to frighten a being so?' she demanded crossly, and would have closed the door in my face had I not boldly prevented her.

'Madam,' I told her, though the appellation flattered the creature with whom I spoke, 'I will know your business with the Frenchman or I will be forced to enquire under what licence you practise your skills.' For I guessed that such a house as this was hardly welcomed by our learned surgeons and physicians who would have the business for themselves if they could.

This threat served its purpose for she sullenly invited me to cross the threshold and enter. I followed her into a parlour which was piled about with the paraphanalia of her trade. However, instead of stopping here to converse further as I had expected, she led me up a stairway at the top of which a door, upon opening, gave on to a large chamber containing what appeared to me to be a number of casks, each almost the height of a man. Several of them, indeed, contained men, for I found their heads to be emerging from the tops of these containers. A servant tended these captives, feeding one with water as we entered, while smouldering coals generated acrid fumes which hung about the place. These last I found to invade my throat and lungs and make me want for air.

'This was my business with the Frenchman,' the woman told me sharply, indicating as she spoke the row of casks before us.

I turned away from the sight immediately and retreated from the chamber back down the stairs, for I had no wish to ingest more of this foul mercurial air than I must. I understood at once that this was the fumigation cure of which I have heard tell. The corroded bodies of these pox-ridden souls were being bathed in the fumes of quicksilver as a means of arresting the progress of the canker.

At length the woman followed me and we returned together to the parlour from which I perceived she managed her house. I needed but little more from her and that I immediately sought.

'If you will tell me in what the cure consists,' I said, 'I will be on my way.'

'So now you would steal the secrets of my art,' she snapped.

'I care not for your secrets, madam, but I will know of Monsieur Vouet's cure. He resided here, I presume?'

She affirmed with a cursory nod.

'For how long,' I asked.

''Twas two weeks, though it should have been more. He would rest no longer than that.'

Two weeks in a barrel! I shuddered at the thought. What an accursed cure for an accursed disease.

'I understand something of this business,' I told her. 'But this I do not. Was he required to ingest mercury?'

Her response was a harsh cackle of a laugh.

'Do you suppose I can afford to fill them with quicksilver?' she demanded, from which I took the answer to be in the negative.

'He had quicksilver within him when he died,' I told her bluntly.

This moved her not.

'Then he must have arranged his own supply,' she told me. 'For 'twas none of mine.'

I left her at once, for I began to feel that house was affecting my brain. Yet I was exceeding baffled. Monsieur Vouet had, indeed, taken a pox cure. But this cure had not required him to swallow quicksilver. How, then, had he come by a gutful, unless he chose to procure it himself as the woman suggested?

I retraced my steps by foot from the pox house towards Covent Garden. My path took me across Bow Street, which reaching, I found there to be a commotion before the Cock Tavern, an establishment run by a renowned mistress, Oxford Kate. Upon the whim of my curiosity, I decided to investigate and, drawing close, was bemused to discover three of our finest cavaliers disporting themselves upon the balcony.

I soon perceived that one of that number was Lord Buckhurst who had not long since suffered to be tried under a charge of robbery and murder but had escaped punishment. With him I found Sir Thomas Ogle and Sir Charles Sedley. All had imbibed sufficiently to enable them to lose their minds and Sir Charles was proudly displaying his manhood for all to see while preaching the virtues of some powder he claimed would have the better part of the women of London lusting after him. Such profanities as issued from his lips and from those of his companions I forbear to repeat, but they were sufficient to incite the common folk attracted by the display to seek to break down the door of the establishment in order to thrash the three miscreants within. Entry not being effected, they resorted to hurling stones and at length drove the naked cavaliers into retreat.

The skirmish being over I continued on my way, reflecting as I went how the King would be pleased at this behaviour of his subjects. And it seemed to me that there was now a generation of our most noble houses that pretended no skill save the seeking of pleasure. No doubt My Lady Villiers would find much in the escapade to revile and I could not but recall her query as to who among these cavaliers surrounding His Majesty was capable of the business of government.

*

Returning to my lodgings I bade Bridget prepare me some nourishment and fetch a bottle from my store with which to wash away the taste of my morning's experiences. She had nought prepared but a rabbit pie which she, the boy and Martha were about to eat for their dinner. Not wishing to deprive them of their victuals I joined them in the scullery and supplied a glass of wine to each which resulted in much merriment, particularly from the boy.

I intended to repair then to my parlour but Bridget would have a word with me concerning Martha. It seemed that the son of one of our city men, having espied her in St James's Park while both were there awatching the pageant of the court, has set about pretending to make love to her.

'He's a beguiling young blade and will ruin her with his promises,' Bridget warned me. 'She is but a fool and will believe all he tells her. If you favour her, do her a service by speaking with Sir Richard Redding.' For this was the boy's father.

I promised Bridget that I would make the matter my business, at which she went away satisfied.

It was time, I knew, to try again if I could solve the Frenchman's journal. So resolving, I took up Delaney's copy of The Reverend Wilkins tome to apprehend, if I could, the nature of Monsieur Vouet's numerical cipher. There was much of interest written upon its pages and I perused it at length, but only one scheme seemed to me to promise fruit. This was, as I had learned, devised by Polybius, a Greek leader of Achaea taken by the Romans. It provided a means of writing letters as numbers, precisely as I sought.

Polybius's scheme was to arrange the letters of the abece in a square of five by five; thus a,b,c,d,e made the first row, f,g,h,i,k made the second row, l,m,n,o,p the third, q,r,s,t,u the fourth and v,w,x,y,z the last. Since this only allowed twenty-five letters one had to be dropped, in this case j. The secret of the cipher was that each row was numbered, as 1,2,3,4,5 and each column numbered also, as 6,7,8,9,0. Each letter was then represented by the of reading its co-ordinate by row and column. Thus A was 16 and z, 50.

What I have described but poorly represents one of an infinity of possible arrangements. The letters in the square might be rearranged is some more perverse order as, too, might the numbers used to mark their rows and columns. But the basis remains the same.

There was one further feature of this scheme and it was this which persuaded me I had found the basis for Monsieur Vouet's cipher. By Polybius's method it was possible to create a cipher utilizing five numerals alone by numbering each row as 1,2,3,4,5 and each column by the same numerals; 1,2,3,4,5. At this A became 11 and z, 55. This curious aspect caught my attention for I had marked previously that the series within the journal contained but a selection of all the numerals. Upon opening it again I was able to confirm that they numbered five, 1,3,5,7,9. There was a symmetry to this that seemed to me revealing of the nature of the Frenchman's mind.

I believed I had the method, but how to discover the exact cipher? On this issue the learned prelate offered no advice.

I must assume by this cipher that each letter was represented by two numerals yet many of the sequences within the journal contained odd numbers of numerals, no doubt with the intention of hindering. Thus I could not with ease begin to identify and count which pairs of numerals occurred most frequently, as I had formerly.

Was I, then, to try every combination? That must surely take me a lifetime and I had not one to spare. Perhaps there was a key within the journal? I searched but could uncover none.

I understood, finally, that I must find a way in, a clue. In short I must guess correctly the meaning of one of the sequences and, from that, derive the cipher by a reverse logic.

I filled a pipe with tobacco with which to soothe and concentrate my mind. Then I took up once more the journal and sought inspiration.

My mastery of the first code had enabled me to understand the form of this record and from its structure I could begin to guess what each series of numerals stood in place of; here a name, perhaps, while there a location. Monsieur Vouet's ports of call of past several months I knew from his open journal so I tried whether the names of any of these cities could provide entry. Alas, my trials proved fruitless, though I tested both Latin and vernacular spellings. What was I missing?

Frustrated, I called Bridget to fetch me another bottle though I knew it would muddle my brain. I felt that the solution to my dilemma lay at the edge of my mind and that if only I could draw it to the centre I would have my answer. Taking a glass, I paced up and down as I probed those outer reaches but that which I sought receded further into the darkness. At length I sensed it was gone.

The trick now, I knew, was to rid my conscious mind of this matter completely upon which I could expect the answer to emerge of its own accord. So thinking, I picked up a hat and took a stroll around the piazza where the stallholders were packing away their wares and battening down their stalls for the end of the day. Seeking refuge from the universal hubbub I, upon an impulse, entered the chapel which sits upon the west side of the piazza. Here I found both peace and solitude. The interior of the chapel was plain and unadorned, having been swept free of all ornament by our late Puritan fanatics. One item only hinted at the earlier ostentation, a cross of gold which hung above the altar. I sat on one of the rough pews that served as seating and stared at this cross for a moment, transfixed without knowing why. Then, with a start, I did know. It was the gold! For was not gold Aurum?

Turning on my heel I hurried back to my own door. I had, I believed, found the key which I sought. According to the Frenchman's own correspondence, a person using the alias Aurum was expecting a delivery of an elixir? If so, this name must surely be coded in the journal.

In my parlour I took up the journal again and tried whether I could match this key to any of the series of numerals. Within a few minutes I had succeeded and in doing so understood my previous mistake. Withal, Monsieur Vouet had chosen to write these names backwards.

This was not the end of my troubles, for I had yet but four of the letters placed upon the grid that held the cipher. I must now use these four to provide clues within other series of numerals and so, by stages, discover the complete key. But now I had started I would not stop and, taking betimes some cold rabbit pie to fortify me, I worked without break. It was well past midnight when I finally rested, satisfied.

My endeavour had, as I expected, provided a list of names and of places. Many of the former were foreign personages with whom I was not familiar, but among the later entries were names which related to Monsieur Vouet's last visit to London. Here were names that I did recognize. And after some trial I was able to locate pages of the journal relating to earlier visits to England and from these I garnered yet more names to add to my list.

Several upon my list I knew in person, many more I did not. Known or not, now I must find the means, judiciously, to persuade some among them to reveal to me their business with the late Frenchman. For against each name was a symbol or hieroglyph the meaning of which I did not yet know.

Among them all, one entry was an immediate cause for reflection. That referring to the mysterious Aurum. I had divined from the way the journal was drawn up that Monsieur Vouet had indicated within it when each transaction had been completed. That relating to Aurum was the first entry not marked thus. It was probable, therefore, that this was the fateful transaction.

There was also one absence. Nowhere in my list did the name of Mr Delaney occur. Was it conceivable then that he was Aurum?

CHAPTER 10

The Questor Unmasked

After such exertions as the deciphering of Monsieur Vouet's journal had entailed, I was not to be found abroad early next morning. Indeed, I was still abed when Mr Starkey presented himself at my lodgings.

'Send him up,' I instructed Martha who awoke me with the news. 'And fetch up some whey.'

Mr Starkey came up presently to my bedchamber and I installed him upon a stool that he might recite his tidings in comfort. For I guessed he was here about the powder.

'It is poison, without doubt,' he told me. 'And most cleverly wrought. For the animal lived one day and a further night showing no signs of distress. Yet this very morning it could not be woke so I do suppose it died in its sleep.'

'And do you suppose it would act in a like manner if administered to a man?'

'I would imagine so, save only that it might act less swiftly by the degree to which the human was larger than the animal. For I have opened the creature and though my skill is not great yet I can find no clear cause for death save an absence of animation.'

Martha had, meanwhile, fetched up a jug of whey and I began to sup some, having tendered a portion to Mr Starkey.

'So in short,' I proposed, 'this powder would render a man dead for all the world as if he had died naturally. Is that not your conclusion?'

'I believe, Mr Wyld, that such would be the effect of administering the powder.'

'Then 'tis a devilish concoction,' I told him.

'Indeed, I had not known before of its like in England. I do but wonder if some Popish influence is to be found in its arrival.'

''Tis not to be discounted,' I agreed. 'Do you know anything of this Frenchman, Monsieur Vouet?'

'I cannot say that I do,' he replied. ' But I have heard mention of such a Frenchman as this and have, indeed, sought him out without success.' He paused as if considering whether to enlarge on this curious claim, which at length he did. 'There is a matter I would discuss with you if you will,' he told me. 'It concerns a certain manuscript.'

At this I was mightily curious and bade him continue.

'I know not how well versed you are in the arts in which I practise but I imagine you are at least conversant with the alchemical cannon, how much is made of the Philosopher's Stone and as much cloaked in mystery and hidden in allusion in its manuscripts. Well, it is my belief that there is much of philosophical worth to be found in these works, much, indeed that may be placed on a sound footing if it can be systematically analysed. I will not trouble you with the sulphurs and the mercuries in which I deal, but in short the key rests in the Stone. Whether this be a miracle only accessible to those who can prove themselves deserving I cannot say. That, however, is the belief of the adepts who make themselves secretive as to what they know and hide their knowledge from the light of common men and as much from our philosophers.

'I have made some progress in this analysis of which I speak, but the final step, bringing with it the Stone, I have not made. Yet I am confident that it has been achieved in more ancient times as certain manuscripts tell. There is one manuscript, moreover, in which I believe the true method is revealed to he who would understand. The manuscript goes by the name of *The Book of Abraham the Jew* and though I know not of its origins, I believe it passed through the hands of a Parisian scribe, one Nicholas Flamel, some two hundred years, and more, previous to today. From thence it passed who knows where, but my own endeavours have led me to the late Cardinal Richelieu of France as being its most recent custodian.

'This manuscript I would examine for I am convinced it will enable me to complete my work. I have sought it long and I had thought to locate it once more in Paris. However my quest has been entirely hampered by secretive conspirers, these companies of adepts, who guard such works against the eyes of any but themselves.

'Even so I strive still, with some success. My latest intelligence is that the work will come to these shores to be delivered into the hands of one of our English adepts and that it would be fetched by a Frenchman such as yours. So you will understand that I am curious to know more of your Frenchman and his business if I can.'

I had listened to this tale in silence and when Mr Starkey had finished I remained silent for a moment longer. 'If you will allow, I would dress before I answer you,' I said finally.

To this he assented.

'Then if you will wait on me below, I will join you shortly,' I promised him. I hailed the girl while Mr Starkey descended. For in truth I knew not how to respond to his request.

Martha soon had me suitably attired and I bade her instruct Bridget to send something commestible to the parlour that I might eat. Upon that I descended and joined Mr Starkey once more, my mind resolved.

'Your tale interests me greatly,' I told him immediately, 'and I would help you, but upon my honour I may say nothing at present regarding the business of the Frenchman.'

'I may read something from that,' he told me with a wry smile.

'It is possible you will,' I conceded, smiling also. 'By the by, I have a question: would you kill to obtain this manuscript?'

'I should not,' he retorted, sharply.

'Please do not misunderstand me,' I pleaded, hurriedly. 'I merely wonder if one of these secretive conspirers would be so moved.'

'I find that hardly possible,' he told me. 'For if the secret be a miracle of God, as they believe, then to sin for it would be to ensure that the transgressor should never be privy to the mystery.'

'But,' I added, 'a conspirator might murder in order to disguise his possession of a lethal sedative, might he not?'

'I imagine that to be entirely likely,' he replied. At which I concluded our interview, leaving him to make of it what he would.

Upon Mr Starkey's departure I sat for some time deep in thought. There were now two mysteries to ponder, one of poison and the other of the manuscript.

I would have thanked Mr Starkey heartily if I could for he had told me what Delaney would not, the true nature of the object Monsieur Vouet had fetched from Paris for him. Of that I was sure. Upon this, I might conclude with a degree of certainty that the person responsible for murder was an alchemist.

Delaney? Though I could not be entirely convinced, I would not believe it was he. Even had I not known him as I did, the manner of the business made no sense if it were so, much less when the second issue was taken into account.

So, Aurum was not Delaney. In which case the secret of the manuscript was of such import that even Monsieur Vouet forbore to record the transaction. Thus I concluded.

Yet in truth I still knew little. In order to know more I must make enquiries of the people on my list, the names derived from the Frenchman's journal. Was there some common bond among them that led to him? What needs of theirs did he serve? In short, what was his business?

There was, by chance, one name on my list that it pleased me to choose as my first. It was that of Sir Richard Redding. I had business with him beside that of the journal, business that might ease the broaching of the latter. It was upon him that I now decided to call.

It might be imagined that the greatest power in this realm resides primarily in the person of the King, to a lesser degree in his courtiers and the population of his court and to some minor degree in the Parliament. Yet the greatest wealth in the realm resides not with the denizens of the court but with those who spent their time further down the Thames; that is in the City where the great merchants and their companies can be found. And to the extent that even a king can hardly obtain power today without gold, it must be agreed that within the City there also resides a considerable quantity of power.

His Majesty was not ignorant of this fact and most of the greatest of these men were knights of his realm. One of these was Sir Richard Redding. He was of the Mercers Company and his wealth was in cloth, much of it traded with the Indies. I knew him by reputation to be an honest man and it was to his mansion in Bishopsgate that I directed the sedan which I took from Russell Street.

I found, upon calling, that he was still engaged in corporation business at the Royal Exchange but upon enquiry there I found that such business as was being conducted was taking place in the Sultan's Head coffee house, whence I immediately repaired.

Upon entering and treading the stairs to the first floor, I found Sir Richard among a group of gentlemen gathered at the great board which ran along the centre of the room. He was engaged in some spirited debate and it was with great difficulty that I was able to convey that I had some private matter to discuss. Eventually, however, he consented to join me in one of the small, curtained booths around the perimeter where we might enjoy more privacy.

'I would speak with you of your son,' I began, after we had exchanged pleasantries. 'For he has been making love to the wench who serves me and it behoves me to ensure that she is dealt fairly.'

Sir Richard seemed much amused by this. 'Why, you must be the third such petitioner this month. I fear the boy makes love to every comely wench in London. His misfortune is to be handsome and they flock to him like lambs to their mothers. No doubt he follows the example of his betters, but I will speak to him. What, pray, is the name of this wench?'

I told him and he repeated his promise to intervene.

I had one of the servants bring us more coffee for our bowls and began to try whether I could draw him upon the other issue which interested me.

'Sir Richard,' I began. 'There is another matter which I hardly dare broach, except that I must. It concerns a French gentleman and traveller by the name of Monsieur Eustace Vouet.' Eliciting as yet no reaction I judged that I might continue. 'Monsieur Vouet was but lately murdered under circumstances that demand explanation and it has fallen upon me to undertake such enquiries as might supply this explanation. During the course of my investigation I have come to understand that Monsieur Vouet served as procurer for a number of patrons, among which number I have counted yourself.'

Sir Richard said nothing at once, but toyed distractedly with his bowl. 'What is the nature of you query?' he demanded, finally.

'Why, it is this, sir,' I confessed, 'I wish to know what he procured.'

Sir Richard appeared bemused. 'So you know not what he was?' he asked.

I nodded.

'Then tell me honestly, sir, who are you?'

'I answer to the King,' I told him. 'Though not in this matter. His Majesty is my benefactor.'

'Can you swear to make no use of what I tell you, save to satisfy your curiosity?'

It was now my turn to study the contents of my bowl. 'I can say this,' I replied at length, 'that if what you tell me has no material bearing on the matter of his death then it will not pass my lips.'

'I believe it will have no such bearing,' he told me.

'Then pray continue.'

'You will have to indulge me a little, Mr Wyld, for in order to explain this business, I must also explain its history. As you know I have a son. He is some twenty years of age, born to me of my wife in the year after we were married, that being 1642, as England began its descent into turmoil. I was already a merchant and she was of an Anglican family, noble by birth but not wealthy, so we made a judicious match. We were not touched personally by the troubles for business must continue whoever rules, but my wife was sorely tested by the religious privation forced upon her. In consequence, she sought refuge in such spiritual comforts as she could find and by and by that led her to the Roman Church.

'I have no personal love for this communion, but I did love my wife and in this I indulged her though it be a danger to us all. And so, in time, I came to know some of the subterranean ways by which the Papists operate.' Sir Richard paused and glanced about him to ensure we were not overheard.

'Two years ago my wife took a tumour. Oh, our physicians crowded around her. They let her blood. They applied their clysters. They administered their potions. 'Twas all to no avail. This growth sucked up her life. Knowing finally that death was approaching she begged me seek help on her behalf by way of an indulgence such as that church grants against punishment for her sins. These matters are not arranged easily within these shores, but, as I said, there are subterranean ways. One of those is Monsieur Vouet.

'Monsieur Vouet is a questor, and so it was to him that I went that I might satisfy my wife's wish. Money was paid, the indulgence was granted and my wife died, appeased, some twelve months ago. So there you have it, Mr Wyld. Monsieur Vouet procured for me an indulgence.'

I allowed myself to reflect upon the import of what I had been told before speaking. 'I am indebted to you, sir,' I told him then. 'And you may be assured that I will find no need to repeat what you have just vouchsafed.' And with that we parted.

Leaving the Sultan's Head I made my way back by the Royal Exchange, skirting the courtyard where a brisk trade was still being conducted at the multitude of stalls gathered there, and thence to river steps and a wherry upstream. Monsieur Vouet was a questor, eh? That was worthy intelligence indeed and made secure the Popish link which I had come to suspect.

Upon my return to my lodgings I took up the Frenchman's journal at once and perused again the entry concerning Sir Richard Redding. Against it was marked one of the signs which Mr Starkey had proposed were Chinese in origin. I guessed now that their import was as a record of the precise indulgence granted. The multiplicity of them recommended this interpretation, I believed. And though I must test the hypothesis further, I was confident it would hold ground.

This new intelligence also made clear why he took such care that his journal should not be read by inquisitive eyes. But what of the alchemical symbols? What did they mean? That must now be my most pressing quest.

CHAPTER 11

Miss Hamilton is Distressed

By the frank confession of Sir Richard Redding I now knew much of the Frenchman's business and could eliminate that much of it with reference to his murder. By this means I believed I could reduce the list of names that still interested me to some ten, namely those which were marked by alchemical symbols in his journal. Yet it seemed unwise to proceed immediately upon the assumption that all the others named in the journal had sought indulgences of him without my making some further test. I knew also that this test should be pursued with a nicety of judgement as not to incite some violent offence, for most of those whose names I had found made a secret of their communion.

Yet I knew, also, that the matter was pressing and that I had little time for nicety. So though it distinguishes me not nobly I must confess that I took advantage of my knowledge as to chose two names from the others who would answer my query not freely, but in fear of what would happen if they did not.

I will not do them the indignity of naming these two, either as to their persons or as to that which they feared. But I did, nevertheless, that same afternoon, obtain the confirmation which I sought. Namely, that those names thus marked, with Chinese hieroglyphs, had purchased indulgences of the Frenchman. And though no philosopher would consider the hypothesis established by so slight an accumulation of evidence, I was satisfied for now to proceed upon it.

Though I had made no firm commitment to Miss Hamilton as to when I might return to her side, I found myself in need of some pleasant diversion and so next morning I rose betimes and prepared once more for court. With Martha's assistance I was soon resplendent in fine linen and sprinkled with rose water, breakfasted and upon my way.

Upon entering the precincts of Whitehall Palace I quickly found myself to be fondly greeted by fellows with whom I had but little acquaintance and while I did not despise their company, wherein I was able to learn the news of the day with all speed, yet I was perplexed.

Sir William Batten, a man with whom I have never before exchanged two words, doffed his hat with a 'How do you do, sir?'

'I do very well,' I replied, and so we passed on our ways.

Moments later I found Lord Buckhurst, the very young scoundrel whose pudendous activities upon the balcony of the Cock Tavern I had witnessed but two days previously was at my side.

'Ah, Mr Wyld,' he said. 'I see you have come to court His Majesty.'

'It may very well be that I have, My Lord,' I replied.

'Well, when you do so, he will not doubt confide in you that I am chastened and to be chastised,' he told me. 'For I have disported myself outrageously, I believe.'

'Ah,' I said. 'Upon the balcony of the Cock.'

'Why, you know already I see.'

'I was a witness, My Lord.'

'And was it not a most remarkable exhibition?'

I agreed that it was and so we, too, parted.

By and by I found my way to the Duke and Duchess's precincts and was by Her Highness's leave able to gain an audience with Miss Hamilton. She did not seem especially pleased to find herself in my company.

'I am surprised, sir,' she said, 'that you have the time to spare for visiting these quarters.'

'And why should I not?' I demanded. 'I have set out on purpose this morning to court your company.'

'Fiddle, sir,' she told me. 'I am but an amusement with which you toy when you may not be occupied elsewhere.'

'What madness is this?' I asked. 'Have I not made love to you these past months in all earnest?'

'So I had thought, sir, but now I find otherwise.'

'And by what means do you descry that I am other than in earnest?' I enquired, mystified and not a little alarmed.

'Why, sir, by those several means as serve to keep me informed.'

'Come, Miss Hamilton,' I said, finally. 'I would know by what means I have offended you, for I must confess that I had not knowingly done so.'

'But, sir,' she replied, 'if you do not know what will offend a lady, then you are not so much of a gentleman as I thought.'

At this I rose, now a little angered, and would have bade her adieu had I not at that instant discovered that she was, indeed, so moved as to display a tear. I quickly resumed my place, anxious to get to the bottom of this mystery.

'You must tell me,' I said, 'for it appears I am not the gentleman you thought, and I do not know.'

'Why, 'tis all over court that you are making love to Lady Castlemaine. Can you tell me that it is not so?'

My Lady Castlemaine! How could I have been so foolish as to neglect that encounter? I would have made my denial upon an instant but I knew that would not do. Some explanation was needed and, indeed, some explanation was due. But what explanation?

'Miss Hamilton,' I said, at length, 'I must first beg you not to believe all that you hear, for upon my honour I am not making love to Lady Castlemaine. I should be a fool, indeed, to court the King's indignation even if I allowed that her beauty enticed me. But I do not allow that. Beside you, she is as rose beside a lily; the rose's thorns will draw blood ere one approaches too close while the lily is protected solely by its innocence. Some men desire to bleed for their loves. I find the perfume of the lily requites mine.'

'Oh, sir, you seek to turn me again with flattery,' she replied but sorrow spoke still from her eyes.

'I speak only with my heart,' I told her.

'Then what is the truth, sir?' she asked.

'You will know that I dined with My Lady this Saturday past, hard upon leaving your sweet company. You will not believe I had no expectation of dining but it is so. I was commanded by My Lady the moment I left these chambers. Why, I was barely within the Stone Gallery when her page came to me. In truth, I thought at first to ignore this command but judged that not wise. And in truth, also, I was curious as to her business with me.'

'They say her business took a full three hours and that you dined alone.'

'I will not deny it was so. And yet I know not what her business was, unless it be to snare me with her thorns. What do they say at court?'

'Must I repeat what is odious to me?'

'Believe me, Miss Hamilton when I say that I am steadfast in my affection. I have not been pricked by the rose. But I would know why My Lady so busies herself, the better that I may defend myself. For it would not serve me well to make an enemy of her.'

Miss Hamilton's cornflower blue eyes were still moist as I caught them with mine, but the sorrow, I think, had almost fled. 'They say, sir, that My Lady will revenge herself upon His Majesty, whose affections turn towards Miss Stuart. They say, sir, that you are her revenge.'

'Then I am to be pitied for I walk upon treacherous ground which will, as likely, swallow me all up.'

'Oh, sir, do not speak in such a way. Your honour shall be your shield.'

'I wish it were so. But My Lady can serve her purpose without ever drawing blood. You, yourself, are witness to that. What then of His Majesty?'

Miss Hamilton lowered her eyes at this slight rebuke. 'Why I believe that His Majesty is so occupied as to have no other care, for the moment.'

'Are we to remain friends?' I asked, taking her hand, which she permitted to let lie in mine.

'I must trust you,' she told me, 'otherwise I should not want to live.'

'Then live. And if you will live, perhaps you may help me. I must know how this matter goes and you are better placed than I to discover. Can you be my ears and my eyes?'

'I will do what I can,' she promised.

'But take care, I beg of you, not to heed all that you hear. My Lady has not done with me yet, I fear, and there will be more that you will find odious.'

'Then perhaps I shall grow thorns of my own.'

'Do you have a boy you trust, should you wish to send to me?'

'I believe so, yes. There is one that loves me.'

'Good. You can find me always by Covent Garden.'

We had been closeted, now, perhaps longer than was fitting and I thought it wise to take my leave.

'When may I return?' I asked, rising.

'I believe we will walk in the park this Sunday after dinner if the weather remains fair. His Royal Highness is much improved in his spirits. If you come to the park you may find me there.'

'Then you shall find me at your service.'

Bowing deeply, I dared to brush the back of her hand with my lips, at which she blushed, but not unbecomingly.

Leaving the Duchess's lodgings I looked about cautiously, anxious now as to what surprise My Lady might have next prepared. No page appeared and, by and by, I let myself believe that one would not.

In the Stone Gallery I met with Mr Pemberton who was about on His Royal Highness's business. He greeted me in ironical jest.

'Mr Wyld. You are indeed an important personage now. We have fresh news of you daily.'

'So Miss Hamilton has let me understand.'

'She will admit you still?'

'I believe she will.'

'Then you have some great power, sir. Indeed, I should wish a portion of it myself.'

'You should have all of mine, were I able to shake myself free of it.'

Pemberton drew me close. 'Pray be cautious. By my word you tread dangerously, if all I hear be true.'

'I think I do tread dangerously,' I confessed. 'But all you hear may not be true.'

'Well, take care, my friend. Otherwise you will need a swift boat to the Continent.'

'I have one ready,' I replied, not entirely without truth.

Upon leaving Pemberton I wished to avoid being further greeted by divers courtiers upon the subject of my new celebrity. With that in mind I made my way by the shortest route to the Privy Stairs and took a wherry downstream to the Somerset Stairs. Yet even upon the water I was not entirely free of my notoriety as I soon understood by the gleam in the waterman's eye which conveyed to me that he was as conversant with court gossip as any courtier. At the stairs I gave the man a shilling, though he only deserved sixpence, and climbed briskly ashore where I was finally relieved to find myself upon the calmer waters of anonymity.

Why had my luck turned thus? This was the thought I carried as I made my way, by degrees, back to Covent Garden. There was no great haste in my step and noting, I suppose, my distraction, some beggars in the Strand began to eye me as prey. I would almost have welcomed them take their chance but something in my gait dissuaded them, which was their good fortune for I would have roused easily in my present state.

As to my luck it was, I concluded, beyond my comprehension. The fates plotted my course and I could not undo what they had done. But how was I to proceed? I had reached no conclusion when I entered the piazza and turned towards my door.

Then, upon a moment, I determined that I must take my chance and allow these events to run their course. I was not without resources. If all went badly then I might need that barque from Dover. If not then I might yet turn My Lady's scheming to my advantage. Had she not opened certain doors that I might otherwise have found closed to me? Why, then, should I not discover what lay behind them?

CHAPTER 12

Villainy in Covent Garden

Safe again in my own parlour, my thoughts turned gradually from the scheming of My Lady Castlemaine to the matter of Monsieur Vouet and his journal once more. My morning's sojourn at court had been so unexpectedly brief that I had now an afternoon in which to make some further explorations in this regard.

Having satisfied myself as to the meaning of the oriental hieroglyphs written in that journal, it had become my principal ambition to uncover the purpose of the alchemical symbols written upon its pages. Their import I could not yet gauge but I believed it to be significant. To achieve my purpose I would have to make some enquiries of the persons marked against these symbols. How that was to be concluded I was not yet certain.

Most pertinent of all these symbols, I quickly concluded, was the mark beside the particular name Aurum. This mark was the sign of the planet Mars, the sign that in alchemy is taken to signify iron. That same mark was to be found alongside one other name that belonged to the Frenchman's last visit to London, marked thus, G. Graunt. I understood this to refer to Mr William Graunt – the French for William being Guillaume – third son of that noble family, who maintained lodgings north of the Strand, and east of St Clement's. So, by and by, I strolled in the direction of those lodgings, intending to see how my luck held.

The home of Mr Graunt was a tall, overtoppling structure typical of the quarter and hemmed in by similar structures to either side. The overhang of the upper storeys so obscured the light as to cloak the street in perennial gloom. This darkness took on a more sombre quality as I came close to the Graunt residence for I discovered it to be in mourning.

I was admitted by a servant who, upon my enquiry, informed me that Mr William Graunt had but lately died, but that his wife, Mrs Graunt was at home. Some moments later I was ushered into her presence. The woman to whom I was presented was of my own age, well maintained and she had, withal, managed a certain air with her mourning.

I bowed. 'Madam,' I began, then faltered. 'I should not disturb you at this moment,' I told her, apologetically. 'I had some business with your late husband, but it was of no import.'

'I do not believe I know you, sir,' she replied. 'Were you a friend of William?'

'No, madam,' I admitted. 'I never had the honour of his acquaintance.'

'He was a fine man, sir,' she told me. 'And much to be missed.'

'I have no doubt,' I agreed. 'When do you bury him?'

''Tis to be upon the morrow at two in the afternoon, for he has been dead these ten days.' She paused, as if meditating upon the sorrow of his passing. 'Will you pay your respects? We have his body by us?'

I was somewhat taken aback by this request as having no acquaintance with the gentleman. Then I remembered that this was likely a family which practised the Roman faith, that being the link between Monsieur Vouet's patrons.

'Thank you, madam,' I replied, it seeming discourteous to respond otherwise.

The body was laid out in an adjacent chamber and upon entry I perceived that it had been embalmed, though not so perfectly as to be able to dispense with the use of incense. The wax-like features I observed there were of a man many years older than his wife.

Standing beside this woman, staring in silence at the features of her late husband, I felt a certain puzzlement, even disappointment. For it was clear to me that I was in the presence of another who had felt the approach of death and sought remission of punishment for his sins through the intercession of the Frenchman. I began to think, in those moments of silence, that this must be all in which Monsieur Vouet traded and that this matter of poison was simply a curiosity, like the powder of transmutation.

After this interlude of silent contemplation, the woman escorted me from the room and I took my leave of her, having again expressed my sorrow at her plight. The same servant led me to the door and, as we took those few steps together, I asked if his master had been ill a long time.

'Why no, sir,' he replied, with some surprise. 'He was took of a sudden, in the night. I believe he never even left a will, sir,' he confided.

'Of what, then, did he die?' I asked.

'Why the physicians could find no cause, sir. They said he must have died upon a whim.'

At this my earlier puzzlement evaporated and was replaced by a most severe conviction. 'I will have need to send to your mistress,' I told him. 'How is she addressed?'

'She is Mrs Genevieve Graunt,' he told me. Upon that I stepped once more into the street.

G. Graunt. 'Twas not Guillaume as I had supposed but Genevieve. In all my dealings with Monsieur Vouet's journal it had never once entered into my consideration that these names referred to any but gentlemen. Yet the Frenchman's serving woman had clearly told me so. And had I but reflected, this business of poisoning has often proved a woman's.

I was convinced I had uncovered a murder in the bosom of this family, a travesty in the midst of tragedy. At another time I might have searched out its roots and thus brought it to light. Not today. How was a case to be carried when this potion was so devilishly wrought? Here was a crime that would escape justice on earth.

Even so, this discovery had furnished me with the information I needed, black though it was. In short, that the alchemical symbol for iron as writ in Monsieur Vouet's journal, the sign of the planet Mars, indicated the supply of a portion of poison to the person to which it was appended. By which logic I could conclude that the person who hid behind the alias Aurum had procured this same potion. My great concerns were that I knew not who that person might be, nor to what end the potion might be used. But as to this last, I was beginning to become fearful.

Or perhaps I was wrong? There was a further means of checking, for this mark was inscripted next to two other names from the journal, in that part pertaining to earlier visits of Monsieur Vouet to London. It behove me, I decided, to discover how these families had fared in the

wake of the Frenchman's sojourn within our city before condemning
Mrs Graunt utterly.

These questions so absorbed me that I was along Russell Street and
almost into the piazza with barely a sense of my whereabouts. I was,
indeed, on the point of entering the square when my reflection was
interrupted by a tug upon my arm and I perceived Ned to be at my side.
He was mightily agitated.

'Stop, sir,' he begged.

'Why, what is it, Ned?' I asked, for I could see that he was trembling.

''Tis Bridget and Martha, sir. They have been set upon by ruffians
and murdered.'

'What?' I cried. 'Show me these villains. I will run them through this
instant.'

'Why, they are within, sir. I have not seen them emerge.'

'Within?'

'Aye, sir. I slipped away upon the commotion and they marked me
not.'

'And did you mark them?'

'Not especially, sir, for I was fearful of my life.'

'The number, boy?'

'Two, sir.'

'And how were they armed?'

'With cudgels, sir, as I believe.'

'Then I had better deal with them immediately.'

'Shall I accompany you, sir?' the boy asked. I could see by his eyes
that he was terrified.

'No, Ned,' I told him. 'You will serve me best if you remain without.
If it should go badly then you must fetch the constable immediately and
inform him of exactly what has passed.'

So saying I began to run towards my lodgings, the heat of my anger
fuelling my desire to confront these murderers with all haste. But then
I slowed, then stopped. It was not by chance, I perceived, that these
fellows had visited my door. They were surely under instructions. Like
as not it was me that they were after.

In truth this did not stay me long. I wanted them as much as they
wanted me. But it did enable me to school myself as to the manner of

apprehending them. And so I entered upon my own chambers with a degree of caution.

I knew that the enclosed spaces of these lodgings would not favour the use of my rapier. But then, I supposed, 'twould not favour the cudgel any better. In either case one strike was all that might be won. Anticipating this I drew the blade and held it at the ready.

I was accustomed to moving with stealth and this enabled me to pass the threshold without being marked. Once within I steadied myself and listened for a sound that might betray the whereabouts of these villains. After a moment I heard some commotion within my parlour. This being upon the first floor, I began to mount the stairs.

The door was open and from the head of the stairs I was able to see that one of these fellows was about my business with an energy. Books were being examined and discarded with no care as to their welfare. I was not surprised, either, to discover that the culprit had a face severely touched by the pox.

'Halt, and stand to,' I shouted at him, entering the room at once and taking my advantage.

The fellow looked up in great surprise and, I thought, a moment's anger. In the same moment he took up his club which lay close to hand and would have laid me out with it, for he moved with the speed of a tiger. I was quicker, and sprang aside so that his blow fell where I was not. Immediately I had him at a disadvantage. This weapon must finish its trajectory be its wielder of inhuman strength, such was its weight. He knew that he was done and in the instant of his knowing I ran my rapier quite through him, penetrating, as I suppose his heart for he was upon the floor without a murmur. I withdrew my blade which he had taken down with him, believing that the advantage was with me.

'Twas not so, for the second of these villains was already upon me having, I suppose, been close at hand. I felt a terrible jolt upon the left side of my head and spun away, staggering and letting slip my blade which fell to the floor. Though disoriented, I sensed him moving to take up the blade and mastering myself with a severe effort I managed to place a foot upon the weapon. This proved of little value.

'Back up,' the fellow snarled, his voice cold as steel. At the same time I heard an ominous click.

Turning now to face him, I found that he intended to murder me. He had a pistol drawn and was steadying the weapon in anticipation of putting me down.

'Who are you?' I demanded, seeking to distract him.

'Silence, fool,' he ordered.

Death was readying itself to enter my parlour for a second time. I looked at the piece which he had pointed at my heart and calculated my chances. It was a flintlock and would probably be true, but there was always a degree of uncertainty, as every wielder must know.

'I hope you know your weapon, sir,' I shouted.

As I had intended, this created a sufficient degree of doubt to distract the fellow for an instant as his eye flickered across the pan. In that instant I feinted to my left. He reacted immediately by letting off the piece in the direction in which I was moving, but by then I had begun to lunge to the right, diving and driving my body towards his thighs in the hope of bringing him down.

The report from the piece filled my ears and I felt a searing pain in my left shoulder as my other shoulder struck him full. I felt the villain stagger but with one arm now useless, I could do little more than flail once I hit the floor. With a jerk and a stumble, the fellow was away. All I saw of him by the time I had pulled myself up again was the back of his head disappearing down the stairs.

I seemed to be alive, but at what cost? My concern was for my shoulder which had taken a ball from the pistol. I ripped off my shirt and examined the wound. The ball was still there, I could see, lodged in the muscle of my upper arm. I knew, then, I had been lucky. My bones were undamaged. Carefully, I bound the wound with the linen from the shirt and began to take stock.

The larger of the two villains was stretched out upon the floor where I had laid him. He would do no more harm. The second was long gone. But what of my servants, Bridget and Martha?

With that thought I set off down the stairs, finding as soon that I had better move with some caution, having both a damaged arm and an uncertain head. With tender steps I stumbled uneasily to the foot of the stairs where I found the boy peering in cautiously from the door.

'Oh, sir,' he cried, and there were tears in his eyes, though whether at the sight of my wounds or because I lived yet I could not say.

'Come, help me,' I told him and put my arm on his shoulder. Together we made our way to the scullery fearful for what deviltry we would uncover.

The room was in turmoil. Stools were flung aside, the table upturned. Then, at once, we perceived muffled sounds and, searching for their source, discovered the two women, living still, bound and gagged and thrust into a pantry where they might rot. I was little able to assist in their release but Ned eventually effected it, upon which the two women vented their relief and anger, by turns, until they had vented enough.

'Now go, boy, and bring Dr Whistler, the physician to me,' I ordered. And with that I slumped wearily to the floor.

Dr Whistler came as soon as he was called. He examined me with care but the result of his examination revealed no more than my own. There was a lead ball in my arm.

'It should be removed in due course,' he advised me.

'Remove it now, man,' I ordered him.

This took him somewhat aback, for he seemed inclined to prefer the consideration of his prescription to the acting upon it.

'I have no assistant,' he observed, by way of avoiding what I asked.

'Take Bridget,' I told him, for she was by now sufficiently recovered to be more concerned as to my wellbeing than for her own.

'You will hardly bear the pain,' he advised me, still determined at avoidance.

'Then send for laudanum and a bottle of West Indian rum. You know as well as I that if the ball is not removed, in due course the arm may go in its stead.'

Eventually I prevailed upon the good physician to do his job and the necessary provisions were fetched. We found strong rope and he tied me to the very scullery table upon which we ate our victuals, I having dosed myself with as much rum as I could swallow. The laudanum I kept for the aftermath.

I cannot say that I recall with any clarity the next several hours for their edges were mostly uncertain, distorted as they became by the pain of the extraction and the spirit which I took to counteract it. Night fell and morning came and then, I believe, I slept. I awoke at evening to find the girl watching over me and then I slept again. 'Twas upon the morrow that I finally returned to some semblance of recognizable sanity.

CHAPTER 13

An Alchemical Circle Revealed

I rose cautiously that morning, which in due course I found to be Saturday. My body was sore but without the heat of fever. Much relieved, I called for the girl and with her assistance examined how I fared.

The wound to my arm was ugly and dark but there were yet no eruptions of pus and the surrounding flesh displayed neither the heat nor anger of corruption. Satisfied, I instructed Martha to bandage it again with clean linen and then had her describe what she could find of wounds to my head.

'There is a great swelling on the left, sir, and much discolouration and bruising.'

'Is the skin pierced?'

'No, sir. I can see no such marks excepting a small laceration,' she told me.

'It seems, then, I might live,' I replied.

'Oh yes, sir,' she assured me.

'In which case you'd best dress me forthwith, for there is business awaiting my attention.'

Upon descending I found the parlour to be shut up. Seeing it, I recalled instructing Bridget to leave it untouched before Dr Whistler began his work upon me. I left it thus, descending once more to the scullery in search of nourishment.

Bridget was alarmed to find me about so soon but I dismissed her worries and bade her prepare me eggs which I ate with brawn and drank a bowl of whey. While doing so, I beckoned Ned to me.

'Ned,' I said, 'I need your help, for my recollection of that ruffian who would murder me wants for clarity. Mayhap the bang on the head he gave me has knocked it clean away. Did you mark him as he left?'

'I did, sir, aye. He was a lean, ugly-looking fellow.'

'But was he not disfigured, for that is my recollection?'

'Aye, sir, about the eye and cheek.' So saying, Ned indicated on his own face with a cutting motion of his finger from his forehead, vertically across the left eye and down to his cheek. 'His face was twisted, sir, leaving him mighty unhappy of outlook, as you might say.'

'Well done, boy. 'Twas as I thought. With that we shall have him if he dares to cross my path again. Now, are you brave enough to help me with the other? For I cannot manage him alone.'

'I'll do my best,' he replied, though his look suggested some uncertainty as to how good his best might prove.

'Then, by and by, we'll find out what he was about, eh?' I told him.

When I had finished my victuals I took the boy and ascended again to the first floor. Opening the parlour door and observing the scene before me brought the recent events heavily upon my mind. There upon the floor was the second of the two villains, or what was left since life had fled his corpse through the hole I had punctured into his chest. I entered and gazed down at his blank features.

'Come, boy,' I said, for Ned hung nervously at the door. 'He'll do you no harm now.'

At this he entered the chamber cautiously and peered at the body himself, nudging it with his foot. Upon that, I believe his curiosity became master of his fear for he was soon as inquisitive as I.

My first thought was to put back the books which had been so carelessly disordered and this we did swiftly, Ned helping. The club was still lying beside the fellow and I picked it up and examined it, to no great effect. 'Twas an adequate means with which a pack of such ruffians might reduce a victim to pulp, but in single combat the weapon showed little merit, as I had recently proved. I handed it then to the boy, but he found he could barely lift the weapon so I took it back and lay it in a corner.

The fellow himself was now stiff with death and not easily handled, even by the two of us together. In the end I took a sharp knife to remove his clothing, for I wished to see what lay beneath. In doing so I was mightily surprised to discover that he had, within a pocket in his breeches, the journal which I had lately discovered among Monsieur Vouet's effects.

At this I stopped my present action in order to find whether aught else of the Frenchman's had been disturbed. The loose memorandum pages appeared untouched and the last portion of poison remained, but I was much angered to find that the correspondence of this Aurum with Monsieur Vouet was no longer in my possession. Upon that discovery I resumed my examination of the corpse but these letters were not about him either. I deduced that the disfigured fellow had them when he left, which put me out of temper.

After that and with much heaving, Ned and I finally stripped the body of its remaining clothing to reveal the ripe and lousy flesh beneath. The smell of him, indeed, was such as to encourage us to complete the task with all haste. Rolling him over, I found upon his back the mark of the lash and there was a small brand between the flesh of finger and thumb of the right hand, both of which spoke of his being convicted a criminal. Neither provided me with a means to identify his paymaster.

Finding nothing more to interest me, I sent Ned for a barrow and paid two shillings to have the corpse taken to the yard outside Bishopsgate where he might be laid under the ground so as to do nobody further harm. And upon him being carted away, I bade Bridget make the parlour fit again, for I had more to ponder. While she did so I took to my bed. Such efforts as I had already made had exhausted me. There were, besides, more exertions to come for which I would need my strength.

Later that afternoon my strength had returned sufficiently for me to contemplate a call. These villains and their visit had posed a question which I must have answered with all speed. The answer lay with another and it was to him that I must go. The distance was not far so I had Ned fetch a sedan to the door and then instructed the bearers to carry me as if I were the King himself. They demanded a King's fee for the privilege but handled me well.

It was to Pall Mall that I went and the home of Lady Villiers where I particularly hoped to catch Delaney. He was at his elaboratory, into which chamber I was swiftly shown.

Delaney displayed alarm the instant he saw me and would have me sit and tell him what had befallen.

'Robert,' I began, taking the stool which he proffered, 'I am shot and I believe it must be on your account.'

At this he protested most strongly.

'But I have not shot you, sir.'

'Perhaps not. Nevertheless it is to you that I come in search of the culprit.'

'What calumny is this, Francis? I have no cause nor reason to harm you. You are, indeed, one of the few men I trust in this world.'

'Robert,' I replied, 'You do not trust me sufficiently.'

'Explain yourself,' he demanded, crossly. 'For I will not have it.'

'It is thus,' I began. 'This Thursday past I returned to my lodgings to find it occupied by two villains intent upon my murder. I was able to dispatch the first, but the second has done me this serious injury of which you see but the exterior sign. That in itself is curious but might be explained without recourse to you. However, this very morning I have specifically found that they visited me on Monsieur Vouet's business. More especially they came with the intention of carrying away his journal and the correspondence which I found at his lodgings. You will admit that raises the question as to how they knew to find such material in my possession. To my certain knowledge only you and I are aware these items exist. So, since I did not arrange their removal myself, I am come to you.'

'Francis. You have my word this was not my doing. Why would I take such action? What purpose would it serve? I desire the return of my manuscript and for that I rely on you. So tell me now, why do you accuse me of this?'

'No doubt all you say is true. Nevertheless you have spoken of this affair to another. So alerted, that person has come to me.'

'But I have told nobody,' he insisted.

'Do you swear that upon the book which you hold most sacred?' I asked.

'Why do you test me thus?' he demanded.

'Because you still refuse to confide in me. This business is no longer a matter of a missing manuscript, heinous a crime though its removal has entailed. There is a conspiracy afoot, poison on the loose and murder has again been commissioned. Therefore I demand that you reveal what you have so far kept from me. Let us start with the manuscript. Tell me what it is.'

Delaney had been pacing in his normal fashion but now he sat down heavily upon a stool. His face was troubled and I think he knew not what to do, what to say.

'Why, it is an esoteric work that I would study,' he told me at length. 'What do its particulars matter?'

'Robert, I will know and you will tell me. Otherwise we will sit here until one or the other falls down dead.'

'It is an alchemical work,' he admitted, finally. 'But I can tell you no more.'

I remained silent, staring at him, waiting.

'Why do you do this?' he demanded again.

'Because I will break this bond that binds you, whatever it be. For it binds you to a murderer.'

At this he jumped up with a start and began to pace again, at once muttering in a low voice which I could not decipher.

'It is called *The Book of Abraham the Jew*,' he shouted at me, at once.

This pleased me, for I knew from Mr Starkey's tale that what he said was true. Nevertheless I was not done with him yet. 'What is this book,' I asked, 'to warrant such devotion and attention?'

'Oh,' he cried. 'It bears that most sacred of mysteries, the secret of the stone. Now let me be.'

'I have barely started,' I replied, simply.

Delaney looked wretched. 'What more do you want?' he asked, sullenly.

'I want the name of a murderer and you have that name.'

'I do not.'

'Who have you told?'

He fell silent again. 'I shall be damned,' he said at last.

'You are damned already by your silence.'

'I have told no one specifically of these items.'

'But?'

'There is a group of adepts,' he admitted finally, 'the existence of which must be guarded. I am one and by me they know of the manuscript and something of the matter in which you are engaged on my behalf.'

'Who are they?'

'Francis, you do me a grave disservice. These men share the sacred secrets of that art beyond which there is no greater. That, itself, demands that they cannot be party to this.'

'Then we have a long night ahead of us,' I warned him.

'Your injuries have affected your mind. You have become unreasonable.'

'What you say may be true, but it will not affect my resolve.'

'Would you have me break a sacred trust?'

'I must and I will.'

'Oooh,' he wailed again.

Again I waited in silence while he wrestled with his conscience. At last he resolved the conflict in my favour and told me what I sought.

'There are eight men, of which I am one. The most learned is My Lord Illminster, holder of the flame.'

'As honest an intriguer as I have knowledge of,' I observed, caustically.

'I know him only by his learning, Francis, to which I find him devoted. Then there are Mr Elias Dugdale, and Mr Robert Wood, both philosophers of the highest renown. Sir Rupert Digby was, I confess, wild in his youth but has travelled widely and become a model of philosophical rigour. You, yourself, know Theodore Willis and John Backhouse and the final person is Sir Charles Mayow. These are the men who know of this business, but I will not believe any one of them is involved.'

'You have told no other?'

'No,' he told me crossly.

'Then by my logic, you are wrong.'

'I have broken their trust,' he moaned, forlornly, ignoring what I said. 'It is beholden of me to inform them.'

'Robert, do not be such a fool,' I shouted, abruptly.

My shoulder was beginning to ache now and I feared the wound would open again, but I had to continue until I had everything from him. 'You have allowed them too much already,' I warned. 'Say no more unless you wish the stain of this infamy to spread wider still.'

I think finally, at that moment, he understood the truth of what I insisted, for he nodded, briefly, in acquiescence.

'Good. Now there is more you must say of this manuscript, for that may yet hold the key. Tell me by what reason it comes to you.'

'I was to become its custodian. Such was determined by a ritual established these two hundred years. It came, as I said, from Paris where it has been in the custody of one Monsieur Dodart, but lately dead. Before him it was held by the renowned French courtier Cardinal Richelieu. Fate decreed that it should cross the sea and I was chosen. It is an honour I was glad to accept.'

'Why not Lord Illminster if he is chief among you?'

'I know not. The ritual was deemed to have laid the burden on my shoulders. That is all I can say.'

'Were all privy to this?'

'Yes.'

'All knew that Vouet was to bring it?'

'That was, as I suppose, a secret.'

Not so much of a secret, I reflected, that Mr Starkey could not hear whispers of it. 'Who, then, shall we say is our murderer?'

'How can I name any?'

'Who among them are Papists?'

'My Lord Illminster certainly, for he makes no secret. Of the others I cannot say.'

'Vouet dealt especially with those of the Roman faith,' I told him.

'But not entirely, Franics, for I am no Papist.'

'Not entirely, then,' I admitted. 'Nevertheless he was a conduit for them.'

Suddenly my resolve broke and I felt too weak to continue. 'Fetch me a sedan, Robert,' I said, 'for I have taxed myself too severely. But promise me first that you will speak no more of this matter.'

To this he agreed, and so I left him and returned once more to my lodgings.

I had to be helped from the sedan when it reached my lodgings and was barely able to climb the stairs to my bedchamber, which I sought. The wound had opened, as I feared, and was spilling my blood once more.

Bridget would have fetched the physician but I told her he was a fool who would poison me as like as cure me. Instead I ordered her to bring fresh linen while Martha sat over me and tended the wound. In time the flow subsided, upon which I instructed her to tie me up with bandages again, but not too tightly.

After that I remained abed. Bridget brought up gruel which I supped and would have taken wine but she refused.

'I will not kill you, sir, though you may kill yourself,' she told me.

''Twill ease the pain,' I insisted.

'I know not, sir, that it will.'

'Then send up Martha, for she will do my bidding.'

'The girl is about some other business, sir.'

In the end she had her way, for I found myself without the strength to argue. And so, at length, I slept, which being the best cure of all was wholly to my benefit.

CHAPTER 14

By Sedan to St James's Park

Sunday morning furnished me with such discomfort in my arm and shoulder I feared I must be fallen finally under the spell of that fever which would take my limb if not my life. In spite of this the wound, when Martha bared it, remained uncorrupted. I therefore resolved, by and by, to believe the pain must be part of the process of healing.

The day had broken fair which meant, as I shortly recalled, that I had an assignation for the afternoon in St James's Park with the fair Miss Hamilton. The situation between us was of so delicate a texture that I would keep this assignation if I were able but I knew not if I had the strength.

'Have we the means to fit Ned for a page?' I asked Martha. For I thought he might assist me in my desire.

'He is too rough for a page,' she replied, guessing my mind. 'Take me, sir, for I can serve you better than he.'

'I'm sure you can,' I told her. 'But you will not suit my purpose. Besides, if I fit you out to wait on me, why, one of those cavaliers will snap you up and I shall have you no more. Fetch Ned, as I say, and we will see how he can be made fit.'

Thus it fell, after some little more grumbling from the girl, that she, Bridget and the boy had much amusement about making him into a page. In the meanwhile I was able to repair once more to my parlour, now returned to its normal state of organization and cleanliness.

My head, which had troubled me since the hammering it took from the villain's cudgel, was at last beginning to clear and I felt able to take a perspective on what had befallen. By this late act of violence, the view before me had changed. It was time for me to make a new account.

I had, as I believed, squeezed all from Delaney that he had previously withheld. I was certain, moreover, that one of the seven men he had named had commissioned Monsieur Vouet's murder and latterly my own. Seven men, of which six were innocent. How was I to pick the seventh?

Lord Illminster was a Papist and a schemer who was, upon My Lady Villiers' word, intriguing with My Lady Castlemaine to bring down the Chancellor. Yet Delaney claimed him a devoted scholar. Sir Rupert Digby had, as Delaney confessed, led an untamed and outrageous youth and was suspected by some of poisoning his wife though I had discovered this gossip to be mere speculation. He was also a noted swordsman and now a philosopher.

Mr Willis and Mr Backhouse were known to me personally yet I would not say that I could vouch as to the character of either. The former was a professor of rhetoric but had no qualification for the part and so had won it, I guessed, by patronage. The other, John Backhouse, had private means to which I was not privy but which were certainly won during the late troubles. On which side his allegiance lay I did not know.

Mr Elias Dugdale was a collector of curiosities with a reputation, if not for dishonesty, at least for making a hard bargain. Such slight dealings as I had had with him had led me to believe he was also a fool. Mr Robert Wood I knew not, either as to his person or his reputation. That left Sir Charles Mayow, adventurer, adulterer, philosopher and now it seemed an alchemist. In my estimation, any of these men – save Mr Wood who I would not slight without reason – might stoop to murder if it suited his purpose.

These seven, with Delaney, were what Mr Starkey had most aptly described as the secret conspirers. Of those that I knew, only Delaney was righteous and it was he who had been selected as custodian of this ancient manuscript. That ritual of selection, methought, revealed a curious insight in its operation.

Delaney *was* righteous, but he was naive of the ways of the world that surrounded him. He was poorly fitted to judge these men with whom he had fallen into association. I, on the other hand, lived in that world and judged them all harshly. Yet neither of us could choose one among them.

Aside from them I found that Mr Starkey, by Delaney's confession, interested me more than previously. His intelligence in the matter of this manuscript had proved entirely accurate. This was something upon which I could form a judgement of him and I judged favourably. I might have further need of him, I supposed, before this matter was over.

And what, finally, of the two villains? The one, dead, had to all appearance been the junior member of the villainous partnership, the other the primary actor. Yet this junior had the ability to read for it was he who had been examining my books. That put me to reflecting further as to the reason for the marks of the lash upon his back. Mayhap he had been a seaman and had received his lashes before the mast. For such are often schooled in the art of navigation, for which a degree of literacy is requisite.

In all, of questions I still had a surfeit. Answers were more elusive.

It seemed Ned could be fitted for a page. With buckle shoes, white linen and clean breeches, all he wanted was a livery coat to perfect him. He pretended himself nervous in this strange attire but I promised him fine sights in the park which steadied his nerve and as soon put Martha out of sorts.

As to myself, I was not so easily fitted. In truth, I began to think myself a fool for contemplating this outing. Against that was a demon which insisted I show myself. I have long found these demons of mine to counsel me wisely and so I persisted in my foolishness.

First I had Martha redress the wound with a wad of linen and then bind it tightly for I had no use for bloody garments. Then I had her choose a loose shirt and light cloak in order that I might disguise as far as possible my injury. Breeches and boots were by stages pulled on and at last I insisted on my rapier being belted tightly about my waist. My sword arm was still whole and I would not go unarmed.

Once attired and ready I tried myself on the stairs and about the parlour and scullery, which made me believe I might succeed. So, finally, Martha went to fetch a sedan, for Ned was too fine today for such a task. The conveyance arrived and we quickly formed our strange procession, he and I, as I was borne slowly towards Whitehall with the boy following behind, I like some impoverished and eccentric duke who must have his entourage, he that entourage.

My little procession arrived at the gates of the palace to find much coming and going. Wishing to draw as little attention to myself as possible I instructed Ned stay by the sedan, which I had already retained for my return journey, while I made to find out what was afoot.

I was soon able to discover the reason for the activity. The King and Queen were riding in the park with the women-in-waiting, a gathering which included many of the finest ladies at court. This had been marked by the gallants and it was they I had found gathered around the gate chattering as they attended the return of the noble outing. Being now a noted gallant myself, I thought to remain awhile among them so that I might learn if I could where the Duchess and her entourage might be found.

So I installed myself. But before I could make my enquiries I perceived the clatter of hoofs which heralded the return of the royal party. The King led, riding hand in hand with the Queen, which was as uncommon a sight as I could have supposed to meet. Her Majesty was finely attired in a short riding petticoat which lent her considerable charm and His Majesty handed her down, having dismounted himself, that they might now stroll within.

Behind the royal couple there was a sea of plumes, each belonging to the hat of one fine lady or another. Towards this the gathered gallants now surged that they might hand down some one or another of them. I, being but a fool, let myself be swept along with this tide and so found myself by no design of my own but I perceive by the design of a lady, beside the mounts of the two competitors for the King's affections, My Lady Castlemaine and Miss Stuart. The latter, adorned with a green plume, knew me not, but the former, with a red plume cocked askew, most certainly did.

'Why, Mr Wyld,' she called down to me, 'how kind of you to lend me your service.'

Upon which I had no choice but to offer my hand and bring My Lady from her mount. This, however, was not the end to my embarrassment. No sooner was My Lady at my side than she offered me her hand to kiss, which kissing, etiquette demanded I must now kiss her cheek also. Thus within so short a span I could hardly have believed it possible, I had been completely outmanoeuvred and once again seriously compromised.

'I suppose you were not waiting upon my return?' My Lady asked, having accepted this greeting.

Fortunately I was absolved from answering this query by her having observed my physical discomfort. The handing down had involved some little exertion.

'You have injured yourself, sir,' she told me.

'I have an injury, My Lady,' I admitted.

'I hope it is not serious, for I would not have you die yet,' she replied.

'Then I must ensure that I do not,' I retorted.

'Come, sir,' she said. 'Escort me to my lodgings for I would have a further word with you in private.'

So commanded, I joined her as she passed through the gate by which her lodgings were gained and we were soon out of earshot. 'Mr Wyld,' she said, 'Lord Illminster would meet you. Have you a moment to see him?'

'When, My Lady?' I asked, taken entirely by surprise again.

'At your convenience, Mr Wyld. This afternoon would suit him, I suppose.'

'I believe I am already committed today,' I told her. 'Tomorrow forenoon?'

'Then it shall be so. Good day to you, sir.' And with the slightest of curtsies and an unreadable smile I was released, mystified and slightly bemused.

I returned slowly beyond the palace gate where the gallants were still about their business. Mine, no doubt, had been well marked and would soon be feeding the court mills. In the meantime I was able to discover that the Duchess and her ladies were expected to take a walk in St James's Park with the Duke within the hour. Learning this I returned to the sedan and collected Ned that we might straightway go there. I desired a period of respite to reflect upon what had just befallen me.

The park was reached from Whitehall by the yard of the home guard and the park gate. Beyond there were gardens which the King thought to model after the French style. Indeed I have heard that he takes advice from the great Le Notre, designer to the French King Louis. These plans were still in an immature stage as to their realization but some avenues of single trees had been laid out and earthworks begun. Elsewhere there were wild stands of trees and thickets where much salacious frolicking was commonly practised as dusk settled and night drew its cloak.

With Ned at my side I walked across the greensward, acknowledging greetings of courtiers and gentlemen with whom I was acquainted as we went. The discomfort in my arm had now eased.

'Well, boy,' I said, 'how do you like the life of a page?'

'I should like it better for comfortable shoes,' he told me.

'Then we must see to it.'

'Aye, sir.'

'And what of the fine ladies and gentlemen? Are they to your taste?'

'The lady with the red plume was mighty fine, sir.'

By which I learnt that the lad had a keen eye. 'Some say the finest of all,' I told him.

'And shall you marry her, sir?'

'No, Ned,' I replied with a smile. 'I shall not marry her for she has her eye on a much bigger prize.'

Thus we strolled until, by and by, I espied a crowd of personages at the head of which were the Duke and Duchess. 'Mark well, boy,' I told Ned. 'For we will join this crowd presently.' And so saying I charted a course that would bring us to them.

As we approached I perceived that the Duchess's father was with them and was engaged with the Duke at some length. The Duchess, who they say is with child, looked mighty well and she greeted me.

'Good day, Mr Wyld,' she said. 'Is it not the finest of days?'

'Indeed it is, Your Highness,' I agreed bowing, though not as fully as I normally might.

'Did you find out who killed that poor murdered Frenchman of yours?' she asked.

'I did not, Your Highness,' I confessed.

'Well you must,' she told me.

I bowed again, and the Duchess passed on, so that eventually I was able to fall in with Miss Hamilton who followed in her train.

'How do you do, madam?' I asked, having bowed once more, as well as I was able.

'Tolerably well, thank you,' she replied, then noted Ned. 'But I see you have your own boy now, sir,' she observed. 'Is that not a fine thing with which to impress a lady.'

'I believe you do me a disservice, Miss Hamilton,' I told her. 'Unless it be that my lad pleases you.'

'But, sir, I have heard already how a certain fine lady was handed down from her horse today.'

'By God,' I ejaculated. 'I will be damned by this noble woman.'

'You will, sir. And I must confess that I find it hard to bear the scorn which I find directed towards me.'

This stung me. 'What must I do?' I asked. 'Shall we elope together and find ourselves a haven far from this tumult?'

'Hush, sir. Do not jest so,' she chided.

'But I do not jest. If you will come, I will gladly go, and the boy shall bear your train.'

At this Miss Hamilton's step faltered briefly and I allowed mine to falter with hers so that we fell back slightly from the crowd. 'You have me at a disadvantage, Mr Wyld, for I know not what to say.' So saying she turned towards me and I do believe was to utter something sweet to my ear, but at that moment she caught sight of my arm. 'Sir, you are bleeding,' she cried. 'Are you hurt.'

It was true. There was some small discolouration on my shirt where the wound lay. The handing down had caused more damage than I had anticipated. I adjusted my cloak to conceal the stain.

'It is but a tiny wound,' I reassured her.

'It seems not so to me,' she replied, clearly troubled. 'How did you come by it?'

By now we had fallen some way behind the company of the Duke and Duchess and so I briefly explained the circumstances while we made up the distance that separated us from the main party.

'So you see,' I concluded, 'my page is here to assist me should I find myself in need of a staff for support.'

'Then I see I have indeed done you a disservice,' she replied. 'I hope you can forgive me.'

'I have done so already,' I assured her with a smile.

We had now rejoined the tail of the party of the Duke and Duchess so I lowered my voice to a whisper. I had a query to put to Miss Hamilton. 'By the by,' I began. 'I am asked to meet with Lord Illminster on the morrow. What does the court say of him today?'

'That you should not meet him, sir,' she hissed. 'For he is the sworn enemy of Her Highness's father and I fear your presence would not be welcome if it were known that you kept his company.'

'My dear Miss Hamilton,' I whispered, 'were it in my power, I would, for this matter is becoming exceedingly vexatious to me. The truth is I believe him to be involved in the matter in which I am engaged. Therefore I must meet him. I will, nevertheless, endeavour to manage the business with tact.'

'Please do, sir,' she begged. 'For the fates are conspiring, I fear, to tear us apart.' There was sadness in her eyes as she spoke these words.

'The fates may be cruel but they are just,' I reminded her. 'Whatever passes, be assured that I remain your faithful servant.'

By now the Duke and Duchess were on the point of returning to the palace and I was wearying once more. Besides, I had no wish to enter those troublesome precincts again today. So, on this unsatisfactory note we parted.

My business at Whitehall was over. With Ned at my side. I returned to the sedan and had the bearers carry me home. As I sat alone in the chair, I, too, felt sad. There was a flow to this affair which it was beyond my ability to control. And in spite of my confident assurances to Miss Hamilton, I feared for the outcome.

CHAPTER 15

A Rendezvous with Lord Illminster

When I awoke on Monday morning the discomfort in my shoulder had eased and I began to believe I should be whole again. Whether I was thereby fit to meet Lord Illminster, I doubted. Nevertheless that was to be my morning's business and I must see it through with whatever strength I could muster.

I had breakfasted, dressed and was preparing to call a sedan to take me to Whitehall when Martha informed me that there was a carriage without. I cursed, imagining it to be Delaney come to hinder my departure. In that I proved mistaken for the carriage brought nobody. Instead it had come to take me away.

'Who sent you?' I demanded of the groom who waited at the door.

'My Lord said you would understand his purpose without explanation,' the fellow informed me.

By this I did, indeed, understand that the carriage was sent by Lord Illminster and that our meeting was to be clandestine.

'And where do you take me?' I asked of him.

'To the country,' was his reply.

'Then I must prepare myself,' I told him.

Returning within I had Martha buckle my rapier about me again and fasten it tight. Then I placed a swordsman's dagger in my boot. Had I a pistol to hand I would have taken that too, for I knew not what to expect of this adventure.

The carriage was a hackney, the groom roughly dressed with the intention, I presumed, of anonymity. When I had climbed aboard he whipped the horses into a trot and we headed past St Gyles' Fields to High Holborn and then headed north. The eaves of the city were soon behind us and the carriage windows relayed pastures broken by woods and coppices to my vision. After the frantic bustle about Covent Garden the absence of human activity was startling and under the present circumstances disquieting.

We drove for many miles while the sun rose higher into the sky, but it was not yet noon when we entered a hamlet and stopped in the yard of a coaching inn. I descended with unsteady feet from the motion of the hackney, determined to discover where we had halted. The establishment went by the name of The White Hart and was, it transpired, on the great road north which led, by divers routes, to Scotland.

Lord Illminster had commanded a private chamber upon the first floor and into this I was swiftly shown. His Lordship was taking a pipe as I arrived but soon put that aside.

'Mr Wyld,' he greeted me. 'I am delighted to make your acquaintance.'

'Your Lordship.' I bowed.

'Pray take a seat sir. Bring us some refreshment,' he added, addressing a servant.

Lord Illminster was of moderate height but thickly built, though not corpulent. He dressed simply but well, with none of the ostentation of a court cavalier. His face was broad and dark, his heavy brow shielding yellow-brown eyes. These eyes, it seemed to me, showed curiosity but no delight in my presence.

'I hope you were not alarmed by my little masquerade,' His Lordship asked me, while his servant fetched in some beer and poured us each a measure.

I shook my head in response and took a draught of the brew. 'How may I be of service, My Lord?' I asked.

'Why, I have it in mind that I may be of service to you, Mr Wyld,' he replied.

At this I was somewhat surprised. 'Your Lordship does me a great honour,' I told him.

Lord Illminster dismissed this with a wave of his hand. 'Mr Delaney has told me of this business of Monsieur Vouet and that you are to assist him in the recovery of the missing manuscript. It is my wish that the book should be recovered with all haste. You will understand, however, if I say that it would not suit me to have my involvement broadcast. I would prefer, also, if Mr Delaney knew nothing of our meeting.'

'You may be assured that I shall be discreet,' I answered, wondering where this was going to lead.

'I expected no less. Now, sir, if I am to be of assistance I shall need to know what progress you have made thus far. Tell me, what have you discovered from the Frenchman's effects?'

Here, then, was the reason for my summons. His Lordship would know my business. Yet I was surprised at the boldness of his approach. Was it, I wondered, a reflection of the esteem in which he held me? I was not worth much consideration in his eyes, then.

I would not willingly cross His Lordship, for he was a dangerous enemy, yet I determined at that moment to reveal as little as I dare to this man who might well have commissioned the Frenchman's murder himself, and my own. 'There was little of note,' I replied cautiously, unsure how much Delaney had revealed to him. 'But I have recovered a memorandum in which Monsieur Vouet maintained some record of his travels.'

'That is all?' he demanded.

'There were letters, also,' I added, remembering that whoever commissioned the murder now had possession of them. To my relief this seemed, for the moment, to satisfy His Lordship.

'Does your perusal of this record put you in mind as to who might have murdered him for this book?' he asked, watching me closely. 'Or where it is to be found?'

'I have yet discovered no clue within the memorandum which might instruct me in that regard,' I told him truthfully.

'These letters?'

'They are cryptic. I know not who wrote them. Mayhap the author is the person we seek,' I added, watching him in turn but his features remained passive.

'What of Monsieur Vouet's business in London? Have you questioned the man's servants?'

This struck me as curious. Why should His Lordship be concerned as to the servants? Then a sudden intuition took hold of me. 'Were you acquainted with Monsieur Vouet personally?' I asked.

At this His Lordship's eyes narrowed and a fleeting look of

displeasure crossed his features. 'By Delaney's word you are to be trusted,' he replied finally. 'Upon that trust I shall confide that I was indeed acquainted with the Frenchman. But perhaps you know this already?' And those yellow eyes fixed me with their stare.

'I did not know,' I told him. 'And I hope you will not consider me impertinent if I ask what business you had with him.'

The displeasure was clear in his face. I was impertinent. But having insisted he wished to help, he could hardly resist at the first opportunity.

'Why, 'twas of a philosophical nature,' he told me, finally, with a gesture intended to indicate that it was of no significance.

The explanation did little to convince me as to its honesty and left me with a wealth of further questions which, perforce I could not ask. I noted, moreover, that Lord Illminster was quite discommoded at the turn of our discourse for he chose this moment to beckon to his servant and bid the fellow order some dinner.

'You will eat?' he asked.

I found in the request no choice but to acquiesce.

Presently some dishes were carried up from the kitchen and laid out at a table beside the chamber window, where we sat ourselves before them. As we began to address the repast His Lordship, who had regained his composure, resumed his interrogation of me. I continued to parry his queries with guarded replies. He clearly sensed my reticence for at length he expressed some exasperation.

'It would appear that you have made but little progress, Mr Wyld,' he observed sharply.

As I picked over the remains of a piece of venison I could but concede that what he said was true. At this he tried a different approach.

'Tell me,' he said, 'how do you propose to proceed, henceforth? Then we will see what assistance I may provide. I have some little influence which may be of service in this matter.'

I was caught at a loss to know how to respond. 'Your Lordship is most kind but I have yet to form an absolute plan of action,' I confessed clumsily. At this my companion eyed me shrewdly and I guessed he was trying to determine if I was a fool or a charlatan. I hoped the former though I feared the latter.

'Then we must hold little hope of finding the culprit,' he retorted, his tone conveying a note of impatience.

'I confess to having little confidence in his apprehension,' I agreed. 'I fear the manuscript is most certainly lost. But perhaps you have some insight yourself regarding the Frenchman that might be of assistance?'

That gave His Lordship a moment's pause. 'I recall nothing which would help your enquiries,' he told me, then.

As before, this seemed to me to pay little respect to the truth, for His Lordship was of the Roman faith and must surely have been aware of the Frenchman's role as questor. There was great irony in this mutual evasion for one in a position to appreciate it. However, I could see no way of pursuing my own questioning and I believe His Lordship then determined to drop the subject too, for the matter of Monsieur Vouet was thence banished from our conversation.

Instead, at His Lordship's instigation, we turned to divers matters of court. I found, withal, that he was well disposed to swap the rumours of the day, which surprised me for I had believed him to be puritanical in this regard. Some recent tale concerning the exploits of the Duke of Monmouth he relayed with evident relish and further tittle-tattle concerning various ladies of honour. I noted, however, that of those matters in which he was directly involved, the Popish party and Lord Clarendon, no mention was made.

'I understand that My Lady Castlemaine has discovered a fondness for your company,' he said of a sudden, catching me quite by surprise.

'Her Ladyship has shown me some small favour,' I agreed. 'However I do not find that I provide anything more than a distraction to her.'

'Her own lips tell a contrary story. I believe by such hints as she allows that she is quite smitten.' He leaned towards me in the manner of a conspirator. 'I should warn you,' he whispered, 'that His Majesty will not look fondly on any such liaison. I advise caution and discretion.'

'Why, thank you, My Lord. I shall be diligent in the pursuit of both,' I answered, detecting in this conspiratorial tone a wish on his part to encourage the affair. Had I not known it to be impossible, I should have believed him commissioned as her agent.

'But the King is quite occupied with Miss Stuart as to notice little else,' he added with a twinkle.

'Not even the fall of his Chancellor?' I ventured, somewhat audaciously.

At this His Lordship's brow darkened and furrowed and I believed he might rise and challenge me, then quite in the same instant he laughed a bellow of laughter. 'I see I have quite mistaken you for a sombre fellow,' he told me.

The table being cleared, there was little more to detain us and His Lordship proposed his man should return me to Covent Garden forthwith. I bade him farewell with a bow and took myself back to the coach where the groom waited. The journey back was uneventful, only I noticed the unevenness of the track working on my shoulder now, having lost my apprehension on the outward part. In all I was thankful to find myself back in my own dwelling by late afternoon, having reflected the length of the journey as the exact purpose of this encounter. My firm conviction was that Lord Illminster's intention had been to discover what I knew of Monsieur Vouet, his activities and his murder. Whether that implicated him in that same murder I could not say. All I could say was that it did not exonerate him.

When I was once more within, I called Ned to me and bade him go to Mr Starkey to enquire whether that gentleman could visit me, the morrow in the forenoon. I instructed him to explain I had an injury which prevented me calling on him. Ned returned with the promise I sought and I looked forward to a profitable exchange. Mr Starkey had proved himself an acute intelligencer and the time had come for me to make use of this ability if he could be so persuaded. I thought, moreover, I had the means to persuade him.

That evening I found myself occupied until late perusing the memorandum and journal of the Frenchman once again. There remained extensive sections of the journal relating to his business beyond these shores which I had not yet deciphered. I set out with the intention of completing this work but soon found the task too taxing. Though I prided myself on being a fast healer, and though the flesh in my arm was now reforming, I still experienced sufficient discomfort to make concentration troublesome.

So instead I took up again the sheets of the memorandum. What I sought in both, and what eluded me, was any mention of Lord Illminster. While it was not imperative that he should be mentioned, I was surprised that he was not there. Unless, as I of a sudden recognized, their dealings were too dangerous to record. It was plausible, I could see, that the Frenchman was a conduit between Catholic France and this Popish party of which His Lordship was a part. Such exchanges would be expected, so why not by the offices of Monsieur Vouet?

I knew, of course, that such speculation was fruitless for there was no means open to me to confirm it. But in the meantime I noted something which I had missed in my first perusal of this memorandum. At intervals within it there were drawn, in no particular context, the astrological sign of mercury which served as the alchemical symbol for quicksilver. That set me to thinking that here might be the evidence I sought that the Frenchman had indeed treated himself in the matter of the pox.

Mr Starkey was as good as his word and presented himself at my door one hour before noon. Martha fetched him up to the parlour where I was presently occupied and I instructed her bring up a jug of small beer that we might be refreshed.

'I was sorry to hear that you are injured, sir,' Mr Starkey told me after we had greeted one another. 'It is, I hope, not serious.'

'Almost, sir,' I told him. 'For I have taken a lead ball in the arm. But God willing I am to recover.'

'A matter of honour?' he asked.

'Nothing so glorious or so foolish. 'Twas some villainy, but I would not dwell on that now. Instead, let me ask you a question. Mr Delaney has some conjecture regarding the quicksilver found fouling the gut of our Frenchman. Have you been able to form any opinion?'

'None that is of value. My own analysis suggests that the material is most common quicksilver, not philosophical mercury which I gauge Mr Delaney had sought.'

'Of a type that might be used to treat the pox?'

'Most certainly.'

'And if it had been philosophical mercury?'

'Then it must have passed the hand of an adept. That is all one can say for certain. But since in my estimation it did not, further conjecture is unnecessary.'

'Does that satisfy Mr Delaney, or is he still troubled?'

'I fear Mr Delaney has a need for signs and portents. But you know him better than I.'

I smiled. 'Where does one acquire such quicksilver?'

'Why, an apothecary, sir.'

'Of course. But we digress. I have another matter upon which I would take your opinion.' I paused to pour us each further beer while I decided how to begin. 'Some days ago you brought me a tale of a great manuscript which you have sought these months and years, in vain. I have further intelligence of this work which I will presently convey to you. However, I must seek first your absolute discretion in the matter.'

'Of course, sir. You have it,' he assured me with enthusiasm.

'I would also seek, in return, some assistance in a matter which I will also impart under the same veil of discretion.'

'If I can be of assistance, be assured, sir, that I will.'

'Then first let me confirm what you already suspected: Monsieur Vouet was the Frenchman that you sought. He was the conduit by which this manuscript was to pass to these shores.'

'Aha,' exclaimed Mr Starkey. 'And what of it now?'

'I'm afraid I must disappoint you, sir, for it has entirely disappeared.'

At this the alchemist looked crestfallen. 'Is that all?' he demanded.

'Near enough,' I admitted. 'I may tell you, I think, though he will not thank me, that the recipient was to be Mr Delaney himself and that he has engaged me to recover it if I can.'

'My own suspicions ventured in that direction.'

'I may also venture that whoever murdered Monsieur Vouet now has the opus you seek. It is especially in this regard that I need your assistance. You have confessed your knowledge of these companies of adepts, these secretive conspirers as you have styled them. There is, of course, one such company upon our shores that would guard this tome from the eyes of the uninitiated. For reasons that it is unnecessary to explain, it is among this company that I seek the murderer.'

'Do you have their names, sir?'

'Indeed I do and I propose in a moment to spell them out. Upon that I desire that you should tell me what you can of each of them, for they claim, each one, to share your ambition.'

'But not my rigour, I fear,' he added, caustically.

I shrugged. 'I have no authority in that regard,' I told him. 'Mr Delaney is, of course, one. However, I am certain he is not an actor, other than in the role which I have described. Prime among them beside Mr Delaney is Lord Illminster.'

'Illminster, eh? Well, I know him to dabble in the arts, having acquired an interest in Paris while evading Cromwell the Protector. He would be the man to bring the book to these shores. It surprises me, indeed, that he did not take it for himself.'

'As it did me when Mr Delaney confessed this. It seems there is some manner of choosing that laid the responsibility elsewhere.'

'I have heard he is ruthless.'

'Then you would count him capable of this deed?'

'As I have already told you, such an act should render him beyond the circle. Further, I cannot say. Who else have you?'

'Mr Elias Dugdale.'

'A quack, sir. He is not your man.'

'Robert Wood?'

'Our wise antiquarian. I would not pick him either, for I believe he could not be so bold.'

'Sir Rupert Digby.'

'Good God, sir, a villain surely if ever there was one? But I know him not as an adept. No curse would stay his hand, I fear.'

'Mr Theodore Willis, our professor of rhetoric.'

'I know of his interest for we have conversed from time to time. He is an able student.'

'Sir Charles Mayow.'

'A man I know not.'

'The last is Mr John Backhouse. Do you know him?'

'We have spoken, but not of the arts, though I have long suspected an interest. He is a man who guards himself well and constantly, but I cannot tell you more.'

'Well there you have them, sir. Your secret conspirers. What do you make of them?'

'Much as I would have expected. Save Mr Delaney I find none I consider capable of progressing the art.'

'Then let us progress. I understand that you have your own byways which inform you with some accuracy. Are they capable of shedding further illumination on what has befallen the Frenchman? There may be some rumour of value, but I will not hear it from where I stand.'

'Well, Mr Wyld, I will see what can be done. One thing, only, I ask. If you do find this book, I beg you to allow me a view of it.'

'If I am able, Mr Starkey,' I assured him. 'I surely will.'

CHAPTER 16

From Drury Lane to Whitehall

Mr Starkey's visit had proved fruitful but upon his departure my mind drifted uneasily to settle once more on my encounter the previous day with Lord Illminster. By no specific logic this unease prompted me, in the afternoon following Mr Starkey's departure, to deal with some unfinished business regarding the sign of Mars in the Frenchman's cryptic journal. There were as I had already observed two names besides Graunt and Aurum, two names pertaining to Monsieur Vouet's earlier sojourns upon these shores, marked similarly with this sign beside them. My conjecture was that the poison had been purchased in each case.

The first name was entered as E. Radcliffe which I had thought to be Eleanor Radcliffe, the widow of the late Earl of Sussex. Nevertheless, after my afternoon's enquiry I could make no sense of that connection. The Earl had died some twenty years previously and his widow was rumoured to have taken up with a Scottish groom riddled with the pox by whom she herself was now infected. There was, besides, no evidence I could find of a Romish connection and so, by and by, I laid this particular avenue aside.

The next morning, being Wednesday, I addressed the second avenue, which proved more profitable. This related to a name entered in the Frenchman's journal as D. Goffe and which I believed to refer to Daniel Goffe, incumbent in a Hertfordshire living who had, besides, the means to maintain lodgings off the Strand. It was well known he had come into a fortune by his wife, now deceased. Less well known were the rumours of a High Anglican mass celebrated by families with putative Roman leaning within his parish. What I did not presently know was when, precisely, his wife had died and the fortune had passed beyond doubt to his name.

I was not averse to calling upon the reverend gentleman in order to pose the question directly but I determined, first, to test the memory of a virtuoso in matters of scandal, particularly where fortunes were concerned. Such was the lady who presided over the tavern in Bow Street upon whose balcony our young lords had recently cocked and crowed.

''Tis uncommon to find you seeking dinner at my table, Mr Wyld,' the mistress, Kate, remarked upon finding me upon her premises. 'Have you fallen out with Mr Dryden, perchance?'

'May I not vary my fare, then?'

'I know not but that you may. What will you take?'

'I am minded to eat beef today if you have any.'

'Then I shall be able to satisfy you,' she replied.

'And a bottle of claret, if you please.'

This being agreed, I took a place convenient as to not being over-heard.

'Come sit beside me awhile,' I urged, when she returned with a plate of meat and a bottle. 'For I would test your memory regarding one of your patrons. I refer to The Reverend Goffe.'

'I cannot tarry,' she insisted, but took the stool opposite at my bidding.

'Then I will be brief,' I assured her. 'Can you recall when, precisely, the late Mrs Goffe passed away?'

Kate's brow wrinkled briefly. ''Tis a curious question which, curiously, I can answer for 'twas on my birthday this two years past, the tenth day of May. Now tell me why Mr Wyld should be minded to make such a query?'

'Upon that I cannot presently satisfy you, but perhaps I may offer alternative fare.' And I related a tale which I had just heard from Lord Illminster concerning a child which was dropped during dancing at court but 'twas not known to whom it belonged. And how none among the ladies of honour could be found to answer for it. This seemed to satisfy the mistress of the house, for I heard her repeat the tale before I had finished my dinner. I was satisfied, too, for the entry in Monsieur Vouet's journal was dated 6 May in that same year. 'Twas a coincidence too rich to discount.

Our interview being over, I joined the company at the main board where I fell in with Mr Robert Southwell who was presently residing in town on business from his estates near Bristol. Having been one of the witnesses at Mr Delaney's evening of the transmutation, he was perplexed at the murder of Monsieur Vouet and quizzed me at length, though I offered him little by way of satisfaction. By and by he told me he was minded to see a play and begged me join him, to which suggestion I found no main objection and so acceded.

The Theatre Royal having been open in Drury Lane these five or six weeks, Mr Southwell wished to see there a new play of Sir Robert Stapylton which is called *The Slighted Mayde*. Since I had not yet seen the piece this suited us both and so, having dined to our mutual satisfaction, we went by Russell Street and were able to find ourselves places in the pit.

The theatre, at this my first inspection, seems well contrived though the passages to the pit were somewhat narrow and inconvenient. Moreover when the music struck up it rang exceeding hollow as if musicians played from beneath the stage. These quibbles aside, there was much to enjoy for the place was mighty full and all were decked in splendour. We soon spied, moreover, that the Duke and Duchess were in their box by which I perceived that we were to be entertained by the Duke's players. In this we were not disappointed and, though the play is not the finest ever writ, the parts of the mortals and the gods were excellently well acted so that we were quite transported in our mirth.

At the end of the play, which was received with great pleasure by the Duke, I found that Mr Southwell intended to return to the Cock Tavern. I excused myself, having some hope that Miss Hamilton was with the party of the Duke and Duchess. With this in mind I was dallying in readiness for the descent of the royal party from the box when my anticipated pleasure was rudely snatched from me. Before me, sneaking quietly from the theatre, I espied no less a figure than that very assassin who had attempted to murder me with his pistol.

The sight of this fellow brought such a heat to my brain that I could scarce control myself. With my hand on the pommel of my rapier I strode swiftly towards him and would have struck him down immediately, he seeing me not. Then, at once, the hand of reason stayed me. I could have his life or his master, not both. And so, the heat still burning fiercely within me, I allowed him to step free. And in a moment I followed in his wake.

My heart was beating now so swiftly and strongly that I feared the sound must reach the ears of my enemy and alert him as to my presence. He, however, seemed oblivious to all but his destination. By now the villain had slipped down Drury Lane. He led me thence, by lanes and passages, to stairs upon the river. I hung back until he had taken a boat then took a second, urging the waterman to take his route from the wherry that had just departed. I promised, moreover, to double his fare were he to ensure that our pursuit was not marked. At this he struck a diagonal course which brought us to the southern bank from which he could follow the passage of the other without the danger of discovery.

We were headed upstream and I soon perceived that our destination must be the palace. 'Twas so, the villain leaving his boat at the Privy Stairs, by which I understood him to be a regular visitor at Whitehall. I alighted presently at the same stairs, paying the wherryman two shillings for his trouble, and slipped cautiously into the palace precincts. Close by were the chambers of the Queen, the Queen's wardrobe and those of the maids of honour. Somewhere among these quarters my quarry had gone to ground.

I was at a loss. I might loiter in the hope of catching sight of him again but he might as soon see me. Frustrated, I retraced my path to the Privy Stairs. I was on the point of returning to Covent Garden when my mind was once more changed for I espied the arrival of the Duke's barge with the royal party but lately at the playhouse.

The Duke alighted first so that he might assist the Duchess. I bowed to the royal couple, my hat in my hand.

'Good day, Mr Wyld,' said the Duke, who seemed in fine spirits.

'Your Royal Highness,' I replied.

'As you can see, we have been practising some naval business,' he told me in jest.

'He misleads you,' the Duchess contradicted. 'For we have been to see a play acted. And now we are to have a ball, this very evening, with dancing. I pray that you will attend, Mr Wyld, for Miss Hamilton is become poor company when you are not near.'

Miss Hamilton, who was with the party, had by now been handed ashore herself.

'Look who we have found,' the Duchess told her, as the party began to enter the palace. 'I have instructed Mr Wyld he should pay suit to you tonight, so you must look your best.'

Miss Hamilton curtsied. 'I am much obliged, Your Royal Highness.'

'Then do not tarry now, all afternoon, or you shall not have the time to complete your toilette.'

By which we understood that we were given leave to spend some moments alone.

'How do you do, madam?' I asked, my hat still in my hand.

'I believe I do very well,' she replied with a smile. 'But I had not expected to see you at court today.'

'I had not expected to be here,' I told her. 'But chance has acted on our behalf. Come.' And I steered the lady towards a cloister where we might gain privacy.

'What brings you here?' she asked as we went.

'Why, I found myself suddenly upon that fellow who would have murdered me. He not seeing me, I have followed him here in order to find out his business but now he has quite disappeared and I know not where he hides.'

At this Miss Hamilton looked mightily alarmed.

'Fear not,' I reassured her. 'Surprise is with me for the moment. But mark, for you may espy him yourself, by and by. He is to be recognized by a scar from forehead to cheek upon the left side of his face.'

'I think I shall tremble with fear, should I find him before me,' she replied.

We were now standing face to face within the cloister when I felt of a sudden the grip of her hand upon my arm. Her features had frozen in a mask. 'It is he,' she whispered.

'Then look to me,' I commanded.

She did so, but her eyes strove to follow my quarry. 'He is gone,' she told me in a moment. 'He did not see, for he is quite occupied.'

I turned around cautiously and was able to see the back of the same fellow I had followed earlier, now returning to the stairs.

'It is indeed he,' I confirmed. 'Pray mark him well. And should you see him again, you must inform me immediately. By him I shall know the master of this treachery.'

Miss Hamilton still held me tightly by the arm and I took the opportunity to place my own hand upon her own. 'Please forgive me,' I pleaded. 'I must abandon you and follow this villain once more. But rest assured, I shall take a turn upon the floor with you this evening if you will permit me.'

'Take care, Mr Wyld,' she told me. But I could read behind her present anxiety a hint of the pleasure that the prospect of the ball now held for her.

With a bow I was away to the stairs myself, though not without caution as to being observed. Having determined that my villain had already departed, I quickly commanded a boat so that once more we danced the dance of the wherries.

This time we headed back downstream and, the tide being on the ebb, we made good speed. We were soon past the Somerset Stairs and the Fleet River. Indeed, I had began to fear he was away to Rotherhythe or Chatham when his wherry stopped at the final stairs before the bridge and here the fellow alighted. A few moments later I did the same and was able to pick him up along Gracechurch Street and by Leadenhall Street to the gate of a mansion into which he disappeared.

I knew not whose mansion he had entered, nor whether this was where he belonged. I perceived, moreover, that it would not be convenient for me to loiter before the gate unless I wished my presence to be remarked. It would be a job for Ned, I supposed. But not today. And so I returned to the stairs once more and took a boat back upstream. In all, I was unsure what profit I was going to be able to take from this excursion but held hope that some would be forthcoming.

CHAPTER 17

A Saraband with Miss Hamilton, a Corant with Lady Castlemaine

'Bridget,' I said, 'Martha. I am to go to a ball at the court this very night. What am I to do?' For evening was already upon me and I could not think.

'Why, sir,' Bridget replied, 'you'll need fine clothes to start.'

'Indeed I shall. Martha, go fetch me silken hose from the mercer. Rouse him if needs must and be sure to tell him I desire the colour to be the blue of a blackbird's egg. See what shirts and breeches of the latest style he has,' I added, giving her two sovereigns and sending her on her way.

When the girl was through the door I addressed Bridget once more. 'I am minded to wear my embroidered vest,' I told her. 'The silver and blue.'

'Yes, sir, it suits you mighty well.'

'My square-toed shoes, too, I think. Pray put them by and see they are in good order.'

'Will you want me, sir?' asked Ned, hopefully.

'I shall need no page tonight,' I told him. 'But you may go and fetch the barber for I shall be in want of a shave.'

Thus the household became busy with the preparations.

Martha returned in good time with the hose and a fine new pair of petticoat breeches. Soon after Ned brought the barber with a bucket of warm water and his razor. I bade the fellow shave me in the parlour where the light was still clear so that he might take my beard alone and leave the rest of me unscarred.

'Now, Martha,' I said, when he was gone, 'prepare me a rub with rose and lavender and tincture of violet for we must ensure that I smell as sweet as a summer bloom this night.'

She was swift away to prepare the rub, bringing linen to apply it and by and by did rub me down from head to toe. The wound in my arm was hard and dark against the white of my naked flesh but not so troublesome as before and I had her bind it gently with a bandage for protection.

'Twas time now to be fitted for the ball. Martha speedily got me into the hose and a new linen shirt trimmed with lace. Then over a fine pair of ribbon-trimmed underbreeches I tried the new petticoat breeches, which went exceeding well. Once I had put on my shoes and she had tied the ribbons I was ready, almost, to take steps, forward and back, upon the floor. It wanted but my vest, its silk lining matching the blue of the hose, and a hat which I had the girl trim with blue ribbon too. Thus I hoped to commend myself in Miss Hamilton's eyes.

'Who shall be at the ball?' Martha asked me as she helped me put on my dress.

'It may be that the whole court will be present,' I replied. 'For it is the fashion, when the days are long, to dance 'til dawn.'

'And who may you dance with, sir?' she asked, coyly.

'That is for the night to decide,' I answered. 'Now curb your curiosity. I promise I will supply you with all the rumour you desire on the morrow.'

So, by and by, I was ready and sent Ned to find a sedan which carried me as far as Somerset Stairs. Though dusk was still an hour and more away, I expected the sunset to find the court upon the water.

I could see before the waterman had pushed off that the river was bustling in anticipation of the evening's entertainment. All headed upstream, my boat joining them. Before long I spied the royal barges in mid stream, pennants barely held aloft on the gentlest of summer breezes. The two barges were surrounded by a flotilla of smaller craft each bearing its own cargo. Some brought courtiers, other ladies while yet others bore gallants and city gentlemen. On the fringes were more craft in which might be spied the beauties from the town in search of adventure or simple city folk enjoying the spectacle of the carnival.

Pulling through these fringes of the flotilla, I had the boatman leave me at the Privy Stairs from whence I was soon taken up again by a boat carrying Mr Pemberton and Mr Arnold, another from the Duke's entourage, who had seen me alight. Both were dressed for the ball.

'Come seat yourself, sir,' Mr Pemberton greeted me. 'You are just in time for the fireworks.' And he instructed his boatman to carry us forthwith into the heart of the flotilla.

As we reached the throng about the royal barges I perceived the sound of musicians striking up a martial anthem; the Duke had brought the music master and some of his players on to the water to greet the fall of night. With this joyous signal, the sky was suddenly embroidered with jewels of light while the music was instantly drowned beneath a barrage of sharp reports. The firework boat had began to divest itself of its squibs and wheels and the other contrivances of the maker's art with which it was furnished.

This distraction continued for many minutes. As it progressed, the acrid smoke from the burnt powder, drifting slowly across the water, made a gauze through which the edges of the scene became indistinct so that we might all be living within some strange dream. Only the vivid punctuations of the reports and the incandescence of the firework remained sharp and incontestable. Then, of an instant, all went silent and dark. At once we heard, from our dream, the mellow strains of some mournful air dedicated to the passing of the day.

The smoke cleared slowly, rolling down the river but my eyes were by now so attuned to the harsh brightness of the fireworks that the evening without them was quite black. From this blackness there emerged, slowly, the twinkle of lanterns, bobbing and dancing on the water. And so, the royal barges leading, the court returned to the palace and disembarked while the townsfolk began to drift downstream and away, following the path of the smoke.

Leaving our own boat in due course, Mr Pemberton, Mr Arnold and I entered the palace precinct from the stairs and Mr Pemberton led us to his quarters.

'I hope you have your Bransles and Corants,' he joked upon the way. 'For I have heard, expressly, a rumour that you will be called upon to dance this night.'

'As to dancing, I am prepared,' I assured him. 'Though had I been forwarned I should have taken the latest fashion from my dance master. I judge the King will bring some new step or other.'

'His Majesty has ever some new dance, it is true, but he will teach the steps to his favourites first.' He drew close to whisper. 'By this he ensnares his courtiers and binds the court to him. 'Tis a strategy he learned from King Louis and it serves him well.'

By now we were within Mr Pemberton's own lodgings where he had put up a light repast. There were some eggs and chicken, a little fish and a fine Rhenish wine that sweetened the palate. My last hours had been so fraught with activity that I had found time for naught since my beef at Kate's. At once I fell upon the meat with an appetite which awoke some slight comment from Mr Arnold. I let it pass but eventually my hunger was sated and I felt ready to converse civilly again.

'Will you take the floor too?' I asked, replenishing my glass with more of the excellent wine.

'We are ordered to come prepared,' Mr Arnold replied. 'For the Portuguese ladies oft find themselves in need of partners.'

'And are we not the ugliest fellows to be found?' Mr Pemberton added.

'None uglier,' I agreed.

'But have you yet heard the judgement upon Sir Charles Sedley?' Mr Arnold asked.

'I have not,' I conceded, though I knew the affair was due.

'He is bound over for his debauchery at Oxford Kate's and the Lord Chief Justice has told him God will judge us all by *his* sins. As to Lord Buckhurst, he finds himself reprimanded for aiding such debauchery when he has but lately escaped punishment for robbery. But I think he will not mind for he knows well his own worth.'

'Then they are not to be flogged?' I asked him.

'I think, sir,' Mr Arnold replied, 'that such flesh as theirs would be quite ruined by the cat. For they are not coarse fellows with skin like leather.'

'Come,' said Mr Pemberton, interrupting this banter. 'The dancing will start on the hour.'

Upon which we three arose and went directly to the room where the ball was to be held.

We arrived to find the chamber crammed about the sides with fine ladies and richly clad gentlemen. The ladies all sat amid their silks and lace while the gentlemen formed small groups before them. The music master had his musicians ready. All now awaited the royal party.

It was near midnight when they arrived. The King and Queen entered first, followed by the Duke and Duchess. In their train came the Duke and Duchess of Monmouth, followed soon by My Lady Castlemaine and Miss Stuart. My own eye passed these by quickly, searching for a glimpse of Miss Hamilton whom I found to be among the group to the rear. Her face shone in the light of the candles as if burnished and about that face her hair, which was caught in ringlets and decorated with jewels, formed a spangled firmament. Her dress, which brushed the floor as she swayed, was a silk of the darkest midnight blue cut low but not immodestly so and at her throat there hung a single jewel which I believed must be a diamond.

When all were arranged in seats, the music master struck up with a tune. At once the King took up the Duchess, the Duke the Duchess of Buckingham, the Duke of Monmouth took Miss Stuart and the Duke of Buckingham took the hand of My Lady Castlemaine, whereupon they formed themselves for a Nonesuch. His Majesty being upon the floor, all the ladies in the room rose with a great rustle and we admired His Majesty's skill and poise as the dancers weaved their way, one betwixt the other, their leather shoes making a patter on the boards as they went.

The Nonesuch being over, the King led Miss Stuart for a single Corant, followed swiftly by other great couples. I soon perceived, withal, that My Lady Castlemaine and Miss Stuart were in some competition to create the grandest spectacle, both in dance and costume. The younger, Miss Stuart, was in frock of emerald green over white lace petticoats and her hair was dressed in lace and jewels. My Lady, in contrast, had left her dark curls to fall freely about her shoulders which were bared and the white of milk. Her dress was another crimson, a shade I had already learned did suit her well and her jewels were the finest in the room. Finer even, I do believe, than the those which adorned the Queen.

After the Corants, the King and Duke took a rest and I found by some small sign from Miss Hamilton, whose eye I had caught now several times across the room, that we were to take the floor with some other of the maids of honour. At this, I had crossed the chamber in a moment to take her hand and lead her out.

'How handsome you are tonight, madam,' I told her with a whisper. 'I do fear I shall quite exhaust you with my gazing.'

'And I see, sir, that blue is a colour which suits you well.'

''Tis the colour of your eyes,' I reminded her with a smile.

We were to dance a Saraband and so we took our places in line where we were joined by several other couples, though I confess I took little note of them. At once the music master struck up and we began to make our steps, forwards and back and then with turns and crossings we drew our pattern upon the floor. Miss Hamilton moved with such poise and elegance, I believed she must charm all who saw. I simply worshipped her with my eyes.

Too soon, the Saraband was over. At this I took the liberty of joining the Duke's party, which the Duchess encouraged, and stood beside Miss Hamilton as she sat with the other maids about Her Highness. Then, after the King had taken a further turn upon the floor, we stood up again to dance a Bransle. This proved a most popular choice and the floor was pretty soon full of couples. The Bransle being a dance of some exertion, our cheeks were soon glowing and our bodies breathless while our steps fell in unison as we matched movement to music in as bold a fashion as we dare. My partner was, I believe, as fully elated as I and ready to match me in every regard.

After the Bransle I escorted Miss Hamilton back to the Duke's party and was standing beside her once more when a gentleman from the King's entourage stepped up to my shoulder and whispered in my ear.

'Mr Wyld,' he said, 'the King, having been shown how well you dance, has particularly asked that you should stand up with My Lady Castlemaine in the next Corant.'

At this I was taken completely by surprise, not having imagined such a thing to be possible. 'I am at His Majesty's service,' I replied and having hastily relayed in a whisper to Miss Hamilton what was requested, I followed him across the floor. As I did so I looked back once, but the expression on her face being too painful to bear, I looked away quickly.

My Lady was adorned with rubies which appeared to me to smoulder in the candlelight as I approached. She was sitting close by the Queen beside whom was also Miss Stuart. The King was presently whispering in the ear of this last lady. I bowed before Their Majesties and My Lady, then offered her my hand for the previous dance had now been completed. She rose with a rustle and I escorted her on to the boards.

'I have been observing to His Majesty how excellently you are fitted for dancing, Mr Wyld,' My Lady told me as we took our position. 'He agrees that you have a fine leg.'

'Are we to dance alone?' I asked her.

'Indeed we are,' she told me. 'The better that we may be seen. For I do believe you can dance the feet off any gentleman in the room.'

And so the music started and we played our parts, which I fancy were indeed excellently executed, and I fancy also that there were few in the room who were not aware that My Lady Castlemaine and Mr Wyld were dancing. No doubt that was the intention.

The music finally came to an end and I escorted My Lady back to her seat. As she sat and I was preparing to bow and retreat, she caught my ear with a whisper.

'You dance like a god, Mr Wyld. Pray do me the honour of your service for the next Bransle.'

'My Lady,' I replied stiffly.

'I shall prepare myself,' she added, a treacherous smile playing about her lips.

At that I did bow and retreat, but my heart was burdened for I knew that the pleasure which Miss Hamilton had briefly enjoyed was soured. Her evening would be quite spoiled by this intervention.

When I rejoined that lady, I perceived that she was discomfited and, after a brief exchange, I understood that it would be fitting if I left her side. I crossed the floor at the next opportunity and regained the company of Mr Pemberton and Mr Arnold.

'Have you been banished?' Mr Pemberton asked, joking.

'I have been used, sir,' I replied. 'And I am to be used again.'

'Then it is fitting that you should remain with us,' he replied. 'For we, too, await our orders.'

In due course another Bransle was called up and I led My Lady out on the floor again. Here the King joined us, partnering Miss Stuart once more and, by and by, the several Dukes brought partners too. I found, withal, that My Lady danced as fine a Bransle as she did a Corant and I divined by her manner that she intended we should be a match for His Majesty and his partner. I had no wish to be part of such a tournament and performed with restraint but I fear this suited My Lady perfectly.

I handed her back to her seat after the Bransle had ended, wishing that now my ordeal should end. It was not to be. Before she sat she remarked, for my ear only, 'Since Miss Hamilton has no further use for you this evening, pray remain at my side. We will take to the floor again presently.'

At this my emotions overcame my reason. 'My Lady,' I whispered crossly, 'you use me badly. For myself I do not care, but I would not see that lady injured further. Therefore I must ask that you release me.'

'Mr Wyld,' she hissed, 'would you make an enemy of me?'

'I would not,' I answered. 'But if I must, then so be it.'

At this her eyes seemed to me to burn like the rubies about her neck. 'Then go,' she said. And I was dismissed.

I made my way back to where Mr Pemberton still loitered. My heart was now troubled and I believe that I trembled too.

'Are you well?' he asked me, concerned.

'I must leave at once,' I told him, my voice barely able to contain my emotion. 'But I have need of your assistance first.'

He would have questioned me then, only my face told him this was no time for questions.

'What is it you seek?' he asked, instead.

'I must speak with Miss Hamilton, alone.'

My friend thought for a moment. 'Go to my chambers,' he told me. 'I will bring her to you.'

'Thank you,' I answered. And with a short bow, I was away.

CHAPTER 18

Colonel Hamilton Gives His Blessing

I made my way swiftly to Mr Pemberton's chambers, my mind a confusion of emotions. Once there I tried to steady myself but that proved impossible. Instead I paced the room muttering incessantly and lamenting my cruel destiny.

I had just slighted the most powerful woman in the land and done so in the presence of the whole court. She would not forgive me, I well knew, until she had exacted her full revenge. Yet in all I knew, too, that I was blameless, unless wishing to protect Miss Hamilton was a sin. So thinking, I condemned harshly the fate that had brought me within My Lady's purview. 'Damn that woman,' I cried, suddenly, out loud. 'Damn her and all her accursed scheming.'

The injury to my arm was throbbing again, partly I suppose from the exertion of the dancing but mostly from the heat of my passions. I took a cursory look at the bandaging for signs of blood but the wound had not reopened, though it might easily do so soon I feared.

I must calm myself and cast this heat of emotion from me. So thinking, I took up a glass and filled it with a draught of Pemberton's Rhenish wine from the table which remained uncleared from our earlier repast. The honeyed liquid, as I sipped it from the glass, did quench some of my passion and I began to think clearly once more.

I had acted in anger and frustration but what was done was well done. I should, no doubt, suffer some fall in favour as a result, but I could live with that. Once my present business was complete, it might be prudent to leave the court and London for a while, to retreat to the country or abroad if necessary. My Lady could scheme but I would be alive to her scheming. I would survive.

And what in all this of Miss Hamilton? Therein lay my greatest concern. In truth I knew not where she stood. And so in fear I waited.

It would, I knew, take Pemberton some moments to discover a strategy suitable to extract Miss Hamilton from the ball without undue attention. I hoped only that she would not refuse my request for then I would be broken.

Time passed, and yet more, so that finally I did begin to worry. How long could it take? Then at once I heard the sound of footsteps approaching.

It was Pemberton who stepped into the room first. Seeing that I was there, he made a sign and the lady entered too. Her face as she came was fixed and stern. I could not read what lay behind this mask.

'I will leave you,' Pemberton said, 'and return presently.'

'No,' Miss Hamilton told him. 'I would prefer that you remain.'

Pemberton looked to me and I nodded, at which he retreated to a distant corner, leaving the two of us to face one another.

I approached the lady. 'Miss Hamilton,' I began, intent on bringing the matter to a head swiftly, 'I have just now made an enemy of My Lady Castlemaine by refusing to partner her further.'

At this Miss Hamilton's mask dropped and she gasped with astonishment. 'Oh, sir!' she cried in dismay.

'I spoke to her thus in the heat of a moment, which was certainly foolish,' I added. 'And yet I must speak, for her actions wounded you greatly. That I could not bear.'

After I had spoken these words her face took on a sorrowful aspect and a tear appeared in her eye. Seeing such sorrow I wanted to take her in my arms, to console her. Yet I could not.

'Do not weep,' I said, drawing closer.

'But, sir,' she cried, 'how can I not weep at such a cruel fate. For your great consideration can only condemn us to greater sorrow.' And at that she did weep, covering her face with her hands as she did so.

'Please,' I said, touching her arm, for I knew not what else I could do. All at once her hand grasped mine, like a child might seek its mother at such a moment. I held it tight, and thus we remained for several minutes. Eventually her sobs subsided but still our hands remained linked.

'Do you love the court?' I asked her, when her tears had subsided and she was able once more to speak. 'For I fear that my action has put your position here in jeopardy.'

'No,' she confessed. 'I do not much love it.'

'Then please listen to what I have to say to you. I did not jest in the park this Sunday past. If you will allow me, I will take you away from this and we will seek some quiet retreat, far from the court and its ways.'

Her eyes were still moist as they looked into my own, searching, but she remained mute.

'Miss Hamilton.' I hesitated. 'Rebecca. Say yes and I will go to your father and ask him for your hand.'

Still she said nothing and still she looked into my eyes. Then, loosing my hand, she reached to her neck and unfastened the jewel which hung there.

'Take this, a token,' she said. 'By it, my father will know you come with my blessing. He will be alarmed, otherwise, for he lives in fear of these days. He will know your name, for I have told him it already.'

I placed the jewel carefully into the pocket in my breeches.

'I will go on the morrow,' I told her.

'God speed you,' she replied, and I thought she might weep once more.

So it was that we parted. Pemberton escorted Miss Hamilton back to the ball and I took my leave of the palace, dreaming as I went of an Eden is some distant corner of the land where we should pass our days in peace.

When I returned to Covent Garden, Bridget sensed immediately that something untoward had disturbed my mien and schooled the girl to hold her tongue, for which I was thankful. Otherwise she would have prated all the night about the ball. When she had undressed me, I did not take my bed immediately but smoked a pipe while I drew together my thoughts. Events about me were moving swiftly and I must hold fast. Yet the day had been long and I soon found sleep pressing. With a sense of relief I allowed myself to succumb.

Next morning, early, I sent Ned to the stables to bid the master prepare me a strong steed fit for a taxing ride. Colonel Hamilton kept his hearth amid the marshes and fens close by Ely. A good horseman would do well to make the journey in two days: it was my intention to be there ere nightfall.

Before I left, however, I instructed Ned that he should spend this day and the next gathering what intelligence he could before the mansion in Leadenhall Street. I bade him watch for the villain especially, but if he could discover who lived within, and what business was conducted there, so much the better. I gave him some small pieces of silver which I cautioned him to guard and spend wisely if he had the need, at which he was mightily pleased.

With that I repaired to the stable and took the mount, which was readied and waiting. She was a bay whom I had ridden before and she knew me well. As soon as we had escaped the confines of the city and were free of its noxious odours we settled into a familiar rhythm and the miles quickly slipped behind her well-shod hoofs. This rhythm so fully occupied my mind that I thought not of the mysteries and threats which encircled me. By this I was refreshed.

The road north to Cambridge passes by Royston and it was in the latter that I rested and watered my mount while I consumed a light dinner of pike and crayfish. I was in Cambridge by late afternoon and there took directions for Aldreth Hall which I found lay just beyond the Great Ouse river on the borders of the Isle of Ely.

Hereabout was a land that had found itself divided during the late troubles. Ely was the home town of Oliver the Protector while its cathedral was the seat of that high church ecclesiastical, Bishop Wren. The men of the region had adhered to either one or the other so that the city and its neighbourhood had become at war with itself. Colonel Hamilton had chosen the side of the Protector.

As a member of Cromwell's Eastern Association the colonel had fought valiantly and was wounded more than once, though never seriously. The campaigns had taken him far from his home but at heart he was a fenman and when many of his fellows followed their commander to London, he chose to return at Aldreth. The death of the Protector and the subsequent return of the King had left him vulnerable, but it seems he had friends enough that no great harm or privation had yet befallen him. And yet, as Miss Hamilton had intimated, he lived his days in fear.

I found my way to the hall by early evening and presented myself at the gate where I was admitted at once. The colonel, when I was shown into his presence, seemed apprehensive.

'Mr Wyld,' he greeted me cautiously. 'This is a strange hour to come visiting.'

'It is, sir,' I admitted, 'but my business is pressing. I will speak plainly, sir. Though you know me not, I come to seek your daughter's hand in marriage.'

'That is plainly put indeed. And yet I do believe I know you for my daughter has spoken of you.'

I bowed at this acknowledgement. 'Miss Hamilton has instructed me to bring you this.'

So saying, I withdrew a small pouch from my pocket into which I had placed her jewel and presented it to the colonel. He opened the pouch and carefully extracted the ornament.

'Then she loves you truly, sir, for this is a most precious heirloom that belonged to my wife, a gift to her grandmother from Queen Elizabeth herself.' He replaced the stone in the pouch and handed it back to me. 'Well, sir,' he said, 'since you have come this far you will no doubt stay the night, by which means you will be able to give me an account of yourself.'

It was agreed that I would presently take an evening meal with the colonel. In the meantime he instructed a room be prepared and sent me a woman with water to wash off the dust of the road. Thus refreshed I rejoined the master of the house within an hour and we drank one another's health from a jug of fenland beer.

Colonel Hamilton was inquisitive as to my means which I admitted were not great but which were, I believed, sufficient to enable me to keep his daughter in comfort. As to my business I was guarded but confessed that I was a servant of the King.

'Then, sir,' he said, 'your position will provide my daughter with more security than my own.'

'Do you have enemies, sir?' I asked.

'We all have enemies,' he replied, to which assertion I could but assent.

At last I believe we came to understand one another. The colonel was no proselytiser or zealot, but a man who had his fellow men at heart. We each of us, if we are honest, must follow our beliefs. He had followed his. Now he was content that he had played his part and thought only to secure his daughter's future in a world that was not the one he had lately inhabited.

'Well, Mr Wyld,' he told me finally, 'I find you as honest as I can find any man after such a brief acquaintance. I know that my daughter loves you. If you love her equally, then she is yours.'

'I do, sir,' I told him.

'I will write to her on the morrow to inform her of my decision. Will you stay, sir, a day or two, that we may come to know one another more fully?'

'I would, sir, did my own business not demand that I return immediately. But I will be honoured to be your guest when my present affairs are settled.'

'Then so be it.'

Upon which we repaired, each to his bed. No doubt my host had much upon which to reflect, as did I.

Next morning I rose with the sun. After a commodious breakfast I bade farewell to the colonel and mounted once more upon the bay which like me was refreshed and anxious for the road.

The beast again served me splendidly. Well before nightfall she had brought me once more within the confines of London. I was, as soon, apprehensive as to what might have passed there in my absence.

CHAPTER 19

The Death of an Alchemist

My return found Ned in quite a state of excitement. He had followed my instructions and spent much of the past two days loitering before the mansion in Leadenhall Street. There he had played the part of a street urchin to avoid conspicuity. From this vantage point he had been able to observe the villain with the disfigured face who he had marked entering and leaving the mansion on three separate occasions, having visited once yesterday and twice today.

By his own intelligence he had also spoken to a woman who served in the mansion, seeking to run errands for some small remuneration. The woman had informed him that Mr Backhouse already had persons within suitable as to performing such tasks, from which he deduced that this Mr Backhouse was the present occupier.

Ned also reported to me that following some hour or so – as he guessed – upon the last visit of the villain to the mansion there had been a considerable commotion of coming and going, during which he saw a gentleman whom he recognized as having previously visited me in Covent Garden. I asked him to describe this latter, who he had found to be tall and somewhat meagrely built which, added to the fact that he had the use of a coach pulled by four black horses, led me to deduce that this last was Delaney. Some business of the alchemists was afoot I guessed, with villainy not far behind.

In all the boy had done exceeding well and I told him take the small pieces I had given him and with Bridget's help purchase that pair of shoes he had desired. Soon thereafter I retired.

*

I awoke the next morning with the delightful recollection that I was now betrothed to Miss Hamilton. From such a position my life must surely become fulfilled in all those aspects in which it was yet found wanting.

In the meantime I had some business to complete. I called Martha and had her dress me, my intention having formed to visit Delaney as soon as I had breakfasted in order to discover what had befallen among his secret conspirers. I was saved this inconvenience by the arrival of Delaney himself who appeared when I had barely begun to take my breakfast.

'Come, sit,' I said, 'and take a morsel with me. I am just betrothed and you shall be the first to congratulate me on the match.'

This news seemed to discomfit him greatly. 'I had not expected such a thing,' he stammered.

'But I have spoken to you of my fondness for Miss Hamilton. Surely you cannot be surprised?'

'Well, no.' And he took my hand and shook it, though with a great lack of enthusiasm. Something was clearly amiss.

'I am pleased to see you, but I judge you have come on business so we had better attend to that immediately. Tell me what troubles you.'

'Mr John Backhouse is dead,' he told me, abruptly.

Now it was my turn to be surprised.

'When did this happen?' I asked.

'He was found yesterday in the afternoon. He has taken his own life in a most unexpected fashion, as you shall presently see for I have instructed that all must be preserved upon your return.'

'You wish me to examine him? Then you believe this to be on account of the Frenchman?'

'He has the stolen letters. I do believe that he has been wholly responsible for this treachery. It leaves only the discovery of the manuscript to confirm the hypothesis in all its aspects. Lord Illminster is of a like opinion.'

'His Lordship is informed?'

'Of course. He has, with me, inspected already the unfortunate man's remains. There is no further need of secrecy.'

'Then my task is over.'

'I believe so, yes.'

'In which case if you will but allow me to take some victuals I will be pleased to see what has passed and how.'

Mr John Backhouse was quite dead. In this Delaney made no mistake. As to the means, it appeared he had consumed a bottle of his own oil of vitriol. The result was quite the ugliest piece of such work I have witnessed. The mutilation and death had taken place in the mansion in Leadenhall Street which I had lately set Ned to observe. It was within this mansion that I now found myself, courtesy of Delaney's coach and four.

The body had been laid out in a bedchamber with little ceremony and a great deal of haste, for even after death the liquor continued its ghastly work. The room had been shut against all visitors and upon our admission the stench of sulphurous corruption was quite overpowering.

Bidding a servant draw the curtains and ventilate the chamber, I approached the body cautiously and, beware of any remaining efficacy to the liquor, perused it at first without touching. The lower features of the face were now barely recognizable as human, such was the destruction that had taken place of the flesh. The mouth yawned and, within, the tongue was a discoloured stump while the lips had in places been eroded almost to the bone. Some of the liquor had spilled over the neck and this was burned too so that the shell of the tract that feeds the lungs was quite visible through the blistered and broken skin.

The decaying effects of the liquor did not appear, by this cursory inspection, to extend beyond these upper regions of the body. The corpse was still clothed and it was impossible to be certain so I called for a knife and carefully cut away the shirt. There was no sign beneath of discolouration and the abdomen did not appear to my eye to be unnaturally distended. This suggested to me that the oil of vitriol had not passed beyond the gullet, which observation I found somewhat surprising. I examined the hands then. Neither showed damage consistent with exposure to the corrosive oil.

'This is an exceedingly hard means by which to extinguish one's life,' I remarked to Delaney after I had finished examining the body. 'Why should he elect such a painful death?'

'I judge it to be an act of penance and contrition for his betrayal,' Delaney replied tersely. 'As he no doubt recognized at the last, his sin has consigned him to the everlasting flames.'

I understood by this that he had little sympathy regarding the late Mr Backhouse's demise.

I had learned all for now that the corpse had to teach and so bade Delaney show me where it had been found. At this he instructed a servant lead the way across a cloistered and paved courtyard to the elaboratory which Mr Backhouse had maintained at the back of the mansion.

This chamber, when we entered, was in a state of considerable disarray. Shards of glass, which were scattered across the floor, spoke of a violent disturbance having occurred and the conclusion was reinforced by an upturned table and stool.

I expressed surprise at this disorder. Delaney, however, had already essayed an explanation.

'The body was found beside this table,' he informed me, indicating the overturned piece of furniture. 'I judge that the death throes induced by the oil of vitriol will have created just such an agony of motion as life left his body as was necessary to create this confusion.'

He bade me to examine a part of the flooring close to the point where the body had lain. 'This is where he dropped the flask of oil of vitriol. You will see that what remained of the liquor has eroded the stone. It is quite clear.'

What I saw there confirmed his view. There was no doubt the stone had been exposed to the liquor. Indeed the thick-walled vessel which had presumably contained it lay in pieces around me, accompanied by parts of an alembic and some other glassware.

'You have found a tidy enough explanation,' I told my companion, straightening up. 'Everything here appears consistent with such a death. You say you have the letters? Pray, show me them, if you please.'

'Why, they are here,' Delaney said, striding across the room to another desk on which papers were collected.

I followed him. There in the centre, among the papers, were three letters. I picked them up, one by one. They were, it seemed, the letters which the mysterious Aurum had penned to Monsieur Vouet.

'Why only three?' I asked. 'There were five.'

'Lord Illminster has taken two others. He wishes to discover if he may, who was their author.'

'So it was not Mr Backhouse?'

'Lord Illminster seems to believe it was not.'

A quick perusal of the desk revealed several examples of the dead man's hand. These showed that His Lordship's conclusion was correct. The letters were in another hand.

'Has Mr Backhouse left any admission?' I asked.

'None has been found and I expect none. The motive is clear to me and to my companions.'

'So all are informed?' I asked.

Delaney nodded in confirmation.

'Then there is no mystery here?'

'None that I can see.'

'Well I'll be prepared to wager you'll not discover your manuscript in this place.'

'Why not?' demanded Delaney, alarmed.

''Tis my belief that Mr Backhouse did not die by his own hand, but by that of another.'

Delaney looked stunned. 'That is impossible,' he exclaimed.

'Not impossible, Robert. The real question, if I am correct, is this: what was the motive?'

Delaney began to argue his case again but I interrupted him.

'Let us see if I am correct,' I told him. 'And first we need to open the body. Who will come straightway, do you suppose?'

'Sir Charles will not, I'll warrant, but perhaps Mr Goddard, who is at Gresham College, might since 'tis not his day to lecture.'

Mr Goddard was sent to and being able, obliged us with his speedy arrival. The three of us repaired at once to the bedchamber.

'My thesis is this,' I explained to Mr Goddard and Delaney as we stood over the body. 'That Mr Backhouse was first murdered and then the oil of vitriol poured into him in order to make it appear that he has taken his own life.'

'There is no sign how he might be murdered,' Delaney complained.

'There is not. Which leads me to conclude that such signs as might have existed have been erased by the oil of vitriol. I would suggest that the breath was wrung from him first, but we will surely find no clear evidence of such a crime now. However if this was the course of events, the oil will not have passed much beyond his throat. So let us discover how it lies.'

At this, Mr Goddard understood exactly my purpose. He swiftly opened the throat of the corpse and the top end of the gullet. When the flesh was laid back it quickly became clear that though the throat was severely burned, the passage to the stomach remained virtually unscathed.

Delaney was not convinced. 'This is no contrary evidence,' he argued.

However Mr Goddard was of my opinion. 'Mr Wyld speaks with good reason,' he told him. 'For if Mr Backhouse lived when he took the poison he would surely have made such a contraction of his throat as to force a portion towards his stomach.'

'Is that the sum of your case?' Delaney demanded, piqued.

'Look, Robert,' I told him, 'by your hypothesis the victim induced in himself such a spasm when he took a draught of the poison that he thereupon dropped the vessel and crashed to the floor, apparently dead. Even allowing that it might act so swiftly, which I doubt, there is yet no sign of burning on his clothing. Neither are his hands marked. The oil of vitriol can only be found about the mouth and neck.'

'That is curious,' he conceded, finally.

'Indeed. And yet everything is consistent with the oil of vitriol being administered as he lay upon the floor, already dead.'

'Perhaps,' Delaney muttered, gruffly.

My interest in the body was over. Mr Goddard sewed up the opening he had made and we consigned the remains to the servants that arrangements might be begun for his interment. His wife, who had been sent for from the country, had yet to return but I recommended that the body be shut up swiftly against her view. As to that, I instructed the housekeeper to send for me when the lady returned that I might offer her some explanation myself.

When we had then bade farewell to Mr Goddard, whose discretion in this matter I for the moment begged, I found I had one further enquiry to pursue of the household. I took Delaney with me and went to search out the housekeeper once more. She was among some serving girls in the scullery, no doubt coining rumours as to the reason for their master's demise. I escorted her into a parlour at the front of the mansion that we might speak without an audience.

'Was it you that found your master?' I asked, for Delaney had told me it was her.

'Aye, sir. He had been taken up this past week with some great enquiry and had shut himself up all day with barely a morsel to eat. I took myself over to discover as to whether I should prepare a supper.'

'But he was not altogether alone? Was there not some visitor, a fellow with a scar, who came twice during the day?' At this Delaney looked at me, askance. I ignored him as I awaited the woman's reply.

'There was, sir, aye.'

'Do you know his business?'

'No, sir, except that it belonged to my master's enquiry.'

'But he had been before?'

'Yes, sir. He has been admitted perhaps five times this past week.'

'And before that?'

'He had not been before this week, to my knowledge.'

'Do you know from whence he comes?'

'I can't say as I do, sir.' She thought a moment. 'Though I have a notion, sir,' she added, 'that he might have some connection with Plymouth.'

That proved the sum of her knowledge, so I dismissed her. Delaney kept his tongue until we were alone again, then he began to upbraid me crossly.

'You are making me a fool, Francis,' he told me. 'Why did you not confess that you already knew something was amiss?'

'But I did not know,' I replied. 'This scarred fellow is the one who would have murdered me. I had my boy watch for him while I was away.'

'At the door of Mr John Backhouse? That can be no coincidence.'

'It cannot, Robert, for I had myself pursued him to this door already, and so I was suspicious. But let us not quibble about this for there are more important considerations now. What do you know of this great enquiry in which Mr Backhouse was engaged?'

'Nothing.'

'Then let us return to the elaboratory and see if we can discover its nature. For it seems to me peculiar that he should be thus engaged one moment, then dead the next.'

Mr Backhouse was not an ordered gentleman and the organization of his elaboratory proved to be a reflection of his self. Sheets of scribbling were mixed with carefully written manuscripts and the verso of many of the latter were also covered with notes. By and by, however, Delaney formed an opinion.

''Tis some crude attempt at the stone,' he concluded.

'Had he the wit?'

'It is to be doubted by this, but he believed he had the method. It would appear he was working in collaboration with another.'

'Who?'

'I cannot say.'

'Then there is no more for us here. But I will tell you who I believe his collaborator to be. It is the architect of this whole affair and therefore a man much to be feared: Lord Illminster.'

'It cannot be,' Delaney retorted crossly.

'We shall see.'

I picked up the three letters, which still lay on the desk before us, and prepared to leave. As I did so I glanced again at them briefly. At once a new concern stirred within me. I knew I had seen the hand in which they were written before, but at the moment I could not say where.

CHAPTER 20

Lady Villiers' Correspondence

Delaney said nothing as we left the mansion and returned to his coach. I climbed in behind him, having first instructed his groom to take us to Covent Garden. We continued in silence while the carriage rattled its way across the ruts into Cheapside, heading by St Paul's towards Ludgate Hill. No doubt Lord Illminster occupied us both.

I had for some time suspected that His Lordship must be the spider at the centre of this web, but that suspicion was supported by no weight of evidence. The villain's connection with Plymouth, on the doorstep of the Illminster estate, was of little substance either, but I knew His Lordship kept a privateer there which I believed to have preyed on Dutch trade this last year. It could make the two who had attacked me his sailors.

Thus a picture is created, piece by piece. And thus my suspicion had become a conviction. That, and a recognition of the ruthless efficiency with which each act had been effected. No other of Delaney's circle of alchemists possessed such brutal determination. Yet I remained perplexed. Why had Lord Illminster designed this last deadly masque? Who was the audience? What was its purpose?

It was then that I recalled where I believed I had seen the hand in which the three stolen letters were written. At this I began to fear more than before. If I was correct, I had a note penned by this hand in my parlour. At the same time I knew it to be impossible, that the writer of the one could not have written the others.

'Tis the letters,' I said with a start. 'The letters are the key. His Lordship must believe me a fool.'

'Lord Illminster? Why?' my companion asked.

'I suppose it to be because I made him think so.'

'By what means do you deduce this?' Delaney demanded, perplexed. So I explained briefly about our clandestine encounter.

Delaney was clearly troubled by this intelligence and displayed such signs of agitation as I knew well were an indication of irritation. He was reluctant to allow that Lord Illminster, a man whom he had judged of the highest calibre, could be the architect of such villainy. But I suspect he was mostly irritated because I had overturned his carefully crafted explanation for Mr Backhouse's death. Though I could not reassure him now, there was no shame in that. I was by nature suspicious. He was not. Nevertheless I did not wish his pride to be injured unnecessarily.

'Robert,' I said. 'If you will allow me I think I can show you in what way His Lordship seeks to delude us. But please permit me to delay that explanation while I satisfy myself on certain matters. We will stop at my lodgings, presently. There perhaps I can say more.'

It was approaching noon, I observed, a Saturday and Fleet Street was crowded so that the coachman had trouble clearing a path. However, by and by we drew to a halt at my door. I ushered Delaney into my parlour and bade him sit – though he would not – while I searched out the note.

The note I sought had been placed in my possession by Lady Castlemaine's page some two weeks and more previously. Fortunately I had preserved it and was now able to compare the hand with that in which the three letters were written. There seemed to be no doubt. The hand was the same.

I invited Delaney to make a similar comparison and his conclusion was as mine. 'The letters were written by My Lady Castlemaine,' he exclaimed, astonished.

'So it would seem,' I allowed.

'Do you doubt?' he demanded and I detected exasperation again overcoming his sorely tested patience.

'The sample is too small,' I told him. 'It is of the utmost importance that I have more to study. Your sister must have letters from My Lady. Will you persuade her to permit me access to them? You can assure her I will be discreet.'

''Tis not a request I would make,' he replied, somewhat sharply. 'She cannot be expected to betray such confidences.'

'Then let us go directly to Pall Mall and I will ask her myself.'

He shrugged. 'As you wish.'

I think he was finally convinced of my delusion.

We arrived at Lady Villiers' door as she was preparing to dine, which proved convenient for all of us. 'There has been a ball,' she told me after we had exchanged our greetings. 'And you have disgraced yourself utterly, my sister informs me. We will dine together and you can tell me all about it.' Her relish at this prospect was barely disguised.

The evening of the ball was still a painful memory to me and I am afraid I denied Lady Villiers much of the detail she sought. However, I believe I was able to persuade her of the probity of my behaviour with regard to her sister.

'I am to be married to the lady,' I concluded. 'Colonel Hamilton has given his permission for me to wed his daughter.'

Unlike her brother, My Lady was unreserved in her pleasure at this news and begged that I bring Miss Hamilton to her at the earliest opportunity, which I agreed I would.

'My Lady,' I said, when our attention to our appetites was waning, 'I have a request of you which Robert believes you will find impossible to contemplate. If so, then I beg at once your forgiveness. I ask only because the matter to which it pertains is particularly odious.'

'What is this request,' My Lady asked, and I could see her curiosity was piqued.

'I wish to discover if My Lady Castlemaine was the author of three letters I have here in my possession. For that I need to peruse some samples of her correspondence.'

'And if she did write these letters?'

'Then she is the mistress of some deadly intrigue.'

'My sister was ever an intriguer,' My Lady told me. 'But then you have sucked that egg, have you not, Mr Wyld? Well, I don't see why not.'

At this Delaney could not contain himself. 'You cannot betray your sister's confidence so casually,' he complained bitterly.

'Pah,' retorted My Lady. 'Such gossip as she relays to me in her letters has been around the court ten times ere it arrives here. Mr Wyld will learn nothing he could not hear for himself if he chose.'

Which reply left Delaney more irritated than ever.

So it was that I presently found myself with several of My Lady Castlemaine's letters to My Lady Villiers which I could place beside the three I had brought from the desk of Mr Backhouse. I begged a glass which Delaney fetched from his elaboratory and spent some half an hour comparing the two sets in detail. Finally I offered a conclusion.

'These three are of the same hand,' I announced, 'but they were not written by My Lady Castlemaine. They are counterfeit. It had to be so,' I added, 'for I had My Lady's note when I examined the letters from Monsieur Vouet's chest. Had those then been in this hand I would have recognized it instantly. These are copies. I have seen better forgeries, but they will no doubt suffice for their purpose.'

Lady Villiers was intrigued by this conclusion and would quiz me, but Delaney required further convincing.

'How can you be sure?' he demanded.

'See for yourself, Robert.' And I handed him the glass. 'These capitals for instance. My Lady writes them with one flowing stroke of the pen but these have been drawn slowly. You may see if you look where the quill has halted in mid stroke.'

So, by and by, I was able to show him how my conclusion was just.

'What does this mean, Mr Wyld?' his sister asked.

'I fear it means some conspiracy is afoot in which your sister will be found culpable. Unfortunately the nature of that conspiracy is for the moment beyond my view.'

'And what is the sense of this subterfuge?' Delaney asked.

'I believe it is to do with the Italian poison in which Monsieur Vouet dealt,' I told him. 'By my deduction, whoever genuinely wrote these letters purchased that potion from him and, I have little doubt, had him killed. From this new deceit I deduce that My Lady is to be found to be the purchaser of poison, in which case I would imagine that some intrigue is being played out at court and that death will be the result.'

'Then you must act,' My Lady told me.

'I intend to, My Lady,' I assured her. 'But I must move with caution for this is at present no more than speculation. Mayhap if I can lay my hands on the villain who acts in these matters I can wring a confession from him that will implicate his master. Until then I am severely constrained.'

'Then you know who that is?'

'I believe so, but for the present I dare not speak his name so publicly as this.'

'Then take care,' she advised. 'And when by God's will you succeed, my sister will be greatly in your debt.'

'I will,' I promised.

Swiftly thereafter I took my leave for I had a great deal to contemplate and much to decide.

There was, it seemed, to be little time for contemplation. I returned to Covent Garden from Lady Villiers to find that a note had been delivered from the palace. It was from Miss Hamilton. She had lately received a letter from her father in which he allowed all that her heart desired and for which she was greatly thankful. I wondered what My Lady Castlemaine would make of that news when it became broadcast at court, which surely it would.

Rebecca, as I was pleased to discover her sign herself, also provided more disquieting news. She had spied the fellow with the scar leaving the Duchess's quarters. This news alarmed me so much that I decided to repair to the palace immediately. Such a visit would, besides, offer the occasion to conclude my arrangements with Mr Killigrew in the matter of my pension. I took with me the one remaining sample of Monsieur Vouet's Italian poison. Miss Hamilton must be alerted to the danger of such a potion, should she ever see one.

The hour was such that the palace precincts were almost deserted when I arrived and I was able to pass through them without interruption. I found Mr Killigrew in his dark chamber perusing his papers as usual. When he discovered me upon his doorstep his demeanour adopted a sorrowful aspect which at once alerted me that all was not well.

'Oh dear, Mr Wyld,' he said, 'I am advised that you are to be removed from the list. It is a sad day when men of your ability are discarded so carelessly.'

'By whose orders?' I demanded, with some degree of alarm.

'Sir!' he chided. 'But I gauge it is hardly beyond your skill to determine by what agency this has been enacted.'

I nodded, grimly.

'However,' he added with a smile, 'no mention has been made to me of arrears. No doubt if you are frugal you can manage with this bill until you have taken care to placate those gods it will be necessary to placate.' So saying he handed me a bill of exchange to the value of £200.

This was a generous act of friendship and I appreciated it as such. Thanking him warmly, I placed the bill in my pocket and turned to go.

'Make your peace soon,' he begged me as I reached the door. 'I have need of you, sir.'

'I may take to the country instead,' I told him.

'I doubt that, Mr Wyld,' he retorted.

So, My Lady had already begun to exact her revenge. I had not underestimated her. But for the moment I must put such concerns to one side. The chase in which I was engaged was fast approaching its end and I would require all my faculties if I was to apprehend the quarry before it went to ground.

I next sought out Mr Pemberton who, after making some bachelor's joke about my betrothal, was able to tell me that the Duchess and her maids of honour were taking a late walk in the park. With that I was quickly on the way to the park myself where I managed to join the party with little difficulty.

Her Royal Highness was in a jovial mood. 'It seems you are to steal Miss Hamilton from me, sir,' she exclaimed with mock dismay.

'Only by your leave, Your Highness,' I replied.

'Well you shan't have it. Not until tomorrow, anyway.'

'Then I must be patient,' I answered.

'So you must. Now go to her before she faints quite away with excitement.'

I bowed and did then join Miss Hamilton, who I found to be smiling most beautifully.

'Madam,' I greeted her with another bow. 'As you can see I have returned safely from my trip into the country. Besides, I have your jewel here which I have guarded with my life.'

Miss Hamilton, however, declined to take the proffered pouch. 'I would be pleased, sir, if you would agree to guard it still,' she told me. 'You may return it to me upon the day that we are married.'

'I shall be honoured to do as you wish,' I replied with a short bow. So saying, I returned the pouch to my pocket.

'May I begin to call you Rebecca?' I asked.

She nodded, happily.

'Then you must learn to call me Francis. And now, Rebecca, I believe it is fitting since we are betrothed for you to take my arm.' Which offer she quickly accepted.

'How did you find my father?' she asked.

'Much to my liking. He has invited me to be his guest and I have promised to return to Aldreth soon.'

As we thus walked and talked I soon managed to engineer a space between the two of us and the party sufficient to speak without being overheard. 'Tell me of the other matter,' I urged, once I was confident we were secure.

'It was the man who you pointed out,' she confirmed. 'I have a notion he was closeted with Lady Hinchbrooke but I cannot be sure.'

Lady Hinchbrooke, another of the Duchess's maids of honour, was at this moment some ten paces in front of us. I absorbed the information quickly, but I knew little of the lady in question and wished I knew more.

'Then I am greatly concerned,' I whispered. 'There is something I must show you.' Guarding that I could not be overseen, I carefully took the container of poison from my pocket and showed it to my companion.

'Should you see one of these you must send for me immediately, whatever the situation.'

'What is it?' she asked, alarmed.

'It is a poison,' I told her. 'Most fiendishly contrived that it leaves no sign.'

Miss Hamilton shivered. 'Am I to believe that we are to be poisoned?' she asked me.

'It cannot be you,' I assured her. 'Though I do fear some political intrigue is to be played out in this way. But come, we should rejoin the party.'

We were soon once more in its midst and engaged in the diverting turns of conversation that animate such walks. So, eventually I took my leave.

'I will come to you again tomorrow if that should please you,' I promised.

Miss Hamilton beamed brightly. 'Please, come as often as you may.'

CHAPTER 21

An Assassin Strikes

It was a little before noon on the following day, as I sat in my parlour contemplating what had befallen and what I feared was about to befall, that a boy arrived from the housekeeper of the Leadenhall Street mansion to inform me that Mrs Backhouse was now returned. With a weary sense of despondency I wrapped myself in a light cloak and stepped out to Russell Street in search of a sedan.

'Twas not simply the service I had presently to fulfil that caused my spirits to fall. All sense of gaiety had left me and I was engulfed by a feeling of helplessness and dread as I waited for events to unfurl.

It was common knowledge that Whitehall was a hornets' nest of intrigue. I could probably, with an hour's diligent enquiry, uncover twenty plots or supposed plots to ruin this or another courtier, lover or competitor. Most were at best fanciful, at worst spiteful. One was deadly. Which, were there rumour of it to be had, would be impossible to tell.

Even the knowledge that it must involve Lord Illminster was of little avail. His alliances were wide, his enemies many. Besides, he could be acting for another and all would be done through agents. And so, as I was carried through the streets towards the Backhouse mansion, my thoughts were mostly dark.

I alighted at the end of Leadenhall Street and paid the bearers, intent on walking the final distance while I tried to compose in my mind a means to convey with gentleness to the widow what had taken place. Yet I could find no way to avoid revealing something of the dreadful fate that had befallen Mr John Backhouse, her late husband.

Upon arrival I was shown into the parlour in which Delaney and I had interviewed the housekeeper on the previous day. The widow joined me there a few moments later. She was a matronly woman, short of stature and plainly got up in her weeds which were yet of the finest cloth.

'Madam,' I began immediately, 'please accept my condolences.'

'Thank you, sir,' she replied. 'This is a grievous blow. I pray God will support me for I am sorely afflicted by it. Yet I cannot understand it.'

'It is with that purpose I am here,' I told her. 'I was privy to the circumstances of your husband's death. Though it appeared he took his own life, 'twas not so.'

'But, sir, they have told me that it is quite plain, my husband killed himself. They say by this I must lose everything unless by the grace of His Majesty I am reprieved.'

'Then pray console yourself,' I told her, 'there is no doubt. It will, as I suppose, be but a short time before all is resolved and he may be laid to rest in consecrated ground. In the meantime take such comfort as you can from my assurance.'

I fear the woman was quite perplexed by this but I believe she did take some succour from my words. Meanwhile there was another matter I must broach.

'I have ordered that your husband's coffin be closed, madam,' I told her. 'I must speak plainly. Death was brought to your husband in such a manner that, though I believe he suffered little, left him mightily disfigured. 'Tis not a death that one might profitably contemplate. If I may advise, madam, tend his memory and leave him thus.'

'But I would gaze upon him one more time. What, sir, shall I find there?'

'Not your husband.'

Upon those words Mrs John Backhouse turned her back to me and became lost in her private contemplation. We rested thus until, at last, I bid a silent farewell and left.

Having no particular need for haste, I decided to return to Covent Garden on foot. The streets were a bustle, the churches full but I passed all without regard. I paused once at a door where dinner and lively conversation might be found, then turned away. What filled my head could not be voiced, yet I could address no other subject with the fullness of my faculties. And so by divers streets and alleys I made my way back to my own door and there had Bridget bring me a bottle of claret and a plate of meat and dined alone. 'Twas like the hour before a storm when the air was filled with portents. My only wish was that the heavens should unleash their fury so that the air might be cleared.

I had promised that I would pay court to Miss Hamilton this afternoon and so presently I busied myself in preparation. Yet even the pleasure that the anticipation of our meeting should bring was alloyed. A shadow had fallen and within it everything was sombre.

It was late afternoon when I finally took a wherry to the palace from which I alighted at the Privy Stairs. Again I found the precincts quiet as I made my way to the Duchess's chambers and gained admittance. And, as once before I had found, the Duchess had her maids seated about her so that they appeared from a distance like blooms. But when I had drawn close, bowed, and been invited to join the party, I found Miss Hamilton to be much distracted and, as I thought, a little distressed.

Normal etiquette being maintained, it was quite some interval before we found a moment for hushed words.

'I hardly expected you so soon, Francis,' she whispered.

'I promised you I should be here.'

'You have not received my note?'

'I have received no note. Why, what has happened?'

'I have discovered the container of the potion.'

'When?' I demanded, astonished.

'But an hour ago. It has been placed in my wardrobe.'

At this I was mightily perplexed and not a little fearful. 'Then mayhap we can prevent this tragedy occurring,' I told her.

'No. It is too late. The container is empty. The potion is gone.'

I felt a cold spell creep upon me. 'In which case the act has been commissioned,' I told her grimly.

'What does this mean?' she asked, anxiously.

I took her hand and held it tightly. 'I fear there is greater mischief afoot than I had anticipated. What has happened with you today?'

'We have prated as usual and dined as usual, only the Duchess's father joined us. We have walked—'

But I stopped her then. Those few words had provided the illumination I sought. A main part of the intrigue I now understood.

'I fear you have already witnessed the poisoning,' I told her. ''Tis clear to me. Its subject can be none other than the Chancellor himself. He fits this pattern in every respect. Does he still loiter in the palace?'

'No. He is away to his residence.'

'We must send to him. But wait. I must think.'

So saying, I began to assess the situation quickly in my mind. How was this to be managed? A cure must be sought, for otherwise we must watch the Duchess's father die. Yet no alarm must be given, either. Whoever had engineered this scheme must believe it to be proceeding rightly. As for the secreting of the empty container within Miss Hamilton's possessions; the implications of this I must reserve for later contemplation.

'Rebecca,' I said then. 'We must find a pretext to gain audience with the Duchess alone. What say you?'

'Why, I believe she will allow such an audience in the matter of our betrothal.'

'Then put it to her immediately, but openly. I would have no suspicion aroused that there is any other reason.'

Presently Miss Hamilton did make such a request, which the Duchess was pleased to grant, and we three repaired to her inner chamber for a private audience.

'Well, Mr Wyld,' the Duchess began, 'what have you to say to me?'

'Your Royal Highness, I beg you not to be alarmed, for I believe I have discovered a plot to poison your father, Lord Clarendon.'

The Duchess rose from her seat with a cry. 'We must send for a sergeant-at-arms immediately,' she declared.

'Your Highness,' I said, 'I beg you hear me out first, for I do fear this matter cannot be so easily settled. You know, I think, that I have acted for your brother, the King, in certain discrete matters. Now it is my wish that you will let me advise you. Our first concern must be for your father. You must go to him and care for him. Take Miss Hamilton with you for she knows something of this matter. If you have vomits by you, apply them to him immediately. I will presently send to you a physician who with God's will can cure him—'

'Then he is poisoned?'

'I fear so, yes, at dinner today.'

'Why, he may be dead already,' she replied rising again in great anguish.

'No, no,' I assured her. 'He will not be dead for this preparation acts by stealth. Go now, but we must make some excuse.' I thought, quickly. 'I think we may say that your father is unwell for that will be enough of the truth to cause no suspicion. I wish suspicion to be avoided for our second concern must be to apprehend the actors in this intrigue.'

Thus it was arranged. Her Royal Highness left immediately with Miss Hamilton and some retainers while I informed Mr Pemberton who alerted the household. In this way the Duchess was gone before anybody knew.

The storm has broken and now we must ride the torrent it would presently unleash. My immediate concern must be to find a physician who could save the Chancellor, though I feared none was fitted. I decided that Sir Charles Scarborough was as suitable as any and so presently called upon him and charged him with the task. Sir Charles was, besides, receptive to philosophical turns of thought which would be an asset, for I had it in mind to take advice of some philosophers in this matter.

'Poisoned, you say,' the physician exclaimed when I told him my news. 'By what infamy, sir?'

'I can but speculate and speculation is best guarded. Let us ensure that he lives first.'

'Do you have reason to suppose he can survive?'

'I cannot say I have. But if you will allow me I will accompany you to his door that I may instruct you in all that I know.'

We travelled in a hackney, which driver I had commanded drive as if the Devil were behind him. During the journey I explained what I knew of the potion and of Mr Starkey's experiment with a dog. I indicated also something of my enquiries concerning previous purchasers of this potion and the speed of its application.

'In short, sir, I believe that the poison takes some three days to act within the human body. As to how, I know not, but if we can by some stimulation keep Lord Clarendon in the world for three days, I believe he may survive.'

Sir Charles appeared to hold little optimism that such a strategy could bear fruit. Indeed I began to fear by his contrary proposals that he would so bleed and blister the Chancellor with cuts and cups that the treatment would kill him before the poison could. Nevertheless there was aught else I could presently do. In this state we arrived at the Chancellor's door and I instructed the hackney await my instructions.

I would have departed at once upon delivering Sir Charles within the Chancellor's residence. Instead I was halted by a retainer on the order of Lord Clarendon himself who insisted I present before him an immediate account. I had expected such an account to be demanded, but it had been my hope that it might be delayed some hours. There was much yet to do.

I was taken by the servant to His Lordship's chamber where I found him already in some discomfort by way of the vomits and clysters which his daughter had induced him to apply.

Lord Clarendon was now in his fifty-fourth year, during which time he had witnessed all the late vicissitudes of the Kingdom which he now served as Chancellor. Much was writ of these troubles on his features which were thereby cast in a somewhat severe mould. However there was a strength in his eye and a dash to him manner for he wore his hair long after the cavalier fashion though he was no cavalier himself.

Upon being shown into his presence I bowed.

'Your Lordship,' I said.

'What is this, Mr Wyld, that you have contrived for me?' he demanded sharply.

''Tis no construction of mine, Your Lordship,' I replied. 'But I do fear it's aim is deadly.'

'Then why am I not laid dead? Until the arrival of my daughter, the Duchess, I felt well. Now the Devil wrings all the juices from me and I am wretched. You must provide me with some just reason why I should submit myself thus at your insistence.'

'My Lord,' I began, then paused. Were the Chancellor dead before me I could justly speak of plots. As he still lived all I had were shades and suspicions.

'Well, sir?'

'My Lord,' I resumed. 'I have been invited by Lady Villiers' brother, Mr Delaney, to pursue an enquiry into a late Frenchman who was murdered by Southwark this three weeks past. The gentleman, a traveller and friend of virtuosi, was a dealer in relicts and potions. Among these latter I have discovered a cunningly contrived Italian poison which takes life without the loser having any reason for suspicion. My enquiry led me by divers routes to the conclusion that some intrigue was afoot within the palace in which this poison would be the main actor. Until today I knew not who would be the target.

'One of the Duchess's maids has this day found a like container in which such poison is housed. The container was empty. The only other event that was unusual was your dining with Her Royal Highness. I have therefore concluded that the two are linked. If I am correct then you are poisoned and we must save you. If I am wrong then you will spend three days in considerable discomfort at my expense. I can, if it would please you, bring to you Mr Starkey, an alchemist, who has fed the potion to a dog and can describe its effects.'

Lord Clarendon frowned and dismissed the suggestion with a curt indication of the hand. 'I have heard it said you have consorted with the King's harlot, My Lady Castlemaine. That does not recommend you to me, sir.'

'I have heard, My Lord, that you sold Dunkirk to the French,' I replied.

Lord Clarendon was clearly angered by this retort but he understood well its intent. 'You speak directly, sir,' was the limit of his rebuke. 'And when I die who shall be called to account?' he asked.

'It is my intent, My Lord, that you shall live. Once that is certain, we may see how the account may be reckoned.'

His Lordship's face did now show such concern as made me believe I had made some progress as to his conviction. I thought I might take advantage of this as to set new wheels in motion.

'My Lord. Sir Charles Scarborough is without. I have told him all I know of this potion and he will do what lies in his power to save you. By your leave, I must enquire elsewhere whether any cure is known.'

At this the Chancellor's complexion became grim. No man would have his days numbered thus, as if by the executioner's axe. He was fearful and so I left him, struggling to face his fear. Upon my leaving Sir Charles entered. Perhaps he could distract His Lordship with his leeches.

CHAPTER 22

Mr Hooke's Counsel

Upon leaving the Chancellor's residence my main intention was to seek out Mr Starkey. He was the only man in London of my acquaintance with any knowledge of this potion. Perhaps he knew also of a cure.

The alchemist was engaged in one of his arcane enquiries and would not at first answer to my hammering upon his door, though I knew well by the light he was within. My continued insistence finally brought him, angrily, to see who disturbed him.

'My Wyld,' he exclaimed upon finding me on his threshold. ''Tis hardly an hour to be calling.'

'It is true, Mr Starkey,' I admitted. For by now the sun had set and darkness was rising. 'Yet the urgency of my cause is such that I cannot allow niceties to rule me.'

'Well, I cannot admit you, sir, for your presence will undoubtedly disturb the balance of the airs and all will be lost thereby.'

'By this loss, sir, you may perhaps save the life of the Chancellor of the Realm. But you must be the judge, which is the most pressing.'

'What care I for chancellors?' he demanded. 'For they care not for me.' But he did let me pass. 'What do you seek from me?' he continued, following behind.

'Lord Clarendon has by some cunning been induced to take the Italian potion,' I informed him once. 'Now I need a cure.'

'Well, I have no cure.'

'Mr Starkey,' I admonished him, crossly. 'You are likely the only person upon these shores with a clear knowledge of these poisons. Have you never heard speak of any who evaded death?'

'The world is plagued by those seeking to evade death,' he retorted.

'Come, sir. Let us speak plainly for you understand my meaning.'

'Then I will speak plainly. I have never heard of a cure.' He paused. 'However, I have heard one tale that may be of use,' he finally conceded. 'It is said that there was a Frenchwoman who, tired of her husband but not his fortune and yet intent on ridding herself of him, fed him the poison in order to achieve this conclusion. However in spite of several attempts, the potion did not have its usual effect. The husband lived and she was decapitated.'

'And to what was this ascribed?'

'Cabbage.'

'Cabbage!'

'Aye, sir, cabbage. For he ate a prodigious quantity of it.'

'Do you believe this tale?'

'I cannot judge. Maybe the airs this plant produces in the belly are beneficial. But if I were the Chancellor I would discover an immediate appetite for the cabbage head.'

'Well if cabbage is all we have, then cabbage we must use.' So saying, I took my leave and returned at once to the Chancellor's residence.

There I sought out the Duchess whom I found with Miss Hamilton in a parlour. Both were grimly set. After greeting them I quickly recounted Mr Starkey's tale.

'It is, I confess, an unlikely antidote,' I finished. 'But for the moment I have no other. I recommend, therefore, that you instruct cabbages to be prepared immediately and then persuade Lord Clarendon to consume them. I have no precise information as to the dose required, only that the quantity should be prodigious. I would suggest that two would suffice for the present.'

'And where will we find these kale?' the Duchess asked.

'No doubt the housekeeper can produce some. Otherwise send to Lambeth for I have heard that many strange plants may still be found in the gardens of the late Mr Tradescant.'

This latter course proved unnecessary. Cabbage heads were found within the kitchens and quickly prepared and in due course the Chancellor was persuaded to consume them. Sir Charles and his leeches had by now been banished for Lord Clarendon would have none of his blood-letting. The physician, whom I found on the point of leaving, was determined to abandon his patient altogether but I persuaded him he must return on the morrow.

'The King will not take kindly to his Chancellor, dead,' I reminded him.

Finally, I, too, left for it was past midnight and I could do no more without sleep. But I feared greatly what the morning might bring.

No news came with the morning so, by and by, I went myself to see how the Chancellor's health lay. He lived still, having eaten cabbages for supper and breakfast and I supposed he would have more for dinner. No doubt there would be some price to pay for all this cabbage, should he live. I wondered briefly if I would not be best served by his dying.

I dismissed this perverse thought and sought out Miss Hamilton, but she was with the Duchess who entertained the Chancellor. Having no wish to submit myself to another examination by His Lordship I left.

I must confess that I held little hope for the efficacy of this antidote. Perhaps consumed with the potion it might have had some mitigating effect. Taken at this late stage, when the poison had already entered the body, I could see no means by which it could intervene. So I went to Delaney.

Delaney was disturbed by my news, though I confess I detected a hint of scepticism in his response. He was not, I suspect, convinced by the logic of my reasoning regarding the administration of the poison. For the moment I was little minded to convince him, or no. However, he appeared reluctant to speculate as to how the poison might operate, which was my main intention.

'Which of our natural philosophers would you judge the most ingenious?' I asked instead. For it was clear I must seek help elsewhere.

'Mr Wren is regarded highly by the men of our new society,' he replied. 'However, it is my belief that Mr Hooke is the most curious of all.'

'Then I will go to him. Will you join me?'

This request Delaney, too, declined. There was, I presently realized, a coolness in his manner with which I was not familiar. I wondered at this and a suspicion entered my mind that in spite of my advice he was falling more heavily under the influence of Lord Illminster than before. If so, it would be to the detriment of my situation for Delaney knew much that I would keep from His Lordship. The state of the Chancellor being most pressing, however, I must put this concern aside.

Mr Hooke was an elusive fellow, but I finally tracked him down to Jonathan's, a coffee house by Gresham College which he was used to frequent. My quarry was an ungainly looking individual who cared little for his appearance. His eyes, however, were as sharp as any wolf's.

'Mr Wyld,' he said, upon espying me, 'I do not expect to find you here.'

'That is because I never am,' I replied. 'However, today I especially require your counsel.'

'I am no churchman.'

''Tis not religious but philosophical counsel I seek.'

'In that case I will serve you if I can.'

'It concerns a potion of which I have heard tell,' I told him and then recounted briefly what I knew of the poison and its effect. 'If such a potion existed,' I concluded, 'how might it act?'

Mr Hooke had listened to me intently. Now he looked clearly at me. 'Do you speak hypothetically?' he asked.

I hesitated, but only briefly. 'I do not,' I admitted. 'The potion has been administered. I wish to prevent a death.'

'Had I the potion,' he advised me, 'I might make some experiments to test how it acted. Now I can only offer hypotheses which are weak things when observation does not support them.' He thought for a moment of two. 'It would seem from this description that the potion induces a narcotic stupor from which death is the conclusion. It must, then, deprive the body of some vital motion without which it cannot function.'

I nodded, listening intently.

'My own observations suggest that the vitality of the body is maintained by the air. The pneumatic engine will extinguish the flame from a fire when the air is removed and it will, likewise, extinguish the life from an animal. Maybe the potion destroys the ability of the body to derive any vitality from the air.'

'How might it achieve such an effect?'

'Now, Mr Wyld, you probe deeply. I have wondered whether the blood is not the vehicle by which the air animates the body. If it could no longer do so, then the body would sleep. A potion that deprived the blood of its efficacity in this regard would have a like effect. But this is gross speculation.'

'I have not option but to speculate,' I replied. 'Let us say that what you suggest is an accurate description of the action of the potion; how might it be countermanded?'

'By stimulating the blood. Vigorous movement might help to encourage reanimation. A superfluity of air will also have an opposing effect, as I have myself observed.'

'Sir,' I said, rising, 'I thank you.' And I left the philosopher with his bowl of coffee and his thoughts, for I could see that his mind was reflecting further on the matter we had discussed. Perhaps some experiment would be the result, and some new discovery to delight the virtuosi.

I returned directly to the Chancellor's residence, seeking Sir Charles Scarborough, but he had abandoned his patient once more. I found him, instead, at home and there recounted my discussion with Mr Hooke.

'Mr Hooke is no physician,' he told me directly. For the Royal College was proud of its status.

'Nevertheless he has a great insight into natural operations. Unless you have some substantive proposal for the Chancellor, then I recommend digesting what he has said and finding some means of acting upon it. Do you have a method of invigorating the blood?'

Sir Charles did not.

'Besides, Lord Clarendon will still have none of me so I waste my time with him. Let him die, if he must.'

It seemed it must rest with me to attempt to invigorate the Chancellor and so prevent his untimely death. Once again I returned to him.

I found the Chancellor weary but in good spirits. 'I live still, Mr Wyld,' he boasted.

'That has much to recommend it, Your Lordship,' I replied. Which jest he took in good part. 'I have taken further advice as to means of countering the effects of this potion,' I quickly told him. 'I now propose a regime of vigorous exercising of the body.'

'That will not sit well with the diet you have recommended.'

'Nevertheless it will oppose any lethargy that the poison may induce.

If I may advise, Your Lordship, I have found that walking the stairs is as beneficial a means as any of inducing heat in the blood.'

'And what dose of this prophylactic would you recommend?'

'A goodly number, until the breath is short.'

'If we succeed, then you shall become my physician, sir,' he told me.

So I left His Lordship and found my way instead to Miss Hamilton's side. However both our moods were sombre and we exchanged but one or two small comforts before I quitted the residence again and returned to my own.

There seemed little more I could do but wait and waiting has never been a part I played well. Therefore I sought distraction. I took some pie which Bridget had prepared for my dinner and afterwards I sent Ned to fetch a man whom I had previously found reliable in the pursuit of certain services. I had immediate need of such a one.

Mr Cowley was a man of many skills. He could teach swordplay to a lord and grammar to his children and might well be found paying court to his daughters when they were of an age to court. Whether the man was a rogue or no, I did not care to judge. His trust I had, and he had mine and that was sufficient. Besides, he knew I would reward him well for his service.

'I have a task, Mr Cowley, which I am unable to pursue myself,' I told him once we were closeted in my parlour. 'I wish you to go to Plymouth in search of intelligence concerning a seaman from those parts.' And I described the villain with the scar. 'You will most likely learn of him from among the crew of Lord Illminster's privateer,' I added. 'For by the *Gazette* she is just now in port.'

'Do you want this fellow fetched back?' he asked.

'If you should chance upon him and do not kill him first, though I do believe he is presently in London. My main concern is whether or no he belongs to Lord Illminster. By that I will advance my cause,' I told him.

'Then I will leave in the morning.'

'God speed you, Mr Cowley,' I told him and with that he departed.

I spent the remainder of the day in restless repose. When evening came I repaired to Will's where I found some distraction among the wits, yet not sufficient to banish for even a moment what troubled me. Thence to bed, but little sleep.

The morrow was but the second full day following the administration of the potion. We must wait all of this and part of the next to discover if the Chancellor would live. I arrived at his residence just before noon to find the household in a state of great anxiety.

Lord Clarendon had attempted to follow my prescription but had eventually been overcome with the effort. This had induced just such a lethargy which I sought to avoid and he was presently confined to his bed. Such was his concern and that of the Duchess that Sir Charles had been recalled and was even now bleeding His Lordship. I was shown into the chamber where I found Sir Charles bitter in his triumph.

'If His Lordship should die it will be down to you, Mr Wyld,' he told me. 'Your regime has induced in him such a state that I cannot be confident he will live. I have ordered him to rest. He will, besides, take no more of your cabbage head.'

'Then we have three potential assassins,' I retorted sharply. 'For either the potion will kill him, or you, or I. Only God can save him now.'

When Sir Charles had finished his letting, Lord Clarendon sent him out for he wished to speak to me alone.

'I know not,' he said, 'whether this be the death you prophesied or some other. But if I am to die, I would know by whose hand. Therefore I insist you speak frankly, Mr Wyld.'

I was reluctant to speak, but His Lordship's demand was just. 'I believe the designer to be Lord Illminster,' I told him.

In spite of his discomfort, a wry smile briefly lightened the Chancellor's features. ''Twould be he,' he said, 'for he carries a terrible hatred for me.'

'By what reason?' I asked.

'Oh, he finds many reasons, Mr Wyld. But chief among them is that I prevailed upon the King to prevent a great blood letting when His Majesty returned to the throne. Lord Illminster would have provided us with blood enough to support the fleet should he have been given his head. He also bears a very personal grudge for he would have married his daughter to the Duke. These Romans are quite unable to rid themselves of their hatred except by the spilling of blood.'

'I pray My Lord that you will not die.'

'But if I should, have you the means to bring him to justice?'

'My Lord, I seek it, but 'tis not yet secure.'

Soon thereafter I left His Lordship's side and Sir Charles returned with his Greek practices. I sought again Miss Hamilton whom I found to be weary.

'I fear this trial is exhausting you,' I said, taking her hand. 'Pray take some rest.'

'But I must stay by the Duchess,' she told me.

'It will soon be over.'

'That is what I mostly fear,' she replied.

'As do I.'

Our brief intimacy was ended by a servant with instructions from the Duchess and I again took my leave. But when I left the household I took with me a great anxiety.

CHAPTER 23

A Trap is Laid

My anxiety was such that sleep was again hardly come by. In the early morning I found eventual respite and thereby rose late so that Martha was still dressing me when a carriage arrived at the door. The groom, upon admission, demanded I accompany him immediately to the Chancellor's residence. I could get no more out of the fellow than this instruction. So presently I went with him in a state of increasing apprehension as to what I should find.

To my great relief the Chancellor was not dead. Indeed he was in ruder health than I left him the previous day. However, my relief proved shortlived.

'Mr Wyld,' Lord Clarendon began, for I had been shown immediately into this presence, 'we have this morning received news that perturbs me greatly. Lord Illminster has informed the King that he has discovered a plot against my life. The instigator of this plot, as he says, is My Lady Castlemaine and he has shown the King letters proving how she has acquired exactly the potion you have described to me.'

'My Lord,' I began, but he instructed me to remain silent.

'There is yet more, much more. Lady Castlemaine's principal agent in this affair is none other than you, Mr Wyld. Lord Illminster points to a recent intimacy between you in support of this claim and a crudely arranged rupture to disguise it. He also says he may show that you have had just such a potion in your possession. However, by his evidence 'twas not you that poisoned me. For that you enlisted one of the Duchess's maids, Miss Hamilton. Upon Lord Illminster's instructions her wardrobe in the palace has been searched and a container, purporting to be that which held the potion, has been found. It would seem, by that account, that I have been grievously misled. I cannot now but fear that all your actions have been expressly to encourage the operation of this potion and that I must soon die. Upon which, sir, you will swiftly find your head upon the bridge and your entrails fed to the ravens. I have a sergeant ready to take you to the Tower. How do you explain yourself?'

My first reaction was fear. My second anger. 'I like the niceness of it,' I told him crossly. 'It seems that my life now rests upon yours. Let us hope for both our sakes that you live.'

'Do you not defend yourself, sir?' he demanded.

'My Lord,' I replied. 'Lord Illminster had created a cunning masque and every turn of the drama is carefully scripted. It is no coincidence that this news reaches us today, the day upon which he will expect the potion to produce its effect. Too soon and you might be saved, too late and it will seem hurriedly concocted. Now we must wait. If you die I will make my case as best I can. If you live then there will be no case for any man to answer and you will be able to decide how, justly, to proceed. I will defend only Miss Hamilton whom I will not see ensnared in such deviltry as this. The Duchess will surely swear she could not have played the part assigned her.'

'I have not yet informed the Duchess of this, for it will trouble her greatly. But let us have Miss Hamilton sent for and see how she answers.'

So saying, Lord Clarendon called a servant and sent her to fetch Miss Hamilton to him. However the servant returned minutes later in considerable distress.

'She sleeps, My Lord and I cannot wake her.'

At this I was immediately alarmed. Lord Clarendon began to speak, but I interrupted him harshly.

'Take me to her,' I demanded. And I believe that the force in my voice was such that even the Chancellor dare not countermand me for he nodded to the servant to do my bidding.

I was quickly shown to the bedchamber in which she lay. I found her, still clothed, reposing on her side. Her breathing was shallow, as in a deep sleep. Yet no amount of disturbance would bring her from this repose. At that a dreadful terror gripped me. I recognized in this sleep exactly the narcotic stupor of which Mr Hooke had spoken.

By now the commotion had attracted the Duchess whom I found by my side.

'The poor child is exhausted,' she told me. 'I have sent her to rest.'

'This is no normal sleep, Your Highness,' I told her. 'I do fear that she walks arm in arm with death.'

'That cannot be,' the Duchess exclaimed in horror.

And yet it was. Slowly, as I sat holding her hand and the Duchess stood beside me, the shallow motion of her breathing ebbed until it was no more. Miss Hamilton was dead. The assassin had missed his mark and struck her down instead. At that moment a great coldness entered my heart and froze it so solid that the tears I should weep could not be released. Instead of the great sorrow that should accompany her passing I was gripped by a terrible, refractory anger. Carefully I placed her hand by her side and then rose to my feet.

'Pray take care of her,' I instructed the servant.

With that I turned from the room, the Duchess with me, and returned to the place where the Chancellor waited.

'My Lord,' I said, as soon as we entered. 'You need concern yourself no more. The potion has taken the soul of another and your life is not in danger.'

'What do you mean?' he demanded.

'Miss Hamilton is dead.'

'Has she killed herself?'

'No, My Lord, she did not,' I instructed him angrily. 'She has been killed by the potion intended to strike you down.'

'Why should I believe this?' he asked.

At this I was unable to contain myself. 'I care not what you believe, My Lord. She is dead and I find her death beyond my comprehension.'

I think His Lordship would have called the sergeant then to take me away, but some sign in the demeanour of the Duchess, who was clearly puzzled by this exchange, stayed him. I then saw that she, too, was angry.

'Mr Wyld,' she said, 'you have instructed us that to your certain belief there was a plot to kill my father and though you would speak not, I gauge that you have knowledge of the conspirators. I must ask you now who you believed would prepare the poison.'

It seemed of little moment. 'Lady Hinchbrooke,' I told her. 'But this was no more than a suspicion.'

Upon this Her Highness glanced at her father and both were much troubled.

'Then, sir,' she told me, 'I think I may assist your understanding. We have these last months entertained a conceit of Lady Hinchbrooke that she would prepare some special sweetmeat for my father when he should dine with us. It seemed a harmless game and the dishes were toothsome enough. This last time Lady Hinchbrooke found a reason to be absent but she nevertheless commanded a custard be prepared with cinnamon and other spices that My Lord should not go without. 'Tis both a great fortune and a great misfortune that he had no taste for a custard that day and so, Lady Hinchbrooke being away, Rebecca ate the custard in his stead.'

This seemed too much to bear. I turned away from the Duchess and her father, fearing I might lose control of my senses. However, by and by, I calmed myself again.

'Well, My Lord,' I asked, 'shall we send for your sergeant?'

'For what reason?' demanded the Duchess.

Lord Clarendon was now, I believe, quite confused as he attempted to explain the weight of the intelligence that had arrived earlier concerning Lord Illminster's plot. The Duchess, however, was quite clear in her mind.

'My Lord,' she said, 'you have known neither Miss Hamilton nor Mr Wyld, except lately. I have a much longer acquaintance with both and I may assure you there can be no truth in the assertion you have just received.'

Lord Clarendon remained troubled. 'I am to live?' he asked me.

'Unless Sir Charles has taken too much blood,' I told him, for in my anger I would not let him be free entirely of his fear.

'Then I must choose,' he replied.

At that he began to pace his chamber and slowly something of his normal composure returned.

'Mr Wyld,' he said at last, 'it seems I am misled. It is my thanks you deserve, not my suspicion. Pray accept my apologies too, for my daughter knows you an honest man and I trust her judgement. I see I must also offer you my condolences for 'tis clear to me now that you loved Miss Hamilton dearly.'

'We were betrothed,' I told him.

His Lordship accepted this information with a nod and resumed his pacing. 'I would have Lord Illminster brought to justice,' he told me, stopping. 'No doubt that would suit you too. How is it to be achieved?'

Now it was my turn to pace the room, moving at first like some automaton conceived out of the mechanical arts which acted like a man but suffered none of his thoughts or emotions save that cold, formless rage that had been released by the pain of Miss Hamilton's death. But gradually, pace by pace, I came to understand that I must tame and direct that rage so that I might at last spend it and so be freed to mourn her passing. With this, by degrees, I discerned the outline of a scheme that would allow me to exorcize it.

'My Lord,' I began as this scheme took shape, 'Lord Illminster must be allowed to commit himself fully in his charges. By this he will undo himself. He must believe he has succeeded and that you are dead. If you are willing, 'twill not be difficult to manage for we all have a death to mourn.'

I turned to the Duchess. 'Your Highness must put the household in mourning. A coffin must be sent for, into which Miss Hamilton's body may be laid and prepared. His Lordship must remain out of sight. Bring together all who know of Miss Hamilton's death and take them, with the coffin and His Lordship in some disguise, to Cornbury. In the meantime I will gather such material as may be necessary to carry the cause in our favour.'

So it was arranged. By early evening the Chancellor's London residence had been all but abandoned and a procession of carriages, one bearing a coffin, had left for the Chancellor's country residence at Cornbury near Oxford. Though no official announcement was made, the Duchess allowed the rumour that her father had died suddenly and unexpectedly. Once it gained the palace, this rumour would became fact and with it, if my hope was fulfilled, Lord Illminster would believe his scheme had run to completion.

Lord Illminster's belief would be further encouraged, I saw, by the sudden disappearance of Miss Hamilton. As for me, I would surely become a hunted man as the chief agent in the murder of Lord Clarendon. How the King would presently deal with My Lady Castlemaine, I did not know. I could not believe he would countenance her being sent to the block, but for now I must leave her to defend herself.

I thought it unlikely, moreover, that a warrant had yet been issued for my arrest. Nevertheless prudence demanded that I assume it had. Therefore upon the departure of Lord Clarendon and the Duchess with Miss Hamilton's body, I returned cautiously to Covent Garden.

All was yet quiet. No sergeant-at-arms had arrived banging upon the door. Even so I judged it would be foolish for me to tarry and I immediately called my small household to me to explain the situation.

'Bridget,' I said. 'Martha. Ned. Listen to me carefully. You must expect a visit from a sergeant soon with a warrant to take me to the Tower. In the next few days you will hear rumours also, in which I am cast a villain. I fear these will alarm you. Nevertheless they will be untrue.'

'What has happened, sir?' Bridget asked me anxiously.

'There has been a murder which I seek to avenge,' I replied. 'Yet by the cunning of this intrigue, it is I am made a chief murderer. Therefore I must use a similar cunning to entrap the main architect. Presently I must disappear so that none can find me. You will not then see me until the issue is resolved.'

'Shall I come with you, sir?' Ned asked me, bravely.

'No,' I replied. 'I must travel alone.' However his words gave me pause to consider that I might have need of him yet. 'Let us make an arrangement thus,' I told him. 'You will go to Will's each day and enquire of a letter for a Mr Cobb. If I have need of you I will send such a letter. Do not trouble to read it for it will simply be a signal that you must meet me by St Andrew's on Holborn Hill. This will be convenient to me as to entering and leaving London unseen. Come at six o'clock or as near as you can judge and loiter for one hour. If I do not come to you, return the next day, and the day after until I do.'

Ned nodded.

'Now go to the stables and have a steed readied for me. The bay, if she be there. Bring her to the north entrance by Lincoln Inn Fields and I will meet you there.'

At which Ned dashed off with my instruction.

'Twas to Martha that I next turned for assistance.

'We must change my appearance so that I may walk unseen within the City as well as without,' I told her.

Not many moments thereafter, following a brisk application of the shears, my curls lay on the floor about me like fallen leaves. The result was untidy and perchance menacing, which suited my purpose and might turn an inquisitive eye aside. But my anticipated return to court must now be accompanied beneath a wig.

For dress I donned my travelling garb, a leather jerkin and breeches of a similar construction to provide comfort and strength, then a good pair of riding boots. My rapier, the girl fastened to me and I took my dagger also. Lastly I took up a purse of gold and over all I placed a travelling cloak. With that I left, to meet Ned at the entrance to Lincoln Inn Fields. It was time for me to undo Lord Illminster.

CHAPTER 24

Lady Hinchbrooke's Confession

I rode out of London by the north, this being my most direct means to the country. Evening was well advanced by the time I left Ned and I pushed the bay hard in search of an inn. The cover of darkness would, I well knew, soon bring out those villains wont to prey on late travellers. After several miles I entered a hamlet where I found an establishment called the Four Bells suitable to my needs. Leaving the bay in the courtyard with instructions that she be stabled and fed, I entered and enquired of a bed for the night.

The place was already filled in anticipation of a local horse fair and I was forced to share my bed with a drunken ostler who made such a rattling and snorting in his sleep, I was mindful to push him on to the floor. By and by this noise subsided and I was left with my thoughts, by which I soon wished for the rattling and snorting to return.

I knew not how I should bear the loss I had suffered. My life had been full of light and now that light had emptied from it, its source extinguished like the flame of a candle. There was no hope of comfort. Indeed, I could scarcely comprehend what had taken place but a few hours earlier. How should I ever be at ease in the world again? Thus my thoughts turned, over and over, until exhaustion put me to sleep.

When I awoke in the morning the ostler had gone and for a brief moment, in the bliss of solitude, my pain was forgotten. Then the mantle of despair fell across my shoulders and I was once more filled with sorrow. I rose to start my first day in an empty world, pleased at least to find that my erstwhile companion had not taken my boots. My rapier was still beneath the bed while everything else was about me for I had laid down in my travelling clothes.

The innkeeper was able to provide whey and some cold fowl upon which I breakfasted and I took straightway to the road. I had no wish to tarry. My destination was still many miles distant and 'twas my intention I should reach it by the afternoon. I sought there Lord Illminster's agent within the Duchess's household, Lady Hinchbrooke. I had learned expressly from the Duchess that she was to be found in Buckinghamshire where she had repaired the previous Sunday upon the excuse that her husband had immediate need of her.

Lord Hinchbrooke was of that reclusive nature as rarely finds need of the court. He had, these many years past, shut himself away with a small retinue of retainers at Hinchbrooke Hall to perfect the art of plant grafting while wars and the world passed him by. Lady Hinchbrooke, his junior by twenty years, had in contrast a pressing need for the court for the late troubles had deprived her during the flower of her youth. She satisfied this need through her position as maid to the Duchess. Though no longer a young woman she pretended youth. In this, sadly, her body ofttimes betrayed her.

Their marriage, an unlikely match, had been made in the year of His Majesty's return. There was much speculation as to the arrangement between husband and wife and what the cost to each was, but so far two sons had been produced, one dying soon after. I could recall no talk regarding courtly indiscretions on the part of Lady Hinchbrooke which might indicate there was none. As likely it indicated that My Lady was discreet.

I found the Hall by the middle of the afternoon, having dined on mean fare close by. Lady Hinchbrooke was there still, and her husband being about his business she found it incumbent upon her to entertain me alone.

'Mr Wyld,' she addressed me when I was shown into her presence. 'I believe you should not be here.' There was a nervousness in her manner which expressed itself in the restlessness motion of her hands.

'In that you err, My Lady,' I replied, 'for I have a pressing need to be here.'

'Well, I will not speak to you and Lord Hinchbrooke returns upon an instant so you might as well go.'

'Then you do not wish to know what has passed?'

'But I do know, sir, that Lord Clarendon is dead and that you are to be held responsible. Lord Illminster has informed me this morning by a letter.'

At this I smiled, which somewhat disconcerted My Lady.

'I see you are pleased with your handiwork, sir,' she said. 'Are you here to murder me too?'

'Lady Hinchbrooke,' I replied. 'Let us try not to make fools of one another. I know of your skill in the preparation of sweetmeats for Lord Clarendon. I know, too, that Lord Illminster is your master. Now I have come to reckon the account.'

At this Lady Hinchbrooke blanched and would have escaped the room only I prevented her by standing before the door.

'Stand aside!' she ordered. 'Otherwise I shall call for assistance.'

I moved not. 'My Lady,' I told her. 'I would do you no injury but if you force me then I shall find no difficulty.'

At this the strength of will left her and her features sank. 'What is it that you want with me?' she asked.

'But little,' I told her. 'You will swear an affidavit accounting your part in the poisoning of Lord Clarendon to which I will bear witness.'

'Do you take me a fool, sir, to sign my own death warrant?'

'You will have ample time to flee, My Lady, if you do not wish to end your life upon the gallows.'

At this Lady Hinchbrooke found new courage. 'No,' she insisted boldly. 'I will not do your bidding.'

'Then let us await the return of Lord Hinchbrooke. Perhaps I can persuade him of the necessity of this course.'

'He will throw you out, a vagabond.'

'Then you will most certainly see the gallows. Do not imagine there is any doubt. It will not be believed that Miss Hamilton is involved in spite of your subterfuge, but if the case should carry and there is any possibility of her being held accountable then I shall implicate you myself. 'Twill not be difficult. And you may be sure Lord Illminster will abandon you if he must to save himself.'

My Lady showed me by her reaction that she did not doubt Lord Illminster would abandon her if necessary, which made me wonder what hold he had over her. At this she finally lost all will to resist.

'What shall I tell my husband?' she asked me.

My instinct was against offering her any comfort but I needed to persuade her to swear her part. 'Tell him that you are betrayed, that you will be blamed though you are blameless,' I advised her.

She nodded. 'What am I to write, sir?'

'That under instruction of Lord Illminster you prepared a poisoned custard for Lord Clarendon and then secreted the empty glass container within Miss Hamilton's wardrobe.'

''Twas not so,' she complained, 'for the custard was prepared by another. My part was to encourage him to consume such sweetmeats.'

'Then say that. My concern is to show how Lord Illminster is the guiding principle.'

'May I be allowed to go to my chamber to write?' she asked, hoping I suppose to escape me.

'I will accompany you.'

She shrugged. 'So be it.'

Thus, presently, the affidavit was written and sworn and witnessed, upon which I took it from Lady Hinchbrooke and made it secure.

'There is one more thing,' I said, then, for I had conceived a new plan. 'I need the letter which you received from Lord Illminster this morning. Please give it to me.'

'By what right, sir? Have I not done enough?'

'My Lady, you will never do enough,' I told her. 'By becoming party to this scheme you forfeit the right to all common courtesies. Now please give me this correspondence.'

At that moment I think Lady Hinchbrooke lost her reason. For she opened a drawer in her writing desk and withdrew a bundle of letters, then thrust them into my hands.

'Here,' she said. 'Take them. I will have no more to do with this man. He has been my ruin.'

At which I found myself to be in possession of the whole of her correspondence with Lord Illminster. I took them for they suited my purpose even better.

I was ready to take my leave, but Lord Hinchbrooke having, meanwhile, returned to the hall it was necessary to make excuses as to my presence. I advised my Lady to say I was on business from Her Royal Highness. I could see by My Lord's disdain that he judged me a scoundrel from my appearance but I cared not. He would soon have concern enough over his wife's future safety. However, before I left I asked for paper and quill and wrote a letter for Mr Cobb by Will's which I saw sent to the posthouse. I would have need of Ned after all.

As I left Lord Hinchbrooke's estate I wondered whether Lady Hinchbrooke would alert Lord Illminster. It mattered little to me that she might, but I schooled myself to be prepared, though on the whole it seemed unlikely. I believe she now feared me more than he and being in danger of her own life would act upon that fear.

I headed back towards Hertfordshire and found another inn wherein to rest for the night. Here I was able to eat a middling good supper of roasted duck and drink a jar or two of ale, which suited me well. This time I had a chamber to myself, which was better to my liking, and I lay down more comfortably, having barred the door with a heavy chest, for I would not be surprised.

Before I slept I took out the letters from Lord Illminster to Lady Hinchbrooke and examined them, curious to discover the nature of the relationship between these two persons. Half a conversation is but half of the truth. Even so I began to believe, by and by, that Lady Hinchbrooke had been so foolish as to allow Lord Illminster to make love to her and had moreover, become bewitched by him. His Lordship, I judged, found this by stages amusing and then of great value for he had persuaded her to take her part in his intrigue and she was utterly helpless to resist. It was thus that she had followed the path of love and now it would take her into exile, or worse. So concluding, I put the letters aside for the morrow when I would have further use for them.

My thoughts remained sorely troubled by the path of my own love as I took my repose but the strong ale I had drunk soon doused them. However my slumber was interrupted twice by the need for the piss-pot and in the morning my head was thick so that I was glad at the prospect of a brisk ride to clear these fumes. Yet I was, withal, of sounder mind than I had been these two days past, by which I supposed the strong soporific had rendered me a valuable service.

It was my intention to meet Ned by evening, having conceived work for him, and I plotted my route on the bay with our meeting in mind. We cantered towards Hertford where I dined and rested and then by divers ways, as lanes and tracks, took a leisurely course towards the confines of London. So, eventually, I entered again by the northern road and found myself upon Holborn Hill at the hour I had arranged, having left my horse at a convenient inn.

The boy was not yet there and I feared my letter had arrived too late but presently I espied him bobbing and running toward me.

'How goes it, Ned?' I asked, as he caught his breath.

'We are besieged, sir, with a sergeant at the door awaiting your return and the constable thereabouts upon each hour, for you are sorely wanted.'

'And what do they say I have done?'

'You have murdered a chancellor, sir,' he responded with a worried look.

'Good. Can you hold a secret secure?'

'I believe so, sir.'

'There is no dead chancellor, Ned, for the one we had still lives.'

'Then he cannot be murdered, sir.'

'He cannot, as I shall presently show. But for now I have an assignment for you. Can you pass the sergeant easily?'

'Aye, sir, for he notices me not.'

'Then return to Covent Garden and find for me three letters.' And I told him where he might find the three letters purported to be written by My Lady Castlemaine which I had hidden. At this, the boy remembered he had a letter in his pocket for me which he had until then forgotten.

'Go,' I said, taking it. 'Find me here in an hour, if you can. I will await your return.'

I repaired to the inn where the bay rested and opened my correspondence. The letter was from Mr Cowley and in it he confirmed what I had suspected. The villain with the scar had been identified by a midshipman on Lord Illminster's privateer who, moreover, reported that he and another had been ordered to London on Lord Illminster's account. 'Twas a job well done.

Ned returned presently with the three letters, which I took from him, after which I cautioned him to return at the appointed hour on the morrow in case I had further need of his service. 'You may assure Bridget and Martha I live still,' I told him. 'But no more.'

Upon which we parted.

The sun had now set and night would soon bear down but I still had business to conclude nearby. I doubted my call would be welcome at this hour, but time was too pressing for me to delay. So I took myself by divers alleys and back ways to a street which lay between Holborn Bridge and Newgate. Here could be found the workshop of an artisan in the imitation of manuscripts and documents; in short a counterfeiter.

Mr Fox, for that was his name, was within but it took some little persuasion to prise open his door which made me believe he had already the news concerning me. I did, however, succeed for I knew him well as having had need of his skill in the past and presently found myself closeted with him.

'I judge you know of my plight, Mr Fox,' I told him.

'I have heard some gossip of that nature,' he admitted.

''Tis not to be wished for and it seems I have need of your services in order to extract myself.'

'That might not be easy, sir,' he advised me. 'For my skill is in great demand just now.'

'No doubt, Mr Fox, no doubt. However, as I say I do have need of your service and I think you will help me,' I repeated.

Mr Fox looked at me carefully, attempting to determine by what lever I would force him to comply if he resisted. I said nothing, and so we rested until finally he acceded.

'Of course, Mr Wyld, sir, of course,' he agreed with a sad smile. 'Now what is it that you require?'

At this I took out the three letters in My Lady Castlemaine's hand from a saddle-bag which I had carried over my shoulder and passed them to him. 'What do you make of these, Mr Fox?' I asked.

The counterfeiter took the letters and read them, then examined them more closely. When he had finished he placed them upon a desk in front of him.

'A somewhat hurried piece of work, Mr Wyld, I should say. Somewhat hurried. Not a piece of work I should be content with myself.'

'I had not thought this your handiwork, Mr Fox. However, I do require you to reproduce such hurried handiwork as this if you are able, save in another hand.'

With this I removed the bundle of letters from Lord Illminster to Lady Hinchbrooke and placed them before me. 'I need the original three letters to be put in the same hand that wrote these letters. I ask only that the work on the new letters appear equally hurried. Can you provide that for me?'

'This is a strange request, Mr Wyld,' he replied. 'A strange request indeed. However, I see no insurmountable problem preventing its completion.'

'And how long will such hurried work take to complete?'

'That, sir, depends upon the remuneration.'

'Shall we say tomorrow at around the same time?'

'Two sovereigns, sir,' he answered promptly.

''Tis but three letters,' I complained crossly.

'Your case is pressing, sir,' he reminded me.

'So be it.' And I tossed him a piece of gold. 'You shall have the second on completion.'

Our business finalized, I left Mr Fox hastily for it was already coming dark and I dare not remain within London for fear of discovery. So I returned to the inn by Holborn Hill and, retrieving the bay, exited once more to find a place for the night. By now the sky was filled with stars and the moon was shining so I journeyed warily. I was little surprised when close by Hampstead I was approached by a fellow on foot, intent on robbing me.

'Halt,' he called, pointing a pistol towards me.

'Be gone, fool,' I told him, wheeling round. 'Or else shoot straight for I will surely cut you down if you do not.'

At this he turned and ran into the shadows and I saw him no more, which was a pity for I might have taken his pistol for my own. Soon thereafter I found suitable lodgings for the night and rested against the coming day.

CHAPTER 25

The King Hears Mr Wyld

I had no pressing reason to distrust Mr Fox but caution was my watchword. Therefore I did not return to his workshop myself the next evening but sent Ned instead, having met the lad as arranged by the Church of St Andrew in Holborn. There was no problem, for he returned with a great bundle which contained new letters and old as well as the correspondence of Lady Hinchbrooke.

'Now, go,' I told him. 'God willing this business will be resolved ere long.'

The hours previous to our meeting I had passed by giving much thought to the progression of my situation, which I persuaded myself was now in my favour. By Ned I learned that My Lady Castlemaine was sent to Richmond while I was still hunted, as was Miss Hamilton. This confirmed my assessment. I judged that Lord Illminster was certain of his case, and the King also. 'Twas time, I decided, to disabuse them both.

Upon leaving Ned and reclaiming the bay I headed once more out of the town and into Buckinghamshire before finding an inn in which to lie. The next day I continued towards the west, skirting Oxford just after noon and passing by Woodstock to Cornbury where I arrived in late afternoon.

I had some trouble making my entry for the retainers judged me by my appearance and thus judged badly. Eventually, at my insistence, they called the Duchess who recognized me not until I spoke, upon which she was mightily surprised.

'Mr Wyld,' she exclaimed. 'Is this some disguise you have found?'

'It is, Your Highness,' I admitted. 'For it allows me passage where otherwise I might find restraint.'

'And now it has not allowed you passage where you might expect it. Well, come in with us. We have been awaiting you with some concern as to your safety.'

Thus I was finally admitted into the great house at Cornbury that Lord Clarendon had made his own. The Chancellor was in his chamber, having remained there for the four days since their departure from London. By this the secret of his survival appeared to have been made secure. He appeared, withal, in good spirits and his health had completely returned.

'Have you achieved our aim?' he asked immediately he found me before him.

'My Lord, I believe I have the means by which it may be achieved.' And I told him and the Duchess of my interview with Lady Hinchbrooke. 'By this, by your continued living and by the death of Miss Hamilton, I believe the King will be persuaded of Lord Illminster's culpability.' The matter of the counterfeit letters I kept for the moment to myself for I was uncertain as yet how they should be managed.

'Then let us throw off this cloak and return to court,' he replied, and I supposed he was impatient after so long.

'Upon the morrow,' I suggested. 'But let us manage your return that it causes Lord Illminster so great a discomfort as to render him incapable of defending himself.'

Which suggestion Lord Clarendon found much to his liking.

The Duchess ordered a chamber be prepared and sent a servant to assist me so that I was, by her ministerings, able to remove the soil of the road from my body and replace it with the scent of rosewater. A clean shirt was found and I presented myself refreshed, in body if not in spirit, before the Duchess as soon as I was able.

'Your Highness,' I began, for I had a request to make of her. 'Once this is resolved I beg you write to Colonel Hamilton. I have not the words to write.'

'I shall do it,' she replied. 'Though 'tis a sorrowful task.'

I paused, embarrassed, I suppose to continue. 'Your Highness, I would gaze upon her again,' I confessed.

The Duchess smiled kindly. 'I have had the embalmers look to her,' she told me. 'Come, I will show you.'

So saying she led me to another chamber where Miss Hamilton lay in her coffin. It was shut, but not sealed, and a servant was called to remove the lid whereupon I was able to see her face once more.

That face was now rendered like alabaster and a great peace had descended upon it but it was the peace of another world, not of this one. All the most vital aspects of her features were now quiet. She was as a beautiful vessel from which the contents had been poured. Seeing her thus, my heart was filled once more with love for her and I could feel a great welling within me, yet still I could not weep. So, after a few moments, I turned away and the cask was shut up again, for her lying here was a secret which must be kept a day longer.

'Her father will want her laid to rest at Aldreth,' I said to the Duchess as we left the chamber. 'I will take her as soon as I am able.'

The time had come for us to present our masque for the court. If we each played our parts then the audience would be persuaded. I hoped I had judged the piece correctly.

We left soon after dawn by coach for Whitehall. I went with the Duchess and we led, with Lord Clarendon following behind. 'Twould be a long journey for we could not halt lest we be discovered, so we ate heartily before our departure. At least we tried, though I failed, for I was in a nervous state of excitement. I had much to gain and much to lose and I could not contemplate that situation lightly.

By my recommendation the Duchess and I would arrive at court first and the coach bearing the Chancellor would tarry. Our arrival would cause such a commotion of excitement, I felt sure, that he would presently be able to slip into the Duchess's chambers unseen, ready to emerge at my direction. 'Twould not matter if this ruse failed, but it would greatly discommode Lord Illminster if it did.

Our arrival did, indeed, cause a commotion though I was not recognized immediately, my appearance remaining that of a vagabond I suppose. We had made our way through the first court and were towards the King's chambers before two sergeants-at-arms attempted to bar my way.

'Your Royal Highness,' the first sergeant began, 'I am under the King's orders to arrest this man.'

'I have particularly promised Mr Wyld freedom of passage that he may take his case before the King,' she told him sharply. 'Would you dishonour my word?'

'No, Your Royal Highness,' he replied, now uncertain how to proceed.

'Then step aside for we have business with His Majesty.'

And so we continued while they followed behind and behind them there grew a great bustling as the rumour spread of our appearance.

'Twas the middle of the afternoon and the King was in his chambers where he loitered and whispered with Miss Stuart, the Queen being present also. A handful of the King's favourites were among the company including my main enemy, Lord Illminster, a coincidence which I hoped would prove propitious.

I entered these chambers under the Duchess's protection and we approached the King together, upon which I bowed while Her Royal Highness addressed him. Our entrance caught the attention of all in the room and I think Lord Illminster would have spoken directly, only he dare not.

'Your Majesty,' the Duchess said. 'I have brought Mr Wyld to you for I understand he is accused of that most treasonable act, the poisoning of my father the Chancellor. He has told me another story which you might find impossible to believe, but I have promised him I will persuade you to hear it.' So saying she curtseyed before His Majesty and left me to the King.

By now Lord Illminster was considerably agitated and he approached the King himself.

'Your Majesty, this man must be taken to the Tower immediately. He is a traitor to your throne.'

'I know Mr Wyld,' the King replied. 'I do not think he will kill me. Why do we not hear him speak?'

At which Lord Illminster had no answer.

'Well, Mr Wyld, what have you to say against the charges which have been placed against you?'

'Your Majesty,' I replied, 'I say first that they are untrue. Second, I would show you exactly why they are untrue and what the truth of this matter is.'

His Majesty indicated that I should proceed, at which I took up some papers which I had with me. 'I am told, Your Majesty,' I began, 'that My

Lady Castlemaine is said to have acquired a potion from a lately dead Frenchman named Monsieur Vouet and that there are letters confirming this liaison. I have here letters in another hand addressed to the Frenchman which I believe show it was not she but another who obtained the poison.' And I handed the three letters I had had made in Lord Illminster's hand to the King.

The King examined the letters briefly. 'My Lord,' he called to Lord Illminster, 'is this not your hand?'

Lord Illminster came to the King's side and took the letters, then his face reddened as a rage took hold of him.

'What trickery is this?' he demanded of me. 'These letters are counterfeit. I did not write them.'

'Well, My Lord,' I replied, 'maybe they are. Your Majesty,' I then said, turning to the King. ''Tis often possible to recognize forgeries of this type with the aid of a glass. If one could be brought we may look and see if Lord Illminster's claim is just.'

I believe I had now caught the interest of His Majesty who was oft inclined to philosophical enquiries. He had his own cupboard of curiosities and from this a glass was fetched. Lord Illminster, meanwhile, could not yet see the purpose of my strategy, but he appeared mightily suspicious.

A table was arranged and the letters placed upon it, whereupon I examined them closely with the glass. Mr Fox had performed his task expertly so that the signs of a forgery were most easily recognized, even by the King when I showed them to him. I offered the glass to Lord Illminster, but he declined my offer.

'Then Lord Illminster did not write these letters himself?' the King asked.

'By this I think not, Your Majesty,' I replied.

'In which case what is your purpose, sir?'

''Tis that perhaps the letters which it is said were written by My Lady Castlemaine are counterfeit also. If they could be brought then we could look at them, too, with the glass to see if they bear these same signs.'

By now Lord Illminster fully understood where this led. 'I don't have them by me, Your Majesty,' he stuttered, upon being asked.

'No matter,' I interjected. 'I have here three other letters which I believe Lord Illminster can attest were found with the first two.'

'And how will we know these are not new forgeries?' he demanded.

'My Lord,' I said, 'you will recall that Mr Delaney, who attended the death of Mr Backhouse with you, saw them also and will, I am sure, be pleased to attest that these three are those same letters. But if you doubt, then please bring us the other two.'

The King was now so engaged by this investigation that he took the three letters from me and examined them himself, without my help. 'It is quite clear,' he told us after a moment. 'They are counterfeit too, Mr Wyld.'

'In which case,' I proposed, 'we may assume that My Lady Castlemaine is innocent of any charge save being implicated in this intrigue by another.'

'What say you to this, My Lord?' the King asked.

'I must allow it appears possible,' Lord Illminster confessed, and I perceived that he was now displaying a degree of nervousness.

'Then who did procure this poison?' he demanded. 'Do you know, Mr Wyld?'

'Your Majesty,' I replied, 'I have lately been to Hinchbrooke Hall where I have spoken to Lady Hinchbrooke. She has sworn for me an affidavit in which she confesses that she was induced to become involved in a plot to murder the Lord Chancellor with poison and that the person who guided her in this was Lord Illminster.'

At this Lord Illminster could contain himself no more. 'This is preposterous,' he declared. 'Your Majesty, 'twas Mr Wyld's concubine Miss Hamilton, as I have shown you, who fed the poison to the Chancellor. I will listen to this no longer.' At which he would have left the chamber, only the King forbade him with an indication of his hand.

''Tis said she had the poison, Mr Wyld,' the King told me. 'How do you answer that?'

'I think you will find that proposition to be unbelievable, Your Majesty,' I replied. 'I have a witness who will vouchsafe that by some mistake on the part of the intriguers it was Miss Hamilton who ate the poison. Were she the poisoner, I do not think she would have done this.'

Now I turned to the Duchess who in turn made a sign to a servant and a moment or two later the Chancellor appeared within the chamber. There was an immediate hiss of whispering as he approached the King.

'Your Majesty,' he said bowing.

'You are not dead?' the King exclaimed, astonished.

'My death was but a rumour, sir.'

'Then you are Mr Wyld's witness?'

'Miss Hamilton ate the poison that was meant for me.'

'And who intrigued to kill you?'

'Your Majesty, 'tis my belief it was Lord Illminster who used Lady Hinchbrooke in this regard. He, it is, who would deprive this kingdom of your Chancellor.'

Now the King was angry. 'My Lord, what do you say?' he demanded of Lord Illminster.

'That this is a plot to discredit me forever. There is no evidence here.'

I handed the King Lady Hinchbrooke's affidavit. 'Here is evidence enough, Your Majesty,' I told him. 'I suspect more could be found within Lord Illminster's chambers, were you to examine them. Beside that I may show that Lord Illminster's agents murdered the Frenchman, Monsieur Vouet, and tried to murder me, as well as killing Mr Backhouse most foully. I think His Lordship has quite discredited himself without the need for assistance.'

The King took the affidavit and read it quickly. 'My Lord Illminster,' he then said quietly, addressing His Lordship, 'by this I believe you have deceived us most treasonably. Sergeants,' he called sharply, at which two of the sergeants-at-arms approached. 'Take His Lordship to his chambers and ensure that he remains there while we decide what is to be done.'

At which a sullen and decidedly uncomfortable Lord Illminster was escorted from the King's chamber.

'Mr Wyld,' the King said when His Lordship was departed, 'it is clear you have been wrongfully accused, which has no doubt been an inconvenience to you. Now go and I will see you on the morrow, when we will look at this case again and make our decisions.'

So I bowed and left, leaving Lord Clarendon to explain how he had been able to rise from the dead.

There was great confusion to be read on the faces of those who waited beyond the King's chamber. 'Twas clear to all that some confrontation had taken place and my walking free, Lord Illminster taking my place in bonds, suggested that a false intrigue had been laid bare. But rumour from the King's chamber had yet to reach beyond and so all were for the moment mystified. Though I was greeted by several courtiers and cavaliers, each no doubt wishing for the benefit of my insight into the matter, I passed all by with no more than a nod of recognition. In truth my only wish was to return to my own hearth and there mourn in peace. And so I left the palace and took a sedan which presently left me before my door, through which I passed, the sergeant having melted away, though by what means he was informed I could not begin to guess.

CHAPTER 26

Lord Illminster's Residence

There was much relief within my household at my return, yet sorrow when I retold the death of Miss Hamilton. When all had been explained and many questions answered, I took leave to have Martha remove my travelling clothes and rub me down, then put me into a clean shirt and breeches. Presently, I shut myself in my parlour to reflect upon the piteousness of my plight. That being but a melancholy pursuit, by and by I called Bridget to fetch up a bottle from my cellar which, consumed, I took myself to bed and slept.

On the morrow I was to return to the King but I was hardly in a fit state, as to my appearance, to wait upon His Majesty. So, early, I had Ned fetch the barber to tidy Martha's handiwork upon my scalp and then visited the periwig-maker. Here I met with confusion for I knew not how I would have myself look in this contrivance. Eventually I came away with the least unbecoming of those periwigs on offer, having left an order to have one made that was more to my liking. 'Twas not myself that I now saw in the glass, however, but some strange apparition wearing my face. Yet, by and by, with Martha to dress me, I was able to find a handsome yet sober enough combination of garb as to be fitting, I believed, for court.

Upon my arrival at Whitehall I proceeded first to the Duchess's chambers where I found Her Highness in mourning as were her remaining maids. She was, besides, in an unexpected state of agitation.

'There is infamy afoot, Mr Wyld,' she confided, as soon as she found me before her. 'Lord Illminster has flown.'

'When?' I demanded sharply, for this news angered me.

''Tis not known, but that he was not to be found by morning.'

'Then he will be away, I suppose.'

''Tis most likely, sir,' she agreed, her mind no doubt straying, like mine, in the direction of the coast where fugitives normally seek their escape.

That escape had clearly dampened Her Highness's spirits and she seemed, withal, more sombre that I had known her before. 'Who shall pay now for this treason?' she asked me.

'None, it would seem, Your Highness,' I replied despondently. Nor would any pay for murder, I reflected, the death of Miss Hamilton still uppermost in my mind.

I believe she may have sensed this turn of my mind. 'By the by,' she added then, 'I have written to Colonel Hamilton to inform him.'

This act of kindness was a relief to me and I thanked her for it.

'She was in my charge,' she replied. ''Tis but my duty. Now go to the King, for I know he awaits you.'

'Your Highness,' I answered, bowing and did then repair straightway to the King.

I found His Majesty with Lord Clarendon and some other courtiers, the Queen and her maids being absent. Having bowed and greeted the King I enquired as to what had taken place.

'It seems by some laxness on the part of the sergeants that His Lordship has slipped away during the night,' the Chancellor told me. 'By this we may assume he confesses his guilt. Your case against him left little room for doubt, Mr Wyld.'

I wondered what form this laxness had taken and who had induced it, for it seemed to me but a trivial matter to make His Lordship secure for one night. 'Is he to be fetched back?' I asked.

'Can you bring him back, sir?' the King demanded.

'I know not that I can, Your Majesty,' I replied. 'But if it is your wish, I will try.'

'Then we had better put you back on the list, Mr Wyld,' the King told me. 'Your removal was upon a foolish whim and sufficient penance has been served by it. Go and see if he is to be apprehended.'

'I will need your warrant to enter his chambers.'

'You have it, Mr Wyld.'

With that I left to serve my commission.

I went from the King directly to Lord Illminster's chambers in

Whitehall. Here was the beginning of the trail and I was curious to know what I would find. A sergeant still stood beside the door and I quizzed him directly about His Lordship's escape. By this fellow's testimony Lord Illminster had disappeared into the air, but I guessed from his want of explanation that the air into which he had dissolved had been lubricated with a suitable quantity of some potent inducement.

The rooms within were in a state as might be expected if the resident had fled hurriedly, with items left carelessly about while the vital was winnowed from the trivial. Yet I soon perceived that this exit had not been so hurried that His Lordship had not found time to erase such evidence as existed of his intrigue. Within a hearth I found the charred remains of papers and from the remaining fragments I deduced that these were the letters he had penned to Monsieur Vouet and those he had had made in My Lady Castlemaine's hand.

Servants remained, but they could tell me little save that their master had returned in a rage the previous day but had presently calmed, having received a note by hand, then busied himself with his papers. I concluded from all this that he had probably walked out of the door when all was quiet and the sergeants looked in another direction. It was clear that others, most probably of his Catholic party, were complicit in the arrangements for it would have been impossible for him to organize his flight alone. The Duchess spoke accurately when she spoke of infamy. But by whatever means he was gone, leaving no indication as to his destination.

There was nothing for me here, then. I must take myself to his residence behind Fleet Street, I decided, and search for more bearings there.

I took two of the King's sergeants-at-arms with me to Fleet Street. Lord Illminster's main residence by the city was to be found between this street and the Thames, close enough to the River Fleet itself that the stink of that foul sewer reached it when the wind was – as now – from the east.

The servants in the house, when I entered, appeared to have anticipated my arrival. I found them to be in a subdued state of nervousness, for which I could find no immediate cause.

Quizzing them, I learned that Lord Illminster had returned before dawn in a condition of great anxiety and had roused all and ordered trunks be packed for a long sojourn abroad. Meanwhile he had busied himself in his own chamber. The coach had been readied as the dawn broke and he had left immediately thereafter, for Southwark – he had allowed it to be supposed – and thence by Canterbury to Dover.

I knew not the day's tides but His Lordship was sufficiently far ahead that it must be doubted if a swift horseman could overhaul him now, even if the waters delayed his passage. Nevertheless I told one of the sergeants to command a rider be sent to the coast with orders to hold him should he be apprehended. Doing so, I wondered if I was beguiled by a ruse on His Lordship's part. He might equally be heading into the country, then by divers routes take a boat from Poole or Plymouth. Withal, I harboured no conviction that he would be found.

I was curious, however, to know more of His Lordship's affairs for I had cultivated such a hatred for him that I would harvest all I could in case of future use. Therefore I demanded a servant take me to the chamber where he managed his papers. At this one of the serving wenches who was present, for all had gathered together to learn what news I brought, gave such a look of alarm that I began to believe some mystery yet lay to be uncovered.

Forewarned, I called the remaining sergeant and took him with me to the chamber on the upper floor to which the servant presently led us. From the landing I opened the door to this chamber cautiously, for it was tightly shut, and peered inside. Like His Lordship's chamber in Whitehall, this room too was in disarray but there was nothing to be seen that could cause alarm. So I entered, cautioning the sergeant to follow behind.

I could not imagine what there was here that had induced such fear in the wench but I searched carefully, finding nothing. However there was a door from within this chamber leading to another. From behind this door we heard, at once, the unmistakable sound of a presence. Upon hearing this the sergeant, who was hard by it, drew his weapon and opened the door. There was but a brief interval of silence followed by a sharp report from which he fell back into the chamber, a bloody wound visible in his chest. By this means I instantly knew who lay beyond.

Taking up my rapier I advanced and soon found myself face to face with the villain whose ill-luck it had been not to kill me when he tried the first time. I understood immediately that Lord Illminster had set this trap, counting on my inquisitiveness to bring me to him. The villain had no doubt imagined it was I who entered the room to apprehend him. Instead it had been the sergeant. Now he had but his cudgel to defend himself, his piece having been discharged. I backed up, allowing him to enter the outer chamber where the sergeant lay bleeding his life away.

''Tis time for you to pay,' I warned him, as he moved forward. And with that I made a quick thrust, forcing him to back up again.

The fellow spoke no word but his eyes watched me sharply. I believed from some signs he gave that he sought to flee rather than fight, for he knew the fight would be uneven. I backed up again, letting him advance and thus drew him into the centre of the chamber, then stepped to my left, so seeming to leave the way open to the door.

My instinct had been correct for the villain swung his club, intending to drive me further from his escape route. To his discomfort I moved in the opposite direction and thrust, so that he found my rapier stuck quite into his arm, in much the same place as I had found his ball in mine.

I twisted the weapon, at which my victim winced and drew back to extract the blade, but did not yet give up the fight. However, I was upon him again before he could recover sufficiently to retaliate and I placed the point of my blade upon his neck, ready to slice his jugular vein should he resist. His eyes now displayed fear as I applied such pressure as was needed to break the skin with my point so that he knew not to move.

'Kneel,' I told him, still maintaining the pressure of my blade at his neck.

He did so, cautiously, at which I lowered my weapon and with one swift movement kicked him sturdily beneath his chin, laying him out upon the floor. Standing over him, my blade now upon his chest, I called to the servants to come and treat the sergeant.

The villain looked up at me from the floor, even now contemptuous.

'Your foul deeds have earned you the foulest of deaths,' I told him and he knew well what I meant. To be cut apart while still alive was not a death to be contemplated by the sane.

At that the light faded in his eyes.

'Kill me,' he pleaded.

'And deprive the crowds of their pleasure?' I retorted, cruelly, for I wished to see him suffer.

Then I ordered one of the servants fetch strong rope and had the fellow bound by his hands and hobbled that he could not run.

A physician had been called to the sergeant, who had been placed upon a bed in the inner chamber which proved to be Lord Illminster's bedchamber. I knew the gentleman not, as to his ability, but I fear no skill could have prevented the sergeant's death, which came to pass within an hour of his injury.

While the physician ministered in vain I saw the villain taken below and secured to await the constable. I, meanwhile, examined Lord Illminster's papers but could find nothing of worth. This appeared to be the place from which he made his alchemical studies for there were shelves bearing like tomes while such papers as I found spoke of his enquiries into this subject. At this, I examined whether the missing manuscript was to be found here but could lay my hand on nothing fitting its description.

I presumed by this that Lord Illminster had taken the prized manuscript with him. Nevertheless curiosity drove me downstairs to quiz the villain by whose hand he had taken charge of it. Perchance he could confirm that it had gone, for he seemed to keep his master's confidence.

The answer, when it came, was not to be expected.

'There was no manuscript,' the fellow told me. 'The Frenchman had it not.'

At which I could not help but laugh heartily.

I returned presently to the palace and to the King to inform him of my discoveries. I found His Majesty taking his dinner with the Queen and the Duke of Monmouth but he was pleased to speak with me while he ate, it being one of the spectacles at Whitehall to observe Their Majesties at their repast. Indeed he invited me to take a dish or two as we spoke.

''Tis clear to me, Your Majesty' I reported, 'that Lord Illminster has made his escape and will be found beyond these shores. However we have taken his chief agent who has murdered three times with his own hands to my own knowledge.'

''Tis some slight compensation,' he acknowledged.

'No doubt His Lordship will inform us when he reaches the safety of his foreign court,' I added. Which observation the King found to be just.

'Mr Wyld,' he said, my own report being concluded, 'I have found it fitting to make some small addition to your pension, about which Mr Killigrew will no doubt inform you. For I have one further task pertinent to this affair for you to perform. 'Twill be arduous to you, no doubt, but as I say I have provided recompense. My Lady Castlemaine is shut up at Richmond where she awaits my orders. I would have you go and fetch her back if you please.'

I saw that His Majesty took some amusement by this commission. It was one that I would decline were I in a position to do so. That not being possible, I stood, bowed and left.

CHAPTER 27

A Funeral in Aldreth

If I must perform this onerous task, then best have it done with all speed I told myself. So thinking I returned by hackney to Covent Garden for riding boots and breeches, having ordered a groom follow behind with a mount from the palace stables, then put myself upon the road to Richmond. The way was easy and the exercise brisk so that three hours brought me to the great park wherein my destination lay. At a walk now, I entered the park by a gate in the wall built by the King's father that his deer should be retained against the hunt.

My Lady Castlemaine was shut up in the King's hunting lodge, where she had been sent by his order upon discovery of her culpability in the matter of Lord Clarendon's poisoning. Whether any had informed her that she was no longer deemed culpable I knew not. But informed or otherwise, there she remained for the King had given her no leave to stray. Now I must release her.

I left my mount with an ostler, the park being well provided with stables and horses and dogs for the chase, then presented myself at the lodge. Presently I was shown into My Lady's presence. By her appearance when I beheld her I judged she still knew not how the situation played. There were the signs of care about her which were not normally to be found.

'My Wyld.' She greeted me with an expression of puzzlement and perchance anger. 'I had not looked to find you here.' Her brow as she spoke was creased by a frown.

I bowed, but slightly. 'My Lady,' I replied. 'I am sent by the King to take you to Whitehall.'

'Then we are not to be hanged?' she asked.

'That lot has now fallen to another,' I informed her coldly.

'Well, I am thankful,' she replied. 'But I would know in what manner this change of heart on the part of His Majesty was brought about.'

Thus it fell to me to recount the events that had followed Lord Illminster's revelations, how the plot was his own, how Lady Hinchbrooke had acted for him and how Miss Hamilton now lay in her coffin. By the time I had finished recounting this tale My Lady's spirits had considerably revived.

'Why, Mr Wyld,' she said, a demon in her eye, 'then our argument has been in vain and you will be able to dance with me again, when we have another ball.'

The carelessness of this remark, for she knew mighty well of my deep affection for Miss Hamilton, was such as to produce that welling of emotion that had so far been unable to flow from within me. Released from the shackles of the rage that had previously held it, that emotion waited but the sting of this callous quip to pour forth. I turned aside, abruptly, and crossing the room to be far from her, I wept.

My weeping so convulsed me that it was several minutes before I could control myself sufficiently to face her. When I did my sorrow had been replaced by a fierce anger.

'My Lady,' I began, re-crossing the room to the place from where she had observed me in my sorrow, 'if you should ever again be so careless with my affection for Miss Hamilton, then I swear I will take a riding whip and chastise you until you call out on account of the pain.'

My Lady Castlemaine opened her mouth to reply, then closed it again. No word came. Instead, for some moments she stared at me, her eyes wide as a fox's.

'Mr Wyld,' she addressed me, finally, 'I am but a cold creature who knows nothing of love, though I hope one day to find somebody who will teach me.'

And I believe in this she was honest.

By and by her coach was made ready and her maids assembled and the journey back to London began. I would ride my mount, but My Lady insisted I accompany her within the coach. This turned into as strange a journey as ever I have taken. By my sharp rebuke and her humble response, the air between us had become cleared and I found myself conceiving an unexpected affection for this creature, though she deserved to be loathed, or pitied.

Nothing more of that exchange was said and her normal demeanour quietly returned so that I soon became the subject of a discussion with her maids as whether I was the most handsome man at court or no. But I believed that I should never have reason to fear her again. And so my onerous commission provided, upon completion at a very late hour, unlooked for rewards.

The day following I set off for Cornbury from where I intended to escort Miss Hamilton's remains to her father at Aldreth. It was eight days now since her last breath had been taken yet I had her ever before me waking and, I believe, as I slept. 'Twas time for her to rest.

I travelled from Whitehall with the Duchess in her coach and her maids followed behind in another, for we were all to make a procession from Cornbury to Aldreth. At Cornbury a hearse had been prepared with six horses to pull it and upon this was placed the coffin in which she lay. Meanwhile I reclaimed the bay, which was still stabled there and rode her onward, taking my place beside the hearse.

Our journey took two days as we made our way by the rural lanes upon which travellers proceed as they travel from Oxford to Cambridge, stopping a night in one of those inns they must frequent. The tracks were plagued with mud and soft earth, the summer so far having been more wet than dry, and so deeply rutted that I began to wonder how we should arrive whole. More than once the strength of the six horses was needed to drag the hearse free of a quagmire. But by and by the journey was completed and we did arrive at Aldreth Hall where Colonel Hamilton awaited us.

The colonel was a sorrowful sight, the signs of his loss being writ about him in lines etched deep. Yet I think our arrival provided relief, for of all the torments waiting is oft the most painful. By servants the coffin was carried away and laid within the hall, then tapers were lit and placed about it and so she rested before her final journey. For the funeral was to be on the morrow.

Once this was arranged, the Duchess and her maids were found chambers within the hall and the colonel ordered a supper be prepared for evening that we might fortify ourselves. I spoke briefly to him when we arrived but he being much occupied, I reserved a full account of what had passed for a time when we could sit together undisturbed.

There being much toing and froing, and the Duchess being concerned to make the acquaintance of the colonel, I sought his library where I took up a book that I might divert myself. The room was cool and though I read little I was briefly at peace. Hearing then but a slight sound as I sat, I looked up and at once believed I saw an apparition. There before me, reaching for a book, was Rebecca. At this I started and jumped from my stool, for I knew not how I should greet such a spectre.

Upon my rising the figure turned towards me and I saw I was mistaken, though the likeness was striking.

'Excuse me, sir,' said the figure, and again it was Rebecca, but not her. 'I did not see you there.'

I bowed. 'I am Mr Wyld,' I introduced myself. 'May I know who you are?'

'My name is Emily,' she replied, at which I understood that this was Miss Hamilton's younger sister.

'Please accept my condolences,' I beseeched her. 'You have lost a sister.'

'And I believe you, sir, have lost a wife, which is much to be pitied also.'

'It is so,' I agreed. And then we spoke little more at that time, for our memories bore us apart.

We ate our supper at a great table where cold meats were provided and fenland ale and it was a melancholy supper at which the conversation was of a dull variety. By and by the Duchess went away with her maids, taking Miss Hamilton with her, and I was left with the colonel for company.

'I had not looked to return to Aldreth under such circumstances,' I confessed to him as we sat by one another sharing a silence.

'It was not to be expected,' he replied.

And then I told him what had passed, how we had endeavoured to save the life of the Chancellor, believing him to be poisoned when in truth it had been Rebecca who had consumed the potion. 'I had her hand in mine,' I concluded. 'And there she went away.'

''Tis not a thing which I can comprehend,' he told me. At which I could offer him no better understanding for I could scarce comprehend myself.

So Friday morning dawned, being the day of the funeral, and I prepared to say my farewell. The coffin was not yet sealed, and before it was I spoke to her for one last time, silent words that she might reply to silently. Then the servants came and the undertakers and the box was sealed and carried to the hearse and the journey to the small chapel was made. Inside those austere walls, for this was a puritan place in all but name, we sang a hymn or two – as was the custom – and words were spoken, then the coffin was taken and put under the ground. A part of my life went into the hole that morning, carried within the stone cold bosom that had once breathed life into Rebecca Hamilton. If there was comfort to be found in the ritual we witnessed by her burial, I could not find it.

Later we returned to Aldreth Hall where a funeral feast had been prepared. Colonel Hamilton gave out his rings to the mourners and alms for the poor. And thus the ritual was completed. Afterwards the Duchess set off with her maids for Cambridge where she would spend the night before the long journey to London. I chose to tarry a while longer.

When all was quiet and there was none left save me, Colonel Hamilton and his daughter I was able to speak more freely of my love. And then I produced the jewel which Miss Hamilton had placed into my care until the day upon which we would be married. That day would now never arrive and it behove me to return to jewel to the colonel. I found him to be of another mind.

'My daughter having seen fit to entrust the stone to you, Mr Wyld, I cannot with honour take it back. What have you else of hers?'

'I have her memory. That is enough.'

'I will not accept it,' he insisted.

'It rightly belongs to you, sir.'

'That is not so. It belonged to my wife, and she left it to her eldest daughter. In time, no doubt, your own eldest daughter, had you one, would have had it. But in the meantime Rebecca expressed no other wish except that you should have it. Therefore, unless you have no use for it, I cannot take it from you.'

Thus, by this logic, I kept the treasure for I could find no further argument against the colonel's.

I remained at Aldreth for two days longer, keeping under these sorrowful circumstances the promise I had once made to be his guest. During that time I rode across his land where the air was clear and fresh and dreamt of what might have been. This was the land upon which Rebecca was raised and by my conceit she was there still, watching from the hedgerows and coppices that grew all about. In the evening we made mournful company, Miss Hamilton having departed on the Saturday morning for the north where she served as maid of honour to the Countess of Carlisle.

It was the Monday when I took my leave. Doing so, I knew not if I should ever see these lands again for they carried now in my eyes a painful burden. Yet there was no reason for me to make haste about my return and I dawdled in Cambridge and again in Bishops Stortford, seeking whatever diversion came my way. Then by and by the need for familiar surroundings grew and I set the bay on the road to London. By Thursday eve the animal was returned to her stable and I was home.

CHAPTER 28

Mr Delaney is Contrite

Upon my return to Covent Garden I found that Mr Starkey had left a note and that Mr Delaney had called several times during my absence. Mr Starkey, by his note, would have me call upon him for he had intelligence to divulge. Delaney left no note but I had little difficulty divining the purpose of his visits. We had an account to settle and such costs as there were to be borne upon this account would be his. No doubt he sought accommodation.

I was in no hurry to make this settlement, though I would not deny it was necessary. So next morning, being Friday, I strolled to Will's to read the news sheets. It was my intention to take my dinner there among such wits as might be found to assemble for I was in need of easy company. I had, though, been settled for but a short span, with barely time to sup a bowl of coffee and read the news from Portugal, when Ned appeared beside me. Mr Delaney had called again and intended to wait upon me should I see fit to return. Reluctantly I submitted that I must receive him and sent Ned ahead to advise him thus.

I found Delaney in my parlour, pacing restlessly as he awaited my arrival.

'There you are, Francis,' he pronounced upon espying me. 'I have looked for you all this week past.'

'I have been burying my dead, Robert,' I replied.

'Yes, I am sorry.'

'But I am here now.'

'Yes. Well.' He appeared uncomfortable and I perceived that he knew not how to begin. 'I hear Lord Illminster has fled to Brussels,' he told me by way of approaching the matter obliquely.

'Brussels? Well I suppose his head will be safe there.'

'My sister assures me that he is unquestionably guilty of treason.'

'There is no room for doubt.'

'And I, it would seem, have been misled.'

'By whom?' I asked, for though I understood his meaning I would not make his task easy.

'Francis, you know perfectly well that I speak of Lord Illminster. He has used me and I have let him.'

'Why do you tell me what I know already?'

'Because I … damn it, Francis can you not help me?'

'No, Robert, I think I cannot.'

Delaney looked at me angrily, then turned his back on me and I knew he was struggling with himself.

'I have come to beg your forgiveness,' he finally confessed, turning to face me once more. 'I should have trusted you when I could not believe His Lordship to be dishonourable. In that I have betrayed our friendship.'

'And much more besides,' I reminded him.

He looked away at this, refusing to meet my eye. 'It is true,' he admitted.

'He would have used you to carry his false case against me. Would you have let him?'

'I …' He shook his head wearily, and a look of abject misery briefly crossed his features.

'Then why should I forgive you?'

'Francis, I can abase myself no further. I am guilty of everything you say. If you cannot forgive me, then I will go and we will speak to one another no more.'

Looking at him, then, I could see he believed I might not forgive him and I could see that he was saddened by the thought.

'You are a fool, Robert,' I told him roughly. 'You are incapable of judging a man's character. You are, besides, arrogant enough to believe that honesty and high standing are necessary bedfellows.'

At this he began to complain but I motioned him to remain silent. 'These faults of yours are clearly hereditary. Were I able, I would remove them with a sharp blade. Since that is impossible, I must accept that you will always be party to them. Therefore I must forgive you. But I beg you, in future, to rely on my judgement in these matters for yours is of no value whatsoever.'

Delaney remained silent for a moment longer. Then he thanked me, humbly, by which I was sure he was contrite. 'I suppose the loss of the manuscript is my punishment,' he added sadly. 'Though you may not judge it fitting.'

I had completely forgotten the confounded manuscript. For, of course, Delaney knew not what I knew thanks to the villain's confession.

'That may not be entirely settled,' I told him then. 'For Lord Illminster never had it.'

Delaney was mightily startled by this news but I quickly convinced him of its truth.

'Then where has it gone?' he asked.

I shrugged. 'Mayhap it never arrived upon these shores.'

'No, no,' he insisted. 'Monsieur Vouet brought it. This I know to be true. All was arranged for the morning upon which I discovered him dead.'

'Then I suppose, like Lord Illminster, it has dissolved into the ether and will presently reappear when it is unlooked for.'

Delaney was in no mood for jokes but he smiled weakly at this one. 'I confess I am completely baffled by your revelation,' he told me after a moment.

'Let us apply a little natural logic,' I suggested. 'If the Frenchman brought the manuscript with him from France, yet it was not in his lodgings, then we must suppose it was somewhere else. 'Twould make sense for him to have found a secure place while he took his pox cure. The only mystery is, where?'

'Your logic has not brought us far,' Delaney complained.

'We shall see,' I replied, though I should confess he was correct. 'I suppose if I am to forgive you, Robert,' I added, 'then I must attempt to help you retrieve this document.'

'Are you still willing to do so?'

''Twill divert me, which would be a blessing,' I confided. 'But if I should succeed there will now be a price.'

'What price?' he asked, alarmed.

'Let us discuss what it will be if I succeed. Rest assured, it will be within your compass.'

And so, by and by we parted.

I had assumed in agreeing to help Delaney again that the key must lie within the cryptic journal which Monsieur Vouet had kept. So when he had left me I took this down once more to examine whether I was right. My perusal quickly convinced me I was not. Nowhere within its pages was his own secret alchemical commission mentioned.

Upon that conclusion I put the Frenchman aside and returned to Will's to take my dinner among the wits. By this I found some semblance of the normality I had once enjoyed, which made me believe that I could drag myself from the state of despair that had lately become my mien.

Back in my parlour with a full stomach I presently set about reviewing everything that I had in my possession, physical and mental, concerning the Frenchman. Only one item remained unaccounted for. 'Twas the alchemical work by Eirenaeus Philoponos Philalethes with the enigmatic inscription supposedly written by Van Helmont the iatro-chemist but which could not have been since he died before the book was published. A book to find a manuscript. It seemed apt. But how was the one to lead to the other?

I examined the book again, searching for some hidden message. Were there words or letters secretly marked which, when extracted, contained a message leading to the manuscript? I could find none. Perhaps the title, *The Marrow of Alchemy* held the key? If so, it held it well. Then I remembered Mr Starkey. If the subject was alchemy, then perhaps I should turn to an alchemist. Since he already expected me I took up the book and, after finding a sedan, went straightway to search him out.

As usual, the alchemist was reluctant to open his door, though when he did 'twas not a matter of unbalancing the airs which disturbed him. Indeed, I found him to be exceedingly glum. As he soon told me, his creditors were upon him again and another spell in gaol was the likely outcome.

'Can you not satisfy them with a part of Mr Delaney's gold?' I suggested. 'I'm sure he will not miss a portion but if he does I will be able to persuade him it serves his interests.'

'Ah,' he replied. And crossing his elaboratory he brought to me a lump of dull, greyish material. 'As you will understand by this, I have managed to return the metal to its original base state. I think they may not be satisfied with lead. Perhaps you could return it to Mr Delaney with my compliments. You may tell him that I have not been able to penetrate the mystery of the transmutation, though I have succeeded in reversing it which may account some progress.'

I examined, curiously, the lump of metal which he placed before me.

'Can you thus abase true gold?' I asked him. For it seemed to me that if gold were so unstable a specie, then we should not place such trust in it as we did.

'Well there, Mr Wyld, you strike at the heart of the matter, for in truth I cannot. And therefore I must deduce that the gold produced by the powder differs in some respect from the other. But as to where the difference lies, that is the anvil upon which we beat ourselves.'

'Then I will tell Mr Delaney of your trials and perhaps he can be prevailed upon to help. Now, sir, I understand by your note that you have learned something of value.'

'It is of no account, I suppose, now that Lord Illminster is unveiled and has fled.'

'Nevertheless I will be satisfied to hear it.'

'It is simply this. I have discovered that there is concern in Paris at the death of the Frenchman who brought the manuscript to these shores and that has led to a certain relaxing of strictures. Thereby it has been allowed to be known that the parcel he was carrying was by ritual long established to be left with a third party and a token provided the new protector by which he might redeem it. As you may judge by these details, they like to preserve everything under a cloak of ceremony. That is all I have, but since it appears in this case the ritual was not strictly followed, there can be no help from this intelligence.'

'Mr Starkey,' I replied quickly. 'I believe that the observance was correct, for I have with me what I now judge to be that token of which you have heard.' With that I told him what I knew and offered him the book which I still held by me.

The alchemist took the tome in his hands and opened it. 'This must be some jest,' he exclaimed, immediately.

''Tis no jest of my making,' I assured him. 'Why do you suppose it should be?'

'Because I know this book from front to back, from top to bottom.'

He looked at me oddly then. 'Can you swear to hold a secret, Mr Wyld?' he asked.

I nodded. 'Unless it harm me to do so,' I assured him.

'I wrote this book,' he confided. 'Though none knows it save you. It has quite confounded those secretive conspirers of whom we have spoken,' he added.

'And what does it contain?'

'It contains knowledge, sir. But if you wish to extract it you have to learn the language, and I am sure that you do not.'

''Tis not my intention,' I agreed. 'However that is by the by. For this book of yours was in Monsieur Vouet's possession when he died.'

Taking the book back, I drew his attention to the inscription and the enigma it contained. 'I am convinced the book is the key,' I repeated. 'Your intelligence shows us there is a lock. Could we but bring the two together then the prisoner might be released.'

By this sudden revelation, I found Mr Starkey to be much enlivened. For the moment his debtors were put behind him. 'Then we must find the third party,' he exclaimed, excitedly.

'Your intelligence does not indicate how this might be achieved?'

'It does not.'

'Maybe that information is contained within the token?'

'Then I had better study it, since it is my work.'

'Please do,' I invited him. But do not be offended if I remain by your side,' I added. 'For if this book be the token, I must keep it within my sight until I can retrieve the manuscript.'

'I judge you do not trust me, Mr Wyld,' he observed wryly.

'In a matter such as this I find it serves everybody's purpose best that I trust no one.'

'Perhaps you are wise.'

It thereby fell to me to amuse myself as best I could among Mr Starkey's reagents and apparatus while he examined the book, page by page. I did not interrupt him nor did I leave him though I was sorely tempted, for my mind when left untaxed was wont to slip into the pit which lay always at my feet. I know not how long this interval lasted, but it may have been two hours or more before Mr Starkey pronounced that he could find no hidden message that might indicate where the manuscript lay.

'Then, sir,' I told him, 'if there be a clue it must lie with the inscription.'

But what clue could these few words, though enigmatic, hold?

'Perhaps there is another Van Helmont,' I suggested.

At that Mr Starkey emitted a great whoop of delight. 'What better place is there to hide a book than among other books?' he exclaimed excitedly. 'Is there not a dealer in books by St Paul's who is called Van Helmont?'

'I know not.'

'Then let me be your guide.'

'I am afraid I cannot allow that in person,' I told him then. 'Please do not misconstrue my motive. I have not forgotten my promise, but I will go alone and try to retrieve this manuscript.'

I knew Mr Starkey was upset by my decision and, indeed, it did not surprise me. But my first duty remained to Mr Delaney. Therefore I left the alchemist with my perceived slight to add to his debtors as a source of discomfort. I intended to repair to St Paul's Yard with all haste.

CHAPTER 29

An Alchemical Tryst

It was but a short distance from Mr Starkey's elaboratory hard by the Tower to the ancient church of St Paul's. I made the journey on foot, the token held close by me. Was the solution to the mystery so simple, I asked myself, for I could not believe it so?

St Paul's Yard was its usual clamour of commerce. The churchyard had, by some tradition which I have never heard explained, become a market containing an array of stalls selling goods of many sorts. Principal among the vendors were booksellers who gathered here to display their wares garnered from all parts of the globe, storing them in the crypt of the great church at night for safety. Among these wares could be found works from Germany and from France, from Holland, China and Spain. Greek Bibles, Moorish philosophies and books from the late King's library all found there way to this place by divers routes as accretions of books were dissipated and then collected again into libraries. Where books were concerned, this yard was a hub of trade.

The churchyard was no mystery to me; my own Euclid had been purchased here. But my visits were infrequent and my library was small for my attention was usually required elsewhere and my present opportunity for study was limited. Consequently I knew not by heart the names of the booksellers, nor yet that one might be called Van Helmont. Enquiry soon proved that such a seller did exist and I presently found myself before his stall where I began to browse among the wares. After a while the seller approached me. He was of medium height, slightly bent with a mass of unkempt grey hair over a leather-skinned face.

'Is there something you particularly seek?' he asked, in a rough sort of accent that seemed to me to be coloured by Frankish guttural.

'Are you an iatrochemist, reincarnated?' I asked.

The old man shook his head. 'No, sir,' he assured me, 'I am not but I can supply his works if they are what you need.'

'That won't be necessary,' I replied. Then I handed him the token, Mr Starkey's book. 'I believe you hold a manuscript which this tome will redeem,' I told him.

The old man took the book from me and examined it, then he examined me. 'You are not the person I was taught to expect,' he answered.

'It is true,' I replied. 'I act for that person. You know that the Frenchman is dead?'

'I am but a conduit, sir,' he answered.

'He is, sir, and the means by which the transaction was to be completed died with him. It has only just been rediscovered. Perhaps we can complete the business now?'

But he shook his head. 'I must be satisfied as to the person,' he told me.

I nodded, then. 'I will send him to you,' I told him.

'Send him alone,' he replied.

I indicated that I would, and so left him to his books while I guarded still mine.

I took a sedan to Pall Mall, then, seeking out Delaney that I might bring this business to an end. He was at home and I showed him the token and instructed him how he was to use it. But before I gave him charge of it, I asked my price.

'Mr Starkey has a great desire to examine this manuscript,' I told him. 'And you owe him a considerable debt. His assistance has been paramount in securing its discovery.'

'Mr Starkey knows of this,' he demanded, aghast.

'Yes, Robert, he does.'

'But he must not.'

At that I laughed. 'I suggest you go and tell him he must not,' I told him. 'Then perhaps he will not.'

'You should have said nothing,' he persisted.

'Robert,' I cautioned him, crossly, discovering he had but a short memory, 'you have withheld information from me when lives were to be lost. I will not have you lecturing me about what I should and should not say. Now you will listen to me: I do not intend to bargain. If you wish this book then you will promise me that you will allow Mr Starkey to study the manuscript. If not I will take it and burn it. The choice is yours.'

Delaney looked at me in astonishment. 'You cannot destroy it,' he exclaimed.

'You are a natural philosopher,' I reminded him. 'You know well that the application of fire to paper is conclusive.'

Delaney was speechless.

'This is not difficult,' I added, for I was beginning to become irritated. 'Your circle is two alchemists short and Mr Starkey is an alchemist. Admit him, then all is squared.'

'He is not a gentleman,' Delaney muttered crossly.

'What does that matter?' I asked. 'Your circle is already brimming with rogues. But that is by the by. If you wish to have the manuscript you will promise me this. That is my price.'

Delaney muttered further to himself and began to pace. 'All right,' he snapped, suddenly, turning to face me. 'I promise.'

At which I gave him the token and left him, glad to be rid of the whole business at last.

I had advised Delaney before parting that it was already too late to visit St Paul's Yard that evening. Consequently I was sure he would go next morning, for he would take the earliest opportunity to obtain his prize. I must confess that in spite of my relief that I was no longer involved I was curious to see how the business was conducted. With this in mind I rose early myself in order to ensure that I might be there in time to witness the transaction, though I must do so by stealth.

When I arrived most of the stalls were yet to be set but when they began to appear, I was mystified and somewhat alarmed to discover that the seller I sought was no longer there. Once I was certain there was no mistake I began to make enquiries from which I quickly discovered that Van Helmont had brought a cart late the last evening upon which to pack all his stock and had driven it away, not to return.

I was mystified for I knew not what this might portend. So, in spite of my vow to put the business behind me, I quickly found a sedan to take me to Pall Mall. Delaney was not at home. I left again, then returned a few hours later, but he was still not there. The next day it was the same, at which I decided he was intent on avoiding me. Thereupon I asked to see Lady Villiers whom I found to be pleased to welcome me.

'My dear Mr Wyld,' she greeted me. 'I have heard everything from my sister. I am so very sorry for you.'

I bowed. 'You are kind, My Lady. It is a great loss, even greater I think for being so unexpected.'

'She will be in a higher place, so fear not. By prayer you will find all the comfort you need, however great.'

I nodded, prayer having brought me yet no comfort though I did not find it fitting to contradict My Lady thus.

'It seems my sister had found that she has no quarrel with you after all,' she continued, sensing perhaps that I might not wish to dwell on my recent tragedy.

'We have, I believe, found an understanding,' I confirmed. 'But, My Lady, I seek Robert. Do you know why he is not to be found at home when I call?'

'I am sure he is here somewhere,' she insisted.

But in spite of her certainty he could not, or would not, be located.

'Perhaps you could ask him to let me know when he is next to be found at home,' I suggested, more than a little annoyed. And soon thereafter I left.

If Delaney would not see me then he must have completed the transaction by some means to which I was not privy. That was clear. Otherwise I should have found him upon my doorstep. Had he, then, completed his side of the bargain? Clearly I must call on Mr Starkey one more time.

Unlike Delaney, Mr Starkey was to be found at home and he invited me in without venturing any protest, which I thought must be accounted a miracle for I could not recall such cordiality before.

'And how are your debtors?' I asked him, for I sensed that his situation was not as it had been when I left him less than a day earlier.

'Why, they are satisfied, Mr Wyld. Entirely satisfied.'

'Welcome news, indeed,' I complimented him. 'Have you perchance seen Mr Delaney?'

'I believe he did pass by, as you mention him.'

'And has he granted you access to that manuscript which you craved the opportunity to study?'

At this a curious smile flickered upon Mr Starkey's lips, a smile that seemed to reflect an inner amusement. 'You will recall,' he told me in reply, 'our discussion about secretive conspirers. I have to confess to you, but only this once, that I am become a secretive conspirer myself. And therefore, if I am to be true to this new profession, then I cannot answer the question you have just asked me.'

'How will you be able to stand it, sir?' I asked.

'It will require great strength, 'tis true,' he acknowledged.

'Then you may tell Mr Delaney that I am satisfied.'

And so I left him.

It seemed that the business was truly over. Delaney had his manuscript and had at my insistence admitted Mr Starkey to his circle. No doubt they would all profit by his admission for he was the most philosophical of alchemists. And now they had closed in upon themselves, like a water lily closes when night draws its veil, taking with them the ancient document so that it appeared from beyond their confines as if it never had existed. When the world was striving towards a new philosophy thanks to men like Mr Hooke who pushed ever forwards and outwards, this appeared to me to be the most archaic behaviour. Who profited from the spells they cast about themselves I could not imagine for it was clear to me by this that they did not. All they achieved to my certain knowledge was the propagation of superstition.

And now, to crown the theatre, Delaney had become as moody as a young girl. No doubt he resented the bargain I had forced him to strike. It was equally difficult for me not to resent his reaction. Though I knew him to be by nature selfish just as he was arrogant and a poor judge of character, yet I could not rid myself of the thought that he deserved to be chastised as roundly I had threatened to chastise My Lady.

I would never administer such a corrective, be it never so deserved. Instead I would let him be. And, by and by, Delaney would emerge from his mood. One day I would find him on my doorstep pretending ignorance that any such season had passed between us. No doubt I would ignore it too. By such frailties do we define ourselves, I as surely as he.

CHAPTER 30

Mr Wyld Seeks a Commission

The following Monday I received a note from Lord Clarendon in which he requested me to call upon him at the Palace of Westminster where the House of Lords was sitting. With no other demand upon my time I found it convenient to repair to Westminster forthwith.

His Lordship had been allowed no respite following Lord Illminster's attempt upon him. No sooner had the Italian venom failed to reach him than Lord Bristol brought in his much promised paper seeking to impeach the Chancellor upon grounds of bribery, personal ambition as to the throne and the encouragement of popery which latter seems a surprising assault from one of the Catholic party.

To Lord Bristol's great misfortune the King discovered himself to be little amused by these accusations and the former was obliged to flee swiftly. He now keeps the company of Lord Illminster in Brussels where his Sovereign's hand may not grasp him. The House of Lords, meanwhile, judged there was no case to answer and so the Chancellor lives still, though his enemies multiply by the hour.

Upon arriving by the palace yard and entering their antechamber I found Their Lordships to be debating some legal matter from their wool sacks. By and by Lord Clarendon availed himself of an opportunity to depart the chamber in order to speak to me.

'I am greatly in your debt, sir,' he told me immediately. 'For without your intervention I might yet have found myself subject to that potion which fatally struck down Miss Hamilton. Such a stealthy concoction is much to be feared. Therefore please accept my thanks, once more.'

I bowed in acknowledgement. ''Tis my greatest regret that the malevolent will which directed all could not be eradicated,' I told him.

'He will not suffer further on this account,' His Lordship confided quietly. 'I have no doubt that after a suitable period of penance, Lord Illminster will find himself pardoned by His Majesty and free to return. Already the memory of his infamy dims. Much as I would like to see him expiring on the end of a rope, I have counselled myself to believe otherwise. I suggest you do the same.'

''Tis a pity for he has done great harm.'

'Well, Mr Wyld, we need not disagree about that. But as for now, my daughter has particularly asked that I determine if there be any service I can offer you in return for your own sacrifices.'

'Save a commission to Brussels, I think not, My Lord.'

His Lordship found slight cause for amusement in my reply. 'Well, in the future, perhaps,' he suggested. 'But do not tarry long or my enemies will have brought me down.'

'I hope not, My Lord,' I told him, though I judged his fears well founded. We spoke, then, a few more words upon which he found himself called back to the chamber to exercise his legal duties.

Being now close by Whitehall, following my departure from the palace at Westminster, I thought the moment opportune to call upon Mr Killigrew and see how matters stood on my account. Among other business that we might discuss, I was curious to know what dispensation the King had seen fit to make on my behalf.

I found that gentleman to be pleased to greet me.

'I take it that the countryside has relinquished its call upon your services, Mr Wyld,' he told me, which was by him a dry observation.

'Events have taken another turn,' I confirmed.

'I am sorry, sorry indeed. There is little enough happiness to be found in these uncertain times. But at least the gods have been appeased. That will count for something.'

'It will make life simpler,' I agreed.

'The King has seen fit to put another hundred on to you too, Mr Wyld, which will no doubt be of benefit when I find myself in possession of the funds to service his debts.'

'And how does the business proceed?'

'In as haphazard a manner as ever. But if you have nothing to occupy you...?' He left his question unfinished.

'The truth, Mr Killigrew, is that nothing will occupy me,' I confessed. 'And therefore if you should find you have a commission which might require a sojourn of several months beyond these shores, I will not be averse to its consideration.'

Mr Killigrew shuffled his papers as a means of organizing his thoughts. 'You will not find the Swedish court to be diverting, I fear,' he muttered mostly to himself. 'For they live off pickled fish which does but little for the sanity. Spain is going down while France rises. That is the main thing. No, sir. Paris is the place where the world now meets so if you find French ways to your liking then I can still offer you an opportunity there. What do you say, sir?'

'I say yes,' I replied immediately. For I would have gone to Sweden, where poor Mr Descartes had perished from the cold, if that be all he had to offer.

'Then allow me one week and I will find business suitable to your diversion.'

I left Mr Killigrew's chamber with a lighter load than I had entered. A sojourn in Paris would serve me well, with the diversions of the French court and the societies of virtuosi to occupy me. It was in this mood that I met with Mr Pemberton who was taking the air of the court as I found him.

'How fares the Duke?' I asked, when our civilities had been completed.

'He sees to his navy which suits him best, I think. But by the company you now keep I suspect you know more than I of his affairs.'

I laughed at this. 'Do not imagine that I can stand too long a time in so rarefied an atmosphere,' I told him. 'I understand from our philosophers that rarefaction is quite deadly.'

'I believe it is.'

So we engaged ourselves in idle tittle-tattle for several minutes more, when by some small commotion we understood that a grand personage passed our way. This turned out to be My Lady Castlemaine who was much in favour again with the King who had, by rumour, despaired of ever bedding Miss Stuart.

My Lady would have passed us by at a distance, but seeing me she diverted from her course and came our way.

'Good day, Mr Wyld,' she said, having approached. 'Mr Pemberton,' she added.

We bowed. 'My Lady,' I replied. 'You are, I trust, returned to your accustomed state of vigour.'

'I am certainly vigorous, sir,' she answered with a smile. 'And you?'

'I convalesce still.'

'Then I wish you well. Perhaps when your own vigour is re-established you will find the strength to dine with me again?'

'I am to depart for Paris within the fortnight,' I told her, by way of an answer.

'That will be our loss and the French court's gain.'

At which she sailed away as a frigate to the Indies.

Mr Pemberton, having observed this exchange, showed no little amusement upon her departure. I demanded his explanation.

'Why, Mr Wyld,' he replied, 'you have slighted the most dangerous woman in the land and yet she eats from your hand like a lamb. Is that not the most marvellous thing to behold?'

The justice of which observation, upon consideration, I could hardly deny.